SHE WAS TRAPPED IN THE HANDS OF EVIL—BUT WHOSE?

Amelia could not believe this was happening to her.

How could she, the reigning beauty of London, be imprisoned in a miserable rundown coach and driven to what was surely the most desolate spot in England?

How could she, who had mocked the power of lords, be held captive by a massively built, beard-stubbled brute of a man, whose manners were as foul as his appearance?

How long must she wait before she discovered who was using this odious man as his agent in an attempt to master her?

And who in the world could possibly save what was left of her honor—and possibly her life—from being lost . . . ?

Amelia

SIGNET Regency Romances You'll Enjoy

Amelia

Megan Daniel

A SIGNET BOOK

NEW AMERICAN LIBRARY

TIMES MIRROR

PUBLISHER'S NOTE

This novel is a work of fiction. Names, characters, places,
and incidents are either the product of the author's
imagination or are used fictitiously, and any resemblance
to actual persons, living or dead, events, or locales
is entirely coincidental.

SIGNET TRADEMARK REG. U.S. PAT. OFF. AND FOREIGN COUNTRIES
REGISTERED TRADEMARK—MARCA REGISTRADA
HECHO EN CHICAGO, U.S.A.

SIGNET, SIGNET CLASSICS, MENTOR, PLUME, MERIDIAN AND NAL
BOOKS are published by The New American Library, Inc.,
1633 Broadway, New York, New York 10019

First Printing, November, 1980

1 2 3 4 5 6 7 8 9

PRINTED IN THE UNITED STATES OF AMERICA

To my parents, Milton and Imogene Meyer, with love

Chapter One

"That seems lovely, Mrs. Harbage," said Amelia, as she looked up from the menu that the housekeeper had proffered for her approval. "My aunt is exceedingly fond of buttered crabs, and my brother will be pleased by the Hessian soup."

The housekeeper beamed down at her young mistress. With a smile, the young lady added, "Perhaps we might add some fresh strawberries, though, with clotted cream? The gardener tells me they are particularly fine just now." Her green eyes twinkled.

The housekeeper, resplendent in the stiff black bombazine gown and snowy mobcap of her calling, ventured an indulgent smile. "And the berries, I fancy, are for Lady Kendall's pleasure, Miss, for I know well you've no taste for them yourself." A telltale quiver appeared at the corner of the housekeeper's mouth. The ample-bosomed Mrs. Harbage had been a part of the household at Standish since Amelia was in leading-strings, and she dared to tease gently now and then. Amy burst out laughing.

"You needn't try to cut a wheedle with me, Mrs. H," she chided. How many times have you had to wipe the cream from my chin?"

"Well, it was always a pleasure, Miss, I'm sure. Would you care to inspect the rooms for the guests now? We could discuss the flowers for the duchess's and her ladyship's chambers."

"I am nearly finished with this tedious job," Amy

1

answered. "Give me a few more minutes, and I shall be with you directly."

Lady Amelia Clerville was seated at a great oak desk in the library at Standish trying to finish up the household accounts. She picked up her pen once more as she heard the swish of the black skirts leaving the room and applied herself with resolution to the heavy ledger. But it was useless, and she shortly closed it again with a snap. Who could concentrate on anything so mundane as figures on such a glorious spring day?

She crossed to the French windows and flung them wide. The sunlight pouring in glinted on her brick-red hair, making it shine like the copper pots in Cook's spotless kitchen. From just beyond the hedge she could hear the swish-swish of a gardener scything the lawn. The breeze shifted, and she grew almost drunk on the sweet smell of the new-cut grass.

She turned back into the room and surveyed it lovingly. It had been her father's room. She fancied she could still smell the sweet tobacco of his ever-present pipe, mingling with the scents of lemon oil and beeswax and old leather. She ran her fingers lightly over the leather bindings of his favorite books, then picked up the miniature of her mother that still held the place of honor on his desk. A loud honking sound overhead carried her to the windows again. A large flock of geese was passing over in formation, the head of the arrow pointed north, and Amy smiled.

It was just the sort of day that Lord Standen used to love. On such a day he would throw his fowling piece over his shoulder, grab Amy by the hand, whistle for her brother Ned, and off the three of them would go into the nearby woods. They'd not return till they had a bagful of geese. Or perhaps they would go angling and bring back a long string of trout for dinner. Other days they'd ride off together across the fields at a hard gallop, Lord Standen teaching the two intrepid youngsters to throw their hearts over any obstacles encountered along the way and adjuring them not to rush their fences. She thought of his mirth, always bubbling just below the surface and frequently erupting into a great bellow. His good-natured laugh was often directed at her.

"Ho, puss! You are a sad hoyden indeed! I see I shall have the devil's own time gittin' rid of you—for what proper gentleman would be wantin' such a brat to wife?" he'd bellow. Then he'd pick her up and carry her into the kitchen for a sweet.

Her eye was caught by the multicolored flowers growing along the terrace edge. The primroses had been his favorite color. And she looked ruefully down at the plain grey cambric gown trimmed in black she was wearing. Its severity was relieved only by a deep-mauve sash and the small white ruffle at the throat. Her unruly curls were restrained by a broad purple ribbon. He would have hated this somber-hued Amelia, looking like "some damned schoolmarm."

He would have hated even more the fact that he was the cause of her drabness. Today the sun was warm and brilliant, but it had rained that day just a year ago when he had been killed. He, who had turned her into the finest horsewoman in the county, had been thrown from his favorite chestnut as he was taking a fence. His death had plunged Ned and Amelia into the conventional mourning he had hated.

She chafed at the restrictions it placed on her. A year with no hunting had left her itching for the yelping of the pack. She wanted to tear the odious grey dresses to shreds, and for weeks she had been looking at swatches of bright silks and pretty sprig muslins.

Amelia grieved deeply for her father. None but she and Ned could truly understand how deep the shock of their father's death went. He had been the warm life-giving sun around which they had revolved. But Amy had been born with a light heart and the gift of easy laughter. It was for these very

3

qualities that he had loved her so. That light had been dimmed by his sudden death. But now it had begun to glow warmly again, and Amy wanted to get on with the business of living once more.

Giving herself a mental shake, she returned to the house once again and went in search of Mrs. Harbage.

I must have windmills in my head to be standing about wool-gathering on such a day, she thought. Her Aunt Louisa, the Duchess of Harcourt, would be arriving this very afternoon, together with Cousin Elinor. Her aunt was truly a dear, and Amy wanted everything to be perfect for her visit.

In the great marble-paved hall she encountered Barrow, the toplofty butler, patrolling his domain. This very superior servant bowed wonderfully to Miss Clerville. He was at his officious best today, knowing that he soon would have a duchess and a countess in his care.

"Perhaps, Barrow, you would bring up a few bottles of my father's finest old madeira. You know how fond my aunt is of it," she said. "Though of course she'd not own it," she added with a twinkle.

"Of course, Miss. Perhaps some of the sherry too would not come amiss," he said. "When would you like the trunks brought up from the box room, Miss?"

"Oh, I think that can wait a day or so, Barrow. I don't expect we shall be leaving for a fortnight at least."

This intelligence seemed to please the stone-faced butler, and he very nearly ruined his reputation with the trace of a smile.

"I shall have Roberts see to it tomorrow then, Miss." And with a perfect bow, he marched silently from the room.

Amy began to think about packing her trunks as she climbed the great staircase. She was to accompany her aunt back to London to make her long-delayed come-out and was looking forward to it. She was just nineteen, and she thought herself passably pretty. She needed to laugh and go to parties and receive pretty compliments from Tulips of the Ton.

She was fully conscious of her good fortune in having the superbly connected Duchess of Harcourt as her sponsor. But really she looked forward to seeing that august lady because Aunt Louie was such a love, what Ned called a "great gun." Oh, she put on a great show of pomp and hauteur when it suited her. Some of her lesser acquaintances thought her as high-handed as a Turk. But Amelia knew better.

The Duchess had an insatiable curiosity about life and a wide-ranging zest for it that encompassed everyone she loved. As the youngest daughter of an earl married to the heir to a dukedom, it was widely said that she had done very well for herself indeed. But the old Duke always knew he'd got the best of the bargain when he married Louisa Clerville. Amy was very like her.

A rustle of stiff silk announced Mrs. Harbage just as she rounded the hall corner.

"I've put Her Grace in the Blue Room, Miss, as you requested."

"Yes, thank you, Mrs. H." Amy surveyed the lovely sunny room with its Austrian blue damask hangings on creamy walls. This had been her mother's room years ago. She could barely remember the beautiful Lady Standen, who had died when Amy was just four. Both of her children had inherited her blunt Dorset common sense and her clear, quick understanding. Amy had her mother's small oval face and large beautiful eyes like dark-green velvet.

Her death had been a severe blow to her doting husband. To salve his pain, Lord Standen had drawn his children ever closer to himself. He could not bear to be parted from them. For the period of some years when the Old King was pleased to send him on several diplomatic missions to the Continent, they had always accompanied him.

In consequence, Amy's education had been such

as many might call wholly unsuitable for a Young Lady of Quality. She spoke German with a decided Viennese lilt, liberally sprinkled with soldiers' cant and horse terms. Once, near Málaga, the incorrigible Clervilles had been discovered visiting a local gypsy camp, Amelia learning to dance the flamenco and play the castanets while Ned accompanied her on the guitar. When Miss Pennywhit, their nurse, had come running and hysterical to retrieve them, Amy flew into a pelter and called her terrible names, in Spanish. Poor old Penny had been puzzled but relieved when the gypsies burst out laughing.

Her French was unexceptionable, having been learned in the finest salons of Geneva, in which city she also developed a quite unladylike taste for rum punch. Her father would never let anyone but Amy mix it for him, so perfect was her receipe.

Even after their return to Standish, their estate in Somerset, she continued the despair of Miss Pennywhit and her numerous governesses, none of whom lasted long. She was lively as a grig and always ready for a lark.

When it was time for her lesson in watercolor painting, she would be out swimming in the pond with Ned and Tom Norreys, Lord Waverly's son, or wandering barefoot through the berry patch with her good friend Katie Sheldon. Instead of sitting sedately at the pianoforte, practicing her fingering, she would run off to the stable to curry her mare or to argue the points of a new bay with the head groom.

She and Ned and Tom and Katie became inseparable, and the four children could often be found racing their horses in the meadow or climbing trees. Amy's curls seemed always to be flying about her face, having escaped from their ribbon. Her frock was usually sadly covered with grass stains, and she lost several pairs of shoes a year.

". . . lilacs, perhaps, mixed with a few of the

primroses and some myrtle leaves." The housekeeper's voice brought Amy back to the present.

"And you always arrange them so beautifully, Mrs. H. I know I can rely on your choice," said Amy.

"And as Lady Kendall is to have the Rose Room, I think perhaps some of those nice ruby roses would be pretty," said the housekeeper as they turned into a lovely room done in deep pink and dove gray. Amy smiled again. This is where Katie had always stayed when they could contrive to get Miss Pennywhit to allow her to spend the night.

Amy thought fondly of Katie and Tom. She had known for years they were in love, perhaps even before they had known it themselves. So it had been with a happy heart that she had attended their wedding last year. They were now become Lord and Lady Waverly, and their estate marched with Standish, so the four childhood friends saw nearly as much of each other as ever. But new responsibilities now sometimes intruded. The terrible foursome had grown up, and many things had changed.

With the death of their father, Ned—Edward, Lord Clerville—had become the eighth Earl of Standen. At only twenty-three, the new Lord Standen was a popular and responsible landlord, manager, and friend. His estate, with considerably help from his sister, ran like one of his fine Swiss clocks. In their early travels, it was always Amy who had asked eager questions about local crops, rotation planting, and exotic livestock strains. Now when a new crop was planted, or an animal bred, it was usually on her advice.

Together the brother and sister were an effective team. They adored and complemented one another, and under their joint management the income from Standish had increased dramatically in the last year, even though Ned had been often away from home.

More and more of the daily management of the estate had lately fallen to Amy, as Ned's absences became more frequent. He would leave two or three times a month now, sometimes for several days. Amy was vaguely worried by these trips and more than a bit hurt that he would never tell her where he was going. He would merely say that he had some business to conduct. He had never shut her out before, but he would close up like an oyster if she ventured further questions.

She supposed the mystery had to do with a woman somewhere.

"What an odious thought!" she mused. Ned was of an age to marry, of course, but she found the idea troublesome. She had had him to herself for so long, and they were so close. She was aware of her irritation at the notion, and it galled her even more. It was so lowering to have to admit to a fault, which this jealousy of Ned certainly was.

Of course she knew that Ned must marry someday. Standish must have an heir, and she truly wanted him to be happy. It had never occurred to her that she might want to marry herself someday. She was quite certain she never would. Her life had been blessed with two extraordinary men. She was convinced that there could never be another to compare to the Standens, father and son, and she could never settle for less. But such deep and dour thoughts were not for today. She put them from her mind.

"Well it seems everything is perfect and in good time, Mrs. H, as always," she said to the housekeeper, who glowed proudly. "I think I shall just go and see to the strawberries myself, shall I?" She grinned and ran lightly down the stairs and out the door.

The dappled sun shone through leaves fresh as clean linen. She could hear a robin from its nest up in the eaves of the house. A gentle breeze mussed her hair and made her laugh.

She soon found herself in the berry patch. She kicked off her gray kid slippers and buried her feet in

8

the cool, moist earth. It pushed up between her toes, and she wriggled them in delight.

She picked a large ripe fruit and bit into it with a grin. The red juice dribbled down her chin. Amy was inordinately fond of strawberries, so she picked a large amount of the very best fruit and carried it off in the front of her skirt.

I hope I get berry stains all over this hateful gray dress, she thought with a little giggle as she headed toward the kitchens with her stash.

From the path she had a clear view of the lane approaching the house. She looked up now to see a small cloud of dust coming toward her. Her heart lifted with pleasure at the anticipated arrival of her aunt, but she soon saw that this was a solitary rider. She shaded her eyes from the burning sun, and her face lit with a smile of recognition.

Atop a very large and very old nag of a horse perched a very small boy. Amy waved and ran lightly out to greet him. She was still without her shoes, and the cool velvety grass tickled her toes. The little stable boy from the Golden Boar in Winsham waved back. He tried unsuccessfully to spur the nag into a brisker pace, finally sliding off the giant's back and dragging it behind him down the road.

"C'mon, Lightnin'! Move yerself! Cain't ye see Lady Amy awaitin' fer us?"

"Hullo, Charley," cried Amy. "I didn't think to see you out here today. How is your mother feeeling?

The small boy cocked his head as if he were trying to remember just how his mother had been when last he saw her. He was a clever lad and a great favorite with Amy, who was teaching him to read.

"She says as how yer not to be worritin' yerself over her, Lady Amy," he said with a proud smile as he remembered his mother's words. "That pork jelly as you had Cook send her has done a powerful lot o'good. She'll soon be right as a trivet, or so she says." Pleased with his recitation, he beamed up at his friend.

He was not more than seven years old, with hair the color of sunshine and a smile that threatened to burst out of the confines of his tiny young face. He grabbed hold of Amy's hand and skipped around the lawn with her, sending her berries scurrying in all directions. Lightning laconically bent his head after one of them and nibbled at it lazily.

Charley laughed and sang snippets of song to Amy, oblivious of the fact that she was a fine lady and he was only a stable boy and the son of one of her tenants. He knew only that she was his friend.

"When I comes fer my lesson tomorrow, think you that Master Ned'll let me ride Pegasus?" The tone of adulation in the boy's voice when he spoke of Lord Standen was obvious.

"If he has returned by tomorrow, I'm sure he'll take you up with him for a short ride." The boy squealed in delight and did a somersault in the grass. "But what's made you bring poor old Lightning all the way out here today?"

"That lazy ole horse!" Clearly Charley thought it a great insult to so much as mention Lightning and the great Pegasus in the same breath.

"I swear I do think him dead, Lady Amy. I coulda run here faster myself!"

"I'll wager you could, Charley." She laughed. "But what brings you? Your reading lesson isn't till tomorrow."

"Oh, I'd not mistake that, Lady Amy, no ma'am. I brung you a letter, I did." He reached inside his too small jacket and tugged out a large and slightly crumpled letter. Amy instinctively noted the fine hot-pressed paper and the elegant masculine hand in which it was inscribed.

"Well then, since you are here, let's see how well you can do with this address." She held the letter down to him. He peered at it for a long moment, his face scrunched up in concentration.

"T-to Lady Amelia Clerville," he faltered, then

10

plunged on. "Standish, near Winsham, S-S-Somerset!" he finished proudly.

"Wonderful, Charley. Now try the back." He turned over the letter and studied it again.

"Hmmmmm. Wishbone Cottage?" he sounded out the words. "Silver Lane, Lyme Regis." He beamed up at Amy, so proud of his accomplishment that he didn't notice that the color had quite drained from her face.

"You shoulda seed the gentry cove what give it to me to deliver. Mortal fine, he were. He were up on the nattiest black stallion I ever seed, and he give me sixpence, he did."

But Amy was no longer listening. She had recognized the address on the back of the letter. She pulled it from Charley's hands, and tearing open the wafer that sealed it, she quickly read the contents.

At that moment, Amelia Clerville, who had never fainted in her life, sank to the ground.

Chapter Two

An elegant black traveling chaise decked out with brass fittings lumbered haltingly into the yard of the Golden Boar. The sun glinted off the important-looking crest picked out in gilt on its sides. It rattled noisily over the cobbles, sending a chicken squawking, and settled in front of the inn. It was impressively flanked by outriders, who, in company with the footmen and postillions, wore the classic amethyst-and-silver livery of Her Grace the Dowager Duchess of Harcourt. The whole assemblage presented a suitably awesome sight.

A tall young footman, looking impossibly cool and elegant in his powdered wig, and obviously hired for his fine physique, jumped down and appeared at the window of the carriage.

"Well, what is it, Thomas?" came a full-throated demand from a rather imperious lady in the depths of the carriage. "Why have we stopped when we are so nearly there?"

"Begging your pardon, Your Grace, but one of the wheelers has thrown a shoe. It shouldn't take above half an hour to fix him up. Would Your Grace care to wait inside?"

"Oh, botheration!" the lady exclaimed. "Well, I suppose we had as well go in. Come, Elinor."

The well-oiled door swung open silently; the steps were let down with only the slightest of thuds. The imposing lady descended grandly and swept into the inn, leaving the faintest scent of oil of roses in her wake.

She was a fine-looking widow of some sixty years in an elegant traveling costume of amethyst *gros de Naples* with the palest of pale-grey trimmings, and she had never lost her exquisite beauty. Her hair was pure white and abundant. It crowned her face like spun sugar. Despite her age and rank she refused to hide its magnificence under a cap or one of the unfortunate turbans that were so popular with her matron friends. The face was not unlined, but such signs of age as lived there were immediately lost when one looked into her incredible amber eyes.

She was followed into the inn by a younger version of herself, a no less stylishly dressed woman of seven-and-twenty in a dress of sea-green Berlin silk and a fawn velvet spencer. She had guinea-gold hair under a modish bergère hat trimmed with roses, and the same remarkably large and warm amber eyes as her mother.

A large red-faced landlord puffed forward to greet his august guests.

"Such an honor to see you again, Your Grace," he said, bowing and dipping, then wheezing and bowing again. "How may I serve you?"

"How do you do, Mr. Jenkins," she condescended to say. "Our tiresome animal has thrown a shoe. I shall require your best private parlor for my daughter and myself while he is being tended. I think the West Room will do nicely."

His flushed face grew even redder. His features contorted into a look of utter despair. "Oh dear. I am so humbly sorry, Your Grace, but the West Room is bespoke by my Lord Tyrone. I have another lovely room just down the—"

"Tyrone!" exclaimed the Duchess. "Why, whatever is Justin doing in Somerset? The West Room will do nicely, Jenkins. You may bring us some refreshments there. You need not announce us."

No one had ever learned the art of making an entrance quite as thoroughly as had the Duchess of Harcourt. She paused in the doorway, letting it frame her as she surveyed the room. It was a very comfortable parlor in an old and comfortable inn. Sunshine sparkled through the mullioned windows, lightening the well-beamed and paneled atmosphere. Her eyes landed on the gentleman lounging there, a brown study in a chintz-covered wing chair before the unlit fire.

Justin Robert Nigel Savile, the Most Noble the Marquis of Tyrone, was a decidedly elegant man of two-and-thirty with the kind of romantic good looks popularized by the infamous Lord Byron. He had a shock of black hair that fell naturally into the fashionable Brutus style. He was dressed with casual polish in a perfectly fitted coat of russet wool over buckskin riding breeches and shining top boots. He had been staring somewhat dejectedly into the empty grate, but as he looked up his face lit with pleasure. The Duchess flowed forward to greet him, one hand upraised gracefully for him to salute.

"So, Justin. Rusticating again, I see. Can we never keep you in London for longer than a fortnight at a time?"

He rose gracefully and flashed her an easy smile. He had never bothered to cultivate the currently fashionable air of boredom, and he now crossed to her with barely suppressed energy.

"Your Grace." He bowed beautifully over the gloved hand and kissed it lightly. "When you are gone from town it becomes an unutterable bore. I could not bear to stay."

"Gammon!" she exclaimed with a rather pleased smile. "Pitching it much too brown, my lord. You shouldn't try to best me, Justin, when we both know perfectly well that you can. I believe you know my daughter, Lady Kendall."

The smooth smile was turned to the younger woman.

"Everyone who is pleased to count himself a member of the ton knows the charming Lady Kendall," he answered. "I'm surprised the Earl trusts you out of his sight, so beautiful as you are looking, my lady."

The amber eyes glowed laughingly. "I fear you are an adept at offering Spanish coin, my lord. I shall not listen to you," she protested. "But are you visiting in the neighborhood? I collect your own estates lie in Kent."

After a barely noticeable hesitation he answered, "I have some business to conduct nearby. What do you here, Your Grace?"

"I've come down to fetch my niece from Standish. I'm taking her back to London with me for the Season. I was to have presented her last year, you know, but the death of her father forced a postponement," the Duchess explained. "But do you not know her brother, my nephew Edward, Lord Standen?"

Lord Tyrone stiffened perceptibly, and the smile faded.

"I believe we have chanced to meet on one or two occasions, in town." His words seemed to come with an effort, and a look of sadness had stolen into his blue eyes.

"I quite look forward to the rigors of presenting a young lady again," said the Duchess. "I think the child will do well. Particularly if you will deign to dance with her once or twice, Justin."

Lord Tyrone was seldom at a loss for words, but he now remained silent for some moments. Finally he spoke. "With pleasure, Your Grace," was all he replied. He looked as if he would say more but thought better of it.

Just then a waiter entering the room caused them to be diverted by the lovely smell of fresh-baked queen cakes and the splashing into glasses of cool red wine. The conversation turned into other channels, and quite soon it was time for the ladies to reenter their carriage.

Lord Tyrone saw them to it, then mounted his own magnificent Welsh black stallion, his horse's hooves beating a tattoo on the stones. Tipping the brim of his curly beaver to them, he rode away.

"Quite a figure, is he not, Mama?" said Lady Kendall with a sigh. She seated herself comfortably back onto the velvet squabs and arranged her silk skirts expertly around her. The chaise resumed the gentle swaying motion that meant they were once again under way. "It must be at least six years since Lady Tyrone died. I wonder that he has never married again."

"And never shall, or I miss my bet," answered the Duchess. "Though of course every matchmaking mama in London has been on the catch for him. He was badly burnt, I fear, by that odious Angela Willoughby he married. Oh, it was loudly touted as a love match," she exclaimed with a show of indignation. "She was always making cow's eyes at him, and it was painfully obvious that he was head over ears in love with her as well. But she soon enough began to show her true colors. Once she knew the knot was quite securely tied, she lost no time in letting poor Justin know that she found his fortune far more attractive than himself."

"Yes, I had heard as much. But she did give him an heir."

"And promptly ran off with the groom, my dear! Justin only just managed to get her back in time to avoid an open scandal. He shut the matter up by buying her silence and a promise of future discretion. I suppose it's really a mercy she died of a fever shortly thereafter," she mused. "No, I don't think we should look to see my Lord Tyrone get caught again in parson's mousetrap."

"Once burnt, twice shy?"

"Exactly. I'm afraid that boy is quite bitter about our sex. Dotes on his son, of course. And he has his ladybirds, I imagine. Just now he's dancing attendance on Lady Cole. He's smooth, well polished, quite an acceptable veneer for the sake of society. But he'll not be caught again."

"A pity. A more eligible *parti* you'd be hard put to find," replied Elinor.

"Oh, my dear. If you could have seen him before that disastrous marriage. I've known him since he was in short coats. So ingenuous, full of fun. Always that lively sparkle in his eyes," she said. "My heart quite grieves for the boy."

Her Grace was looking out over the familiar countryside, the green myrtle and the cowslip blooming prettily along the roadside, the quiet woods and delightfully unquiet waters that were southern Somerset.

"Oh look, Mama, we are here."

The carriage turned easily through the lodge gates of Standish. It crunched over the gravel and headed proudly up the long drive. The house was bathed in the light of early afternoon, the pink brick glowing rosily in the sun. Heavy cables of wisteria climbed the beautiful Tudor facade, dripping heavy purple blossoms over the leaded windows.

The Duchess smiled fondly on the home of her childhood. The beautiful plane trees shading it gently on the south were unchanged since her youth. She had always liked them best like this, dressed in the fresh green of early spring.

They alighted from the carriage, and she breathed deeply of the sweet country air. It seemed very quiet, and she could hear the murmur and splash of the stream behind the house as it played over the pebbles and rippled off to meet the River Axe downstream.

She wondered vaguely why Barrow had not come out to greet them, nor anyone else for that matter. As she stepped up to the small porch, a young chambermaid appeared at the door. She bobbed a curtsy and turned a pair of large and crying eyes to the two ladies.

"Oh, Your Grace," she finally managed to stammer out. "It's terrible news."

Vague sounds began to swim above Amelia's head and seep into her mind, the sound of familiar voices, reassuring and comfortable. She felt the cool silk brocade of the parlor settee on which she was lying. The burnt feathers that were being held under her nose made her cough, and she regained full consciousness with a start. A rough old hand was chafing her wrist.

"There now, my little love, it's all right now. Your Penny's here by you, Missy. Penny's here," Miss Pennywhit cooed softly, murmuring meaningless sounds of comfort. The well-loved old voice brought remembrance. A great ache began to spread outward from the region of Amy's heart and made her whole body shudder as with a sob.

She turned her head to see the stricken face of her Aunt Louisa, sitting stunned in a chair nearby and holding the letter. Amy tried to smile. She held out her hand for the letter. Lady Kendall took it from her mother and gently gave it to Amy. She read again:

My dear Miss Clerville,

It is with great sadness and regret that I must inform you of the death of your brother, Lord Standen. He was thrown from his horse on the road near Lyme Regis. I can assure you that his death was quite quick and painless.

His valet, Mr. Parker, was also somewhat injured and is recovering at Wishbone Cottage, the home of the local surgeon. You need have no fear for him and can expect to see him at home again in about a fortnight's time.

For reasons I hope I can someday express to you,

I prefer to remain nameless at this time, but I am,
I assure you,

> Your most obedient servant,
> A friend

Amy read the letter through several times. Penny
was watching her carefully, but she now seemed quite
restored. Lady Kendall sat down beside her and quietly took her hand.

"Oh, Nell," said Amy in a voice of unspeakable
sadness.

"Shall I send for Dr. Chambers, my love?"

Amy looked up vaguely. "What?" Her expression changed subtly, and she flushed even more.
"No, no. I beg you will not, Elinor. I am perfectly all
right now." Her eyes began to glisten, and she started
to chatter, her voice gradually rising in pitch.

"So silly of me to have fainted like that. I cannot
conceive what came over me. One would have
thought I was a Bath miss. You know I cannot abide
those insipid, missish airs. Why you, Aunt Louisa,
must think me a silly widgeon indeed. There is absolutely no reason to—"

"Amelia!" said the Duchess in a voice forceful
enough to stop the flow of chatter that was fast becoming hysterical.

Lady Kendall reached for a glass, and Amy felt
the fiery brandy slide down her throat. In a kindlier
voice, her aunt said, "You are to go to your room
now, Amelia, and have a rest. Nurse will give you a
few drops of laudanum to help you sleep."

She nodded to Miss Pennywhit, who was helping
Amy to her feet.

"Come along now, Missy. There's a good girl.
We'll just have a little nap now, shall we, love? You
just come along with Penny now, Missy." Amy allowed herself to be led from the room.

"Oh dear," said the Duchess as she sank into her

chair once again. "How much more will that poor child be called upon to bear?"

"I'm so glad we are here, Mama. She will need our help and support."

"My great fear is that she will not allow it. You know what she is, Nell. The deeper the hurt, the less she will allow it to show. She is so terribly proud. If only she would cry, but I fear she will not. Do you know, she never shed a tear for her father, not once. They are still all locked up inside her."

"Perhaps she will now, Mama, when no one is around. But I'm afraid I need to cry right now, Mama."

"Oh, so do I, my love, so do I." She held out her arms to her daughter. The servants faded from the room, leaving the two ladies to help each other as best they could.

Chapter Three

Amy did not cry that night. When the laudanum had at last worn off she lay in the dark, dry-eyed and aching, conscious of nothing save the pain of her loss.

"Oh, Neddie!" she moaned to herself, as she remembered her handsome brother and his always laughing voice. "Why you? I try to understand, but I don't."

As soon as the sky began to lighten perceptibly, she was out of her bed and prowling restlessly about the great house. Her reaction to tragedy and grief had ever been a need for action. She paced the rooms like one of the wild cats in the menagerie at the Royal Enclosure. She tried to sit but was soon on her feet again. She wandered into the drawing room. At length she picked up the fatal letter and reread it as she paced. Now she began to analyze it, it struck her as distinctly odd.

Who had written this strange letter, and what had he to do with Ned? If her brother had been thrown from his horse, how came his valet to be injured as well? These questions began to gnaw at Amy's mind. She would have been glad of an opinion from her aunt, but the Duchess was not yet up. Only Miss Pennywhit was hovering about; hearing Amy awaken, she had risen from the truckle bed she had set up in Amy's dressing room. She kept silent but was watching nervously for any signs of a return of the hysteria of the previous afternoon.

But Amy was not hysterical. She was curious.

And when that happened she would not rest until she had her answers.

The nether regions of the household had been slowly coming to life, and Amy descended to the butler's pantry just as Barrow was shrugging himself into his morning coat. Nurse was hard on her heels, the skirts of an ancient dressing gown flapping after her.

"Barrow," Amy snapped, and the hapless butler turned around with a decided start. "Have John saddle Medusa and bring her around in fifteen minutes. I am riding to Lyme Regis."

Penny began to cluck, "Oh, my pet! Are you quite yourself?" But Amy had disappeared back up the stairs. The old nurse shook her wispy gray head. "Oh, I do hope Missy isn't taking one of her queer notions. She's had a bad shock, and what must she do but go haring off across the countryside before she's even had her breakfast."

A look of resignation came into the old face. "But there, I never could stop that one doing anything once she'd set her mind to it."

"I could send John to accompany her," suggested the sensible Barrow, with a note of real concern in his voice.

"Aye, and if I read her mood aright, he'd not keep up with her past the first stile." She nodded sagely, and there was wisdom as well as sadness behind the watery old eyes. "Grief does funny things," she said. "The child must cope in her own way. We cannot do it for her," and she turned back toward the stairs.

"I fear her Grace will be most displeased," Barrow lamented.

"Aye," said Miss Pennywhit, but after a pause she added, "But perhaps not. She knows the child near as well as I do."

A very short while later found Amy riding wildly across the green countryside. She sat anchored to Medusa's back while the beautiful mare flew over the rolling hills at a full gallop. Her hooves pounded on the earth and clattered on the stones of the low pack-horse bridges. Amy had thrown off her hat, and the freshening breeze lashed at her hair and caused the skirts of her black wool habit to billow about her. She turned toward the south and the blue cliffs of Lyme Regis.

And finally the tears came. First they trickled, then streamed down her cheeks in rivulets. The wind whipped them back onto her hair. She was crying for her mother, for Ned, for her father, but most of all for herself. She had never felt so alone in all her life.

Giant sobs wracked her body and threatened her horsemanship. She pulled Medusa up under a giant oak and buried her face in the animal's soft mane until her sorrow spent its fury.

She wasn't sure how long she had stayed there, drawing comfort from the warmth of the animal and the release of her sorrow, but when she rose at last and resumed her journey, she felt surprisingly calm and at peace. She rode more sedately now, and a half hour later she saw that she was approaching her goal. She could see the great yellow hill of the Golden Cap standing guard over the little harbor town. The morning sun polished the ancient Cobb to a high gloss and shimmered on the turquoise water of the bay. Amy loved the sea and stayed a moment to drink in the lovely scene. Then, almost reluctantly, she spurred Medusa on, down the hill and into the town.

Some moments later she stood confronting the brass knocker of Wishbone Cottage. She quickly pulled a black ribbon from her pocket and tried to bring her unruly locks into some order. She gave her eyes a last dab with a damp handkerchief, and with a deep breath of resolution, she lifted the knocker.

The oak door slid open to reveal a tiny house-keeper disappearing under the huge cloud of a white mobcap. A pair of brilliantly blue eyes glistened in an antique face, illuminated by a welcoming smile.

"Yes, Miss. Good day to you, Miss. And what is it I can do for you?" came a squeak.

"Good morning. I am Miss Clerville. Is the doctor in?"

"Oh, it's that sorry I am, Miss, but he be gone over to Bradpole. It Miz Collins's baby, ye see. I do 'spect him back in the mornin', Miss."

"Oh dear," muttered Amy. "Have you a Mr. Parker here in your care?"

The old face cracked with pleasure. "Oh, aye, Miss. That we do. Such a nice young man. Now, he was in a proper state when they brought him here! That were a nasty bullet hole, all right. And his leg broke right through, an' all. But you're not to worry 'bout him now, Miss. Not at all. He'll do just fine, that one will. A right fine, strong gentleman. The fever's gone now, an' the doctor wouldn'ta gone off unless he were in a fair way to bein' hisself again, I promise you, Miss."

Amid this stream of chatter the old lady had not noticed Amy's strange reaction to her words.

"May I see him, please?"

"Well, I don't know, Miss, the doctor bein' away an' all." She gave Amy a measuring glance. Even though the young lady was unaccompanied by so much as a groom, and her hair was blown all anyhow, the old lady knew Quality when she saw it, and a longstanding habit of catering to its whims was not easily overcome.

"Still an' all, Miss, he didn't say as how the poor young man was to have no visitors. Seems to me a pretty thing like you is just what's needed to brighten up his day. He's been a bit in the dumps, you see." She paused once more, then seemed to come to a decision. "You just come right along with me, Miss. Cheer him up proper, you will."

The miniature housekeeper flitted up the stairs like a hummingbird. Amy, her mind in a ferment, followed.

"Only look who I've brought you, Mr. Parker, to cheer you up." The patient lay propped up in bed in a light and airy chamber, his left arm and shoulder heavily bandaged and one leg raised under the covers.

"Lady Amy!" he groaned when he saw her. He quickly pulled at the blankets to cover his bare chest.

Amy tried to be gentle. "I knew Ned would want me to look after you, Parker. How are you feeling?"

"Oh, I'll be fine, Miss. I've seen worse than this before." He tried to sit up, but the housekeeper bustled over to him. Peeping out from under her cap with a stern look, she said, "Now, Mr. P, you're not to overdo, just because you have a pretty young visitor. You lay right back now, there's a good boy. What'll the doctor say if you start to bleedin' again? Sit you down, Miss, and I'll bring you a nice cup o' tea."

When the old woman was gone, Amy sat firmly in a chair by the bed.

"Now, Parker," she said with resolution, "I wish you will explain to me exactly what has happened."

"I thought they'd written to you, Miss, to explain. About the accident and all."

"We both know, Parker, that my brother was one of the finest horsemen in the country. I find it hard to believe this tale of his being thrown from a horse that he had himself trained from a colt, especially a tale coming from such a strangely anonymous source."

"Nevertheless, Miss, I can promise you—"

"Parker! One does not get a bullet wound in one's shoulder from a riding accident."

"Damn that woman!" he exclaimed, then added with a blush, "Begging your pardon, Miss, but I'd hoped that housekeeper could keep her mouth shut."

"Luckily she has not. Now I am waiting for the full story, Parker."

"We all hoped as how you'd be put off by the

letter, Miss, but Master Ned, he woulda known better. He always thought you'd be like to come around asking awkward questions after him." The valet hesitated again, but one look at the determined expression on her face made him continue.

"You always were the stubbornest girl I ever saw!" he muttered with the freedom of a longtime family servant. "I suppose you'd better have his letter, then. He wrote it a while back. Said I was to give it to you if anything happened to him, and I thought it was really necessary." He paused, eyeing her gloomily. "It don't seem you'll go away without it."

"I most certainly will not!"

He pointed to his somewhat ragged-looking coat on a nearby chair.

"If you'll look inside the lining on the lefthand side, you'll find it,"

Amy found the spot and pulled out a few loose stitches at the bottom of the lining. From this hiding spot she pulled a large and crumpled letter. She winced at the sight of the familiar script. Opening the pages gently, she slowly smoothed them out and read.

My Beloved and Too Clever Sister,

If you are reading this it means that you've been up to your usual tricks. You are too clever by half, sister dear, and I was sure you'd not fall for whatever story they've cooked up to account for my untimely demise. You would have ferreted out the truth by hook or by stile, and in so doing you might have endangered the lives of some very special people and hurt our chances of beating Bonaparte in this damned war

Ah yes, the war. But what has that to do with me, say you? I'm not a soldier, it's true. But you know that had our father lived I would have been. You know well how I've been itching to join against the French and help send Boney to the rightabout. But my first obligations were to you and to Standish. At last I have had the chance to do my part.

I'm sure you have wondered about my absences from home of late. I knew you were hurt when I could not explain them to you. I found the secrecy between us as intolerable as you did, but it was necessary. You see, I have been slipping quietly into France to gather information there, information that has helped our armies now fighting in the Peninsula.

My knowledge of the Continent and my fluent French, together with our proximity to the discreet little harbor at Lyme Regis, rendered me a perfect candidate for this job. I have been overjoyed to do it. It has been important work, and if it has cost me my life, well, then I have neither lived nor died in vain, and that is the truth, most beloved sister.

I have been privileged to meet some of the finest men this country is fortunate enough to count as her citizens. They will carry on the job, and if you ever have the opportunity of aiding them, it will be the greatest honor you could pay to my memory. But they must not be jeopardized in any way by further inquiries from you at this present.

So I am asking for your continued silence and at least a semblance of belief in the concocted details of my death.

I do realize the enormity of such a request to the likes of Amelia Clerville! Whether you call it curiosity, a thirst for knowledge, or a meddlesome nature, I know the direction of your mind! I beg your forbearance and can only promise that when Europe is at last rid of the little Frenchman, you'll have the whole story of my activities. I ask your promise now to restrain your lively mind on this head until that time.

I have one other last request to make of you. I believe you have never refused me anything it was in your power to give, and I beg you will attend me this one last time. I wish you will not mourn overmuch for me. You have had too much sadness in your life already. You have been robbed of too much of your youth. I will have no more of it! I wish that you will go to London with Aunt Louie just as we planned. Enjoy the balls and the parties, the pretty clothes and the rides in the park. I will know, and I will be happy. And if you should meet a man that you can love, then go to him, Amy. Just name the first boy after me!

I would also have you know that you need not marry for any reason other than to follow the dictates of your heart. Of course my title must go to Cousin Jasper, along with the estates in the north, but Standish is not part of the entail, and I have arranged that it will be yours. My solicitors can give you the details of the trusteeship, but I have made it clear that Standish is to be managed as you see fit. You always were better at running the place than I was. Made me look a regular quiz by comparison!

Now, dry your tears, little one, and convince poor Parker of your utmost discretion. I'm sure he's all in a stew. I have no fear. I have trusted you with my secret as I would have trusted you with my life.

Adieu, most loved of sisters. Our parents and I shall be watching you with all the love in our hearts.

Your most loving brother,
Ned

Parker had been watching her face. He had noticed the ravages made by the morning's tears and was happy to see her smile several times as she read. She went through the letter twice, folded it carefully, and laid it tenderly in her lap.

"I promise," she whispered. "I promise, Neddie."

After a moment she looked up. "How did it happen?" she asked softly.

"Well, Miss, I'm not sure I understand it all myself. Our ship left Lyme Regis and headed for the usual spot. There's a little inlet on the French coast, just south of Cotentin. Master Ned had made some good contacts there, and we were expecting to pick up something important. The ship anchored a ways off shore, and we rowed in on the tide.

"We got to the shore and there they were, Miss. It was like the Frenchies were waitin' for us. They opened up with pistols, and Master Ned was hit almost at once. I just managed to get him back into the boat and push off when they got me with a couple as well."

He paused, and a look of sadness and pain stole into his face. "I didn't yet know as how he was dead, Miss. All I could think of was bringing him away from there. I wish it'd been me, Miss. Oh, I do indeed!"

Amy reached out instinctively for his hand, and he continued.

"They followed us into the water, but I was rowing for all I was worth, and we left them behind. I got Master Ned to the ship and brought him home. That's all, Miss."

"It was very brave of you, Parker, rowing all that way with a bullet in your shoulder," she said gently. "I'm sure you did everything you could, and Ned would be very proud." After a moment she added, "You say they were waiting for you?"

"That's the truth of it, Miss. I'm much afraid that they've got one of their own fellows well rooted hereabouts, and not one of us suspecting him. Someone has to have given us away to them. The devil of it is my being laid up here. I can do nothing!" he exclaimed in frustration.

"Well, you'll not worry about that now. You'll do just as the doctor and that wonderful old woman downstairs tell you. When you are stronger we shall figure it out between us."

The valet was not comforted by these words. That well-known look of obstinacy was stealing into Amelia's face. He knew she'd not rest until she'd run her spy to ground.

"You'll do nothing foolish, will you, Miss?"

"I have promised Ned that I will not, Parker. I shall merely keep my eyes and ears open and see what I can learn." Parker knew he would have to be satisfied with that. To herself she added a promise that

29

whoever was responsible for the death of her brother would not go unpunished.

"I brought these away for you, Miss," said the valet, retrieving a small leather pouch from the drawer of a burlwood night table. She recognized it at once as a coin purse of Ned's. She emptied the contents onto her lap. His gold repeater, still faithfully ticking, a pair of seals with the Standen crest, and his garnet signet ring. The last had been a gift from their father only last year, no more than a month before his own death. She stared into its wine-red depths. It seemed to glow with a life of its own, while Neddie now had none. Suddenly she could not bear to look at it.

"Here, Parker," she said, holding the ring out to him. "I think Ned would want you to keep this." The valet took it uncertainly. She reassured him, saying, "We shall let it be a token of my pledge to help in any way I can." She let a small sigh escape, and a melancholy smile. "Even if I can best help by doing nothing."

"I thank you, Miss, as I'm sure his lordship and all Master Ned's mates would too, if they could."

"I want you to know too, Parker, that you will have a place at Standish as long as you wish. And now I think you must rest."

He had become conscious of the pain in his leg, and he closed his eyes for a moment. When he opened them again, Amelia was gone.

Chapter Four

Grief and rain arrived together at Standish. The morning was drab and drizzly as Amy sat brooding in the pretty little breakfast room. The frivolous bamboo furnishings and the bright flowers climbing up Chinese yellow wallpaper could not offset the heaviness of the leaden sky or of Amy's mood.

The weather had turned decidedly nasty in the week since her visit of discovery to Lyme Regis. Sooty clouds running before the wind crossed the sky, depressing the malachite countryside as they depressed Amy's usually buoyant spirits. The heavy masses emptied themselves on the earth until she felt that the very sky was crying with her.

When their fury had been nearly spent, they made one last violent attempt at destruction, throwing down hailstones as big as marbles, knocking the blossoms from the trees and pummeling the newly sprouted crops into the earth. Now the storm had settled into a boring and persistent drizzle.

Amy was in truth thankful for the unsettled weather, since it made impossible the many visits of condolence that she had, with great dread, expected to receive. She had, of course, seen Katie and Tom, and one or two others, but she couldn't bear the thought of having to share her very private grief with so many other people in so public a manner. The funeral had been a terrible ordeal for her. She found herself irritated by the well-meaning sympathy of people who she was sure could never truly understand her pain.

Her aunt and Elinor did understand, and they gladly relieved her of the burden of answering the stacks of mail that were unceremoniously dumped on the doorstep each day. Amy threw herself into the work of the estate, spending whole mornings closeted with her bailiff.

Whenever the sun peaked through for a few hours she was on her horse, riding out to inspect the storm damage and visiting her tenants, giving reading lessons to the children or working with the beautiful new colt that she and Ned had just purchased.

This morning she sat glumly over her breakfast, watching the clouds melting onto the lush green countryside beyond the bay window and thinking how glad she would be to take herself off to London, where every prospect would not remind her of the brother she had lost.

She was drawn from her reverie by the entrance of her cousin, and her face brightened considerably. Elinor's face, however, showed a definite grimace as she stared horrified at Amy's breakfast plate heaped with grilled bacon, kippers, eggs, tomatoes, and toast, accompanied by a large cup of steaming coffee. Amelia's appetite was certainly not depressed. Elinor turned quickly away and asked a servant to bring her some dry toast and a cup of tea.

"Are you all right, Nell? You look quite pale," asked Amy with concern.

"I am perhaps not quite myself just at the moment, but I shall be fine directly. It passes quite quickly, you know," she said, an enigmatic smile stealing into her amber eyes.

Amy looked at her oddly a moment, and noticing her very pretty morning dress of worked French muslin in a delicate shade of straw, she exclaimed, "What a very becoming gown, Nell. I don't believe I've seen it before. Is it quite new?'

Elinor grinned a little sheepishly. "Why, thank you. Yes, it is new. You see, I find that all of my other gowns have become a trifle tight of late." Her tone was light as she seated herself and began to pour out her tea from a delicately flowered pot.

After a short moment, Amy's eyes grew wide with understanding, and a broad smile replaced her former dejected look. "Nell! You don't mean . . . ?"

"Yes, love. At long last I do mean that Kendall may soon have an heir."

Amy jumped up and ran around the table to hug her cousin. "Oh, Nell. I am so pleased! When will it happen? Why did you not tell me sooner? It will be a boy. I know it will!"

Elinor laughed her pretty laugh and begged Amy to sit down again. "It did not seem just the time to tell you when we first arrived," she said gently, "but I did want to let you know as soon as I felt I could do so. We would love to have you stand as godmother, Amelia, if you've no objection."

"Oh Nell, I should be so very pleased," she answered sincerely in a thickened voice. "And I shall be the most insufferably doting godmama!"

"I do not doubt it a bit." Her cousin laughed. In a soft voice she added, "If it is a boy, I think we shall call him Edward."

Two soft green eyes met two glowing amber ones in a moment of perfect sympathy and understanding.

"I shall sorely miss having you in town with me, Nell."

"Well, you needn't miss me at all," replied Elinor brightly. "I should be moped to death to be imprisoned in the country at this time of year. I shan't be confined until the end of the summer, so I have persuaded John and the doctor that there is really no reason for me not to enjoy much of the Season, as long as I am careful not to overdo." A girlish smile stole into her radiant face. "There is little fear of that. John won't let me do a thing for myself. He is like a little boy with a new and very delicate toy."

The two young women fell to talking about this happy news and of the gaieties of a London Season, and the Duchess found them laughing and making plans when she entered a short while later. She was pleased to see a genuine smile on her niece's face at last.

"Ah, I see you have shared your news, Elinor."

"Oh, Aunt Louie, is it not splendid?"

"Yes, indeed, as long as the child decides to take after our side of the family." She turned to her daughter with an indulgent smile. "Your John is a truly estimable man, my love, and, I'm sure, an excellent husband, but a plainer gentlemen I've yet to meet!"

"Oh Mama, to me he is the handsomest man in the world."

"No doubt," answered the Duchess drily. "They do say that love is blind."

She was answered with a light laugh, and Elinor said, "I've been trying to give Amy an inkling of the rigors of a London Season. Do you think, Mama, that she will be able to enjoy all the pleasures of town? Need she curtail her activities very much?"

"I have given that question long thought, and I don't really believe that it is necessary." She turned to Amelia. "We shall discreetly publish Edward's wish that you not go into mourning, my dear. The fact that you have already been in black gloves for a whole year for your father will, I think, make our decision more acceptable. Also, of course, your presentation under my auspices will offer you a certain protection. However, I feel you must be prepared for a few malicious comments from the very high-sticklers as well as from the merely jealous."

"I shall not mind, Aunt Louie. But must I remain in my weeds?" She looked down with a moue of distaste at the plain black levantine morning dress she wore.

"I think not, my dear. As long as you are circumspect in the styles and shades you allow yourself, and perhaps retain your black gloves for the most serious occasions, I think you will do very well in colors."

Amy's eyes began to shine. "Can we leave soon, Aunt Louie? You know I love Standish, but I feel that I simply must get away." She paused, and a shadow of sadness crossed her face. "There is too much of Ned here." Imploring eyes lifted to the Duchess's face. "When may we go?"

"I know you are eager, dear, but I think we must allow a month to pass. The Season will not even then be fully begun, and we shall still have plenty of time for all the requisite shopping."

Before the look of disappointment on Amy's face had a chance to deepen, Barrow entered the room.

"Sir Julian Deventer, Miss."

Amy smiled with genuine pleasure and did not notice the look of surprised distaste on her aunt's face. "Show Sir Julian in, Barrow."

The gentleman was promptly ushered into the room. If one did not look too closely, he looked younger than five-and-thirty years. He was dressed with careful propriety and somberness, as befitted the occasion of a formal call of condolence. His dark coat, plain gray pantaloons, and black cravat made a striking contrast to the cheerfulness of the breakfast room.

His bow to the Duchess was very polished and correct, but as the introductions were made and an opportunity offered for closer scrutiny, that lady noticed that his long, manicured fingers sported one or two too many rings, the fobs dangling from his waist were of garish taste, and the signs of dissipation in his once-handsome face were unmistakable. She was struck by the air of familiarity with which he kissed the hand of her niece.

"I would have come sooner, Amelia, but I have been away for several days. I have only just returned to hear the terrible news. I felt I must come to see you at once."

"That was very kind of you, Sir Julian. Won't you join us in a cup of coffee?"

As he seated himself at the dainty lacquered table, he smiled across at her. "I'm sure I need not say, my dear, that I should be proud to have you call on me at any time that I can be of assistance."

Two pairs of eyebrows shot up, and the Duchess and her daughter looked at each other sharply, much surprised, not to say distressed, by the easiness of the gentlemen's manners toward Amy.

"I thank you, sir," the young lady said and smiled prettily. "I hope I may carry that promise to town with me. I know so few people there."

The cup of coffee that he had been in the act of raising casually to his lips stopped abruptly in midmotion. "What? Do you still go to town, then? But surely . . . I mean, I had thought . . ." his voice trailed off into the silence of the unasked question.

"Why yes, sir. It was my brother's express wish, you see. And to tell the truth, I find that I cannot bear to stay in Somerset."

A frown had immediately replaced the surprise in his face. Now it deepened into a scowl. This new intelligence did not accord at all with the plans he had formed for Miss Clerville. He sat thus a moment and finally said, "Do you really think it wise, my dear? I can tell you that the biting tongues of the damned town tabbies may make you soon repent of breaking their code of conduct."

"I believe, sir," said the Duchess archly, "that my credit in society is quite good enough to carry my niece through tolerably well."

"Of course, Your Grace," he replied smoothly. "I assure you I did not mean to imply that it was not. But I have good reason to know the effects of spiteful tongues. I would not have Amelia suffer so."

"I believe Miss Clerville will be quite safe in my

care, sir," she said in accents icy enough to freeze even the hardened Sir Julian.

The atmosphere in the room had grown somewhat less inviting. After a few more moments of civil but innocuous chat, the gentleman rose to take leave of the ladies.

"I shall take the first opportunity of calling on you in town, Miss Clerville." He raised her proffered hand to his lips and kissed it lightly. Turning to the other ladies, he sketched a bow. "Your Grace . . . Lady Kendall. I bid you good morning." And turning quickly, he strode from the room.

"Well, Amelia! I cannot say that I am at all pleased by your choice of friends," said the Duchess as soon as Sir Julian had quit the room. "His manners are very familiar. I daresay you have known him for quite some time?"

"Why no, Aunt Louie. I don't believe we've met above a dozen times, but I have always found him a very lively and amusing companion. I am sorry you do not approve."

"Approve!" she exclaimed. "Do you not know Sir Julian Deventer's reputation? Why, he is known to be one of the most shocking libertines in London. The tidy fortune that he inherited with the title he dissipated long ago. He is one of the most notorious gamblers in town," she said with disgust. "It really will not do for you to be seen with him, Amelia."

Now Amy's ever-sensitive pride had been pricked. "Oh, I have heard the stories about him! And I know what all the bibble-babblers in the village who have seen me speaking to him say about us. I declare, Aunt, it is a pity that a young lady cannot carry on a civil conversation with a gentleman in a public place without setting them all to blathering. But I must say I had expected better of you!"

Elinor's voice broke in gently. "You must understand, dear, that you are now the very natural prey of every fortune hunter in the country. It will not do for you to encourage the advances of one so openly, or to allow such familiarity in a gentleman you hardly know."

"Do you think I would care a rush for his lack of fortune or his reputation if I truly cared for him?" she asked, her eyes blazing. She rose abruptly, nearly knocking over the gilt bamboo chair, and crossed to the window to try to regain her temper.

"I cannot believe that Ned was very pleased by your friendship with Sir Julian."

The gentle words were well calculated. Amy's anger flew away almost at once as she thought about her brother. Yes, it was true that he had not at all liked Sir Julian Deventer. Somehow that gentleman had generally contrived to call when Ned was away on one of his trips, so the dispute had never really come to a head. But Amy knew that Ned had been displeased by the friendship.

"You are right. He did not, though I was never certain why. Is his reputation really so very shocking?"

"It is the worst, my dear," replied the Duchess.

"Well," said Amy with a sigh, "As I said, it would not matter to me what he had done if I loved him." The Duchess's face looked ashen for a moment, until Amy added, "But I do not, Aunt Louie, not in the least. He has beguiled my days with interesting chatter and flattered me with pretty compliments, but having known Ned, you cannot truly believe that I would settle for Sir Julian Deventer."

"I have always credited you with a deal of good sense, Amelia." She patted her niece's hand. "I see that I may continue to do so."

The door opened once more, and the dignified Barrow slid silently through it. His voice was considerably warmer now than when announcing the previous visitor as he said, "Lady Waverly."

All three ladies smiled, and Amy ran to the door

to greet her friend. The sun seemed to come out as that young lady bounced into the room.

"Katie! I'm so glad you've come," cried Amy.

"Good morning!" Lady Waverly bubbled with a bright smile. "Your Grace," she said as she made a pretty curtsy to the Duchess. "Why, Lady Kendall, you do look radiant this morning. What a very pretty gown."

Amy looked at her cousin with a twinkle. "May I tell her, Nell?"

"Yes, of course, Amy."

"Elinor is to have a child, Katie! Is that not splendid. And I am to stand godmother!"

Katie clapped her hands in delight and kissed Elinor on both cheeks. "Oh, I am so pleased for you, my lady. I'm sure the child will be just as beautiful as you are."

"Let us hope so," said the Duchess drily.

"I've come to tell you the wonderful idea I've had, Amy. You know that I had planned to hold a ball before we all left for town. Well, of course that is out of the question just now, for you could not be there. But we mustn't all desert the country with nothing special to mark our passing. What say you to a small, cozy dinner party for our very particular friends?"

"Oh, it does sound lovely, Katie. I've been dying to get out of the house." She turned a pleading face to the Duchess. "Do you think it would be acceptable, Aunt Louie?"

"I cannot see why anyone would object, my dears, to an informal gathering of young people, if it is kept quite small and discreet."

"Oh, it shall be, Your Grace, I promise."

"It sounds quite unexceptionable, then. I see no reason you should not go, Amelia."

"Oh, thank you, Aunt Louie," she said, giving her aunt a hug.

"But will you not come too, Your Grace, and of

course Lady Kendall as well?" asked Katie with a pretty plea.

"I think my presence might give your party rather a different complexion, my dear. I thank you, but I believe a simple young people's party would occasion the least comment."

Katie flashed her most beguiling smile on the Duchess. "You are right, of course, Your Grace, but I do hope you will honor us at Waverly House while you are in town.'

"Whenever you should feel the need of the sobering presence of an old lady to dampen your youthful spirits, I should be happy to oblige."

"Such fustian, Aunt Louie. I'll wager when Katie holds her ball, you'll be the first one to stand up for the waltz" said Amy with a mischievous smile. "In fact, I shall dare you to! I know you, Aunt Louie. You never could resist a dare."

"I always was rather fond of dancing," replied the Duchess a trifle wistfully.

Turning again to Katie, Amy asked, "Shall I wear my lavender silk? It's the only truly pretty mourning gown I have."

"Oh, you do look so divine in it. Let's go and have a look."

They rose and started to cross out of the room. Elinor and her mother watched them go with fond smiles as Lady Waverly's voice floated back to them.

"My new rose sarcenet has finally arrived from London. You must see it, love. It is the silliest dress imaginable, and I adore it. But perhaps the white satin, you know the one, with the cherry ribbons, would feel more festive. What do you think? Of course there is my dark-green velvet . . ."

Chapter Five

On the morning of Katie's party an egg-yolk sun burst through the clouds at last. The mist rose from the grass, and Amy's spirits rose with it. A long brisk ride on the beautiful Medusa had gone far to restore the color to a face paled by grief and grey weather.

She skipped in the front door, her arms loaded with masses of lilacs, Katie's favorites. Their fragrant heads spilled over in a foam of purple-and-white blossoms. She had, on impulse, picked them as a surprise for her friend.

"Good morning, Jack," she said brightly to the footman stationed in the classically elegant front hall. "Would you please have these sent over to Lady Waverly?"

"Right away, Miss," he answered, beaming fondly at her. There wasn't a servant in the house who did not love Amy, and they all shared her grief. There would be smiling in the servants' hall this afternoon when Jack reported that young Miss seemed to be in spirits today.

Divesting herself of her lovely burden, Amy grinned to discover that the heady scent of the lilacs clung to the heavy folds of her riding habit. Her boots clicked across the hall and up the curving staircase.

She was still glowing when the evening came and she descended to the proud smiles of Nurse Penny-whit. Her feet were silent now in soft evening slippers of Denmark satin.

"I daresay the Queen herself couldn't look any finer than our Missy tonight," the beloved old nurse cooed to Barrow. That dignified servant did not deign to answer, but the pride in his old eyes could not be denied, and he nodded ever so slightly.

Amy was a vision in lavender crape. The flowing silk was cut with a simplicity that spoke volumes for its quality, and was trimmed with silk braid of the softest slate grey. It fitted Amelia to perfection, moving softly with her graceful form. Her mother's black pearls at her throat and a grey-and-silver ribbon threaded through her curls enhanced the picture, which was completed by long black gloves of the softest kid leather.

"Oh dear," sighed the Duchess, taking in her niece with a swift shrewd glance as Amy entered the yellow drawing room to take her leave. "I see just how it will be!"

"Why, what's the matter, Aunt Louie?"

"Well, I mean to say, just look at yourself, my dear."

Amy turned a worried glance to the large gilt pier glass over the mantel and began to fuss with her flaming curls.

"I can see that I shall have a long and very boring string of moonstruck young bucks in and out of my drawing room at all hours of the day and night just as soon as you have made your first appearance," lamented the Duchess. "And I can tell you, my dear, that there are few things in this world more boring than a young man in the throes of calf love."

Amy gave a light laugh of relief, and her brow cleared. "Such nonsense, Aunt Louie. I only hope that I am not left to sit with the matrons all through my first ball because no one has asked me to dance."

Elinor now joined in with a tinkle of laughter. "You need not have the slightest fear of that, my dear. Only look as lovely as you do tonight."

"When they begin reading you poetry over the

42

teacups, Amelia, I shall abandon you to your fate, and so I warn you," concluded her aunt.

Amy's smile shot forth, and she gave her aunt a lively hug. Then, donning a black velvet cloak lined with palest lavender, she stepped out to the waiting carriage.

It was a small and congenial group that Tom and Katie had thoughtfully gathered. Most of them had been known to Amy since her earliest childhood, and she was completely at her ease. Her face reflected the glitter of the dozens of wax tapers, their warmth flickering in her glowing eyes.

She was chatting comfortably with a pretty young matron in almond-green sarcenet with a dainty lace-ridden cap perched atop her curls.

"And do you still go to London, Amelia?" asked Lady Thornton.

"Yes, ma'am," Amy replied. "My brother desired that I should go, and my Aunt Louisa has kindly renewed her offer to bring me out."

"I am glad, my dear. I am sure there is no reason for you to bury yourself away in the country for yet another Season. And I am persuaded that no one can take exception to that which the Duchess of Harcourt has granted approval." The lady's pretty eyes sparkled. "Why, just think what all the town beaux would be missing if you stayed away."

Amy's soft laugh carried across the pink-and-gold room to where Katie was seated, and the latter smiled to see her friend in spirits.

"You are kind, Lady Thornton," said Amy. "But I am persuaded we shall all be cast into the shade by your Sukey. I always knew she would turn out the best of us all."

"Well, yes, I do believe she'll do," replied the fond mama, her fine grey eyes full of pride as she beamed at her pretty young daughter across the room. "I must admit I do look forward to the gaieties of London myself." A mischievous gleam lit her eye. "A daughter can be convenient," admitted the attractive widow.

Amy's tinkle of laughter was heard again. "Convenient for the gentlemen, I collect you mean, ma'am, for now they will have two pretty Thornton ladies to dance attendance upon. But it is also convenient for me, dear ma'am. I shall be glad of so many friends in town."

"Never fear for that, my dear. You will find yourself with friends enough quite soon, and most of them in pantaloons, I doubt not. Ah, and here is Sir Julian Deventer, right on cue, come to pay his court to you. I collect that you require no assistance from me to charm him silly."

Lady Thornton rose, and with a vague nod to the approaching gentleman and a soft rustle of her green skirts, she glided across the room.

Amy had felt a pang of conscience when she saw Sir Julian enter Katie's drawing room a short time before. She knew that he was no favorite with Katie, and he could only have been invited in the belief that it was Amy's wish to have him there. She would not disappoint Katie in her gesture, and though her eagerness for the gentleman's company, after her aunt's astute comments on his character, was decidedly tepid, she exerted herself to enjoy it.

"You do look positively royal this evening, Amelia," he said smoothly as he made her a practiced bow and kissed her gloved hand lightly.

"I thank you, sir," she replied and curtsied prettily. "I can promise you that I am royally glad to be here. Lady Waverly's parties are always a delight and just such as I have been needing."

"Any evening graced with your lovely presence is bound to be a delight, my dear. And how pleased I am of another chance of seeing you before you are swallowed up by the town."

"I assure you I am no Jonah, sir," she said lightly,

"and though I know London is the great whale of cities, I am a very swift swimmer."

He laughed at her witticism, and she noticed that he held her hand still. She disengaged it gently and studied his face with attention as he dropped more flowery compliments into her ear. Strange that she had never before noticed the hard lines of dissipation which now seemed so marked in his face. Her aunt was a shrewd judge of character, Amelia knew. Proud as she was, she could not but admit that if that lady held such a low opinion of the gentleman, it could not be entirely without basis. She had previously discounted the rumors and stories that the gossip mongers in the neighborhood delighted in bandying about concerning Sir Julian, and enjoyed her idle flirtation with him. But she now pondered her aunt's comments on his character, albeit with a pleasant smile on her face, until Katie came bounding up to them.

"Oh, Amy! I've such a grand surprise for you, and he has just arrived! I knew if anyone could help restore your spirits it would be he." She turned a brilliant smile on Amy's companion. "You'll forgive me, Sir Julian, if I steal her away for a while."

Amy turned to the doorway, and her face lit with pleasure as she saw a jolly-looking gentleman a few years older than herself who had just entered the room.

"Ferdie!" cried Amelia as she raced across the room and flung her arms about the neck of the gentleman in question. The young man beamed down at her and held her at arm's length, surveying her with a broad and approving grin.

"I say, Amy! You're looking as fine as fivepence." A slight frown creased his brow. "A bit thin, though. Don't let my mother get sight of you. She'll be filling you up with arrowroot jelly and other vile stuff quick as the cat can lick her ear."

A gurgle of laughter erupted from Amy, and she reached up and mussed his hair, already something less than neat. In fact, the Honorable Ferdinand Brice's hair was the despair of his barber and his valet. With a texture akin to that of a furze bush, abetted by his constant habit of wantonly running his fingers through it, he usually resembled nothing so much as an absent-minded scientist whose experiments with the novelty of electricity have gone amiss and who is now in the process of being fried to a neat turn.

A sad look darkened his happy face for a moment. "Terrible news about Ned. Best of good fellows an' all, y'know. Needn't tell you, Amy. Call on me. Any time. Old friend and all, y'know," he stammered uncomfortably.

Amy knew that Ferdie, too, had loved Ned, almost as a brother, and she squeezed his hand.

"Oh, Ferdie! How glad I am that you are here," she said with real warmth. "I haven't seen you this age. How long have you been in Somerset? Why have you not been to see me?"

"I only just arrived these two days since. Give a fellow a chance, girl!"

"You must come riding with me, Ferdie. This week! If the weather holds fine we can ride to the abbey. Do you remember what jolly times we all used to have there with Neddie and Sukey and those silly Gillray boys?"

"Jolly indeed! You and Sukey and Katie used to lead us fellows a merry chase round the ruins," answered Ferdie as his ebullient laugh bubbled up.

He was indeed a jolly fellow. His addiction to creams and jellies, trifles and gooseberry tarts had taxed the talents of Weston to outfit him in the manner befitting his station. He was very prone to popped buttons and burst seams, but that circumstance had never been able to dampen his *joie de vivre*. His round cherubic face, of a perennially reddened hue, was beaming now at Amy.

The laughing pair was interrupted by the approach of Lord Waverly. "Here, old boy," he said to

Ferdie. "Got to do the polite, you know. Come and introduce your friend to his host."

Ferdie ran his fingers through his hair and cried, "Damme! Beg pardon, Tom. Seein' Amy again has sent my manners flying." With that he turned to a dark-haired gentleman who had just entered the room. The stranger, standing stock still framed by the Grecian pilasters of the doorway, seemed to be surveying Amelia with a concentrated stare that discomfited her. As the attention of the group was turned to him, he favored them with a nod and a formal bow.

"Justin," hailed Ferdie. "Come and meet your host."

The tall gentleman strode across the room with long strides. It seemed to Amy that the room had shrunk and become so still that she fancied she could hear the soft "shush" of his gleaming boots on the Turkey carpet. Ferdie assumed what he felt to be an air of great elegrance.

"May I present Justin Savile, Marquis of Tyrone. The Earl of Waverly and Lady Waverly." As the Marquis took Katie's hand, Ferdie's uncomfortable formality dropped away. "Damme, Tom," he exclaimed to Lord Waverly, "I still can't get used to that handle of yours. Plain old Tom suits you too well, and I've seen Katie here too many times with mud on her nose to be able to call her Lady Waverly very easily."

"You are too mean, Ferdie," Katie objected with a little pout that was belied by the smile in her eyes. "Here am I trying to be the great lady for his lordship, and you insist on giving away my secrets!"

Tyrone smiled as he bowed gracefully over her hand. "Your servant, my lady." Turning to Tom and shaking his hand, he added, "My lord, please forgive my intrusion at your party. Mr. Brice seemed so certain you would not mind."

"Oh pooh," exclaimed Katie. "Of course you are

47

most welcome, my lord. It is we who are honored. We are very informal here in the country, and a new face is always so welcome."

During this exchange Amy had a chance to survey the newcomer more closely. She saw an elegant gentleman of above average height and powerfully built. He obviously had no need for buckram wadding to enhance his splendid physique. A square face was softened by a pair of deep-set eyes the color of sapphires. They seemed to hold a guarded look as he spoke.

"And this is Amy," said Ferdie in proud accents. "Or Lady Amelia Clerville, as I should say. Is she not something special, just as I said?"

Amy blushed at his praise and turned a warm countenance to Tyrone as he made a very correct bow. She answered with a curtsy and extended her hand graciously, always ready to meet a new friend.

"Your servant, Lady Amelia."

She was startled by the coldness of his tone, and when his glittering blue eyes caught hers she felt inexplicably frozen to the bone.

"My Lord Tyrone," she replied correctly, her head tilted to one side and eyeing him curiously as he bent over her hand.

As he rose again, he saw her cool eye studying him, and a cynical smile stole across his handsome features.

"My lord, do come and meet our other guests," said Katie, and Tyrone, with an irritating little nod to Amy, allowed himself to be led away.

Amy turned her attention to Ferdie and Sir Julian, who had rejoined her. But as they chatted, her eye strayed to the dark gentleman being introduced around the room.

With an eye for men's fashions cultivated by her brother, she saw that his dark-blue coat was of the finest Bath cloth and the best cut. His neckcloth was simply folded, but dazzling in its whiteness, and his Suvaroff boots gleamed like a mirror. In short, she could see that everything about the Marquis of Tyrone was of the finest.

Her reflections were curtailed when his handsome face looked up to discover her watching him. His glance quickly took in Sir Julian, standing next to Amy with a proprietary hand under her elbow. With a raised eyebrow, his cold gaze rested another moment on her face before he returned his attention coolly to Lady Waverly.

Well! thought Amy hotly. What a great cock-o'-the-walk he seems to fancy himself. I dare swear he is used to the whole world toadying to him. Well, he shall have none of it from me! She determinedly turned her back on the Marquis and favored her other companions with a killing smile.

When they adjourned to the elegant dining room with its groaning table, Amy found herself seated between Ferdie and Sir Julian Deventer. She chatted gaily through the two courses and several removes, savoring particularly a crimped salmon with oyster sauce, a matelot of rabbits, and a dish of artichoke bottoms au gratin, and teasing Ferdie lightly about his third cheesetart and second helping of Rhenish crème. She was thoroughly enjoying herself for the first time since Ned's death.

Tyrone, on the other side of the table, took advantage of the chance of unobtrusively studying her lovely face, glowing in the warm light of the crystal chandeliers and beautifully enhanced by the huge centerpiece of lilacs that sat before her. He was a bit surprised and more than a little worried by what he saw.

He wasn't sure exactly what he had expected to find when he met Amelia Clerville. He had gone to a deal of trouble to arrange this introduction. A recent visit to Wishbone Cottage at Lyme Regis had convinced him that it was necessary.

Lord Tyrone had lost one of his best men, and a good friend, when Edward Clerville had been ambushed in France. He was determined that such a thing should not happen again.

So it was with astonishment and chagrin that he was told by Parker, Clerville's valet, that Miss Clerville was privy to dangerous information about the spying operation. If she was unable to hold her tongue about her brother's work, many of Tyrone's other men might be seriously endangered.

Parker seemed to have implicit trust in the girl, as Clerville himself must have had to write such an ill-advised letter. But the Marquis's cynical attitude toward the untrustworthiness of her sex made it impossible that he should eye Amelia with anything other than misgiving. Her light laugh floated down the table to where he was seated. The apparent lack of concern over the loss of her brother which he read into that laugh filled him with indignation. Her fine eyes were turned on Sir Julian Deventer, a gentleman whom the Marquis had good reason to mistrust. Clerville had been a fine man, he thought with distaste at the sight before him. He deserved better.

His attention was claimed by Lady Thornton, who was seated at his right hand, and his eyes reluctantly left what he thought of as her coldly beautiful face.

Amelia turned back to Ferdie Brice as she asked, "What has brought the Marquis of Tyrone into Somerset?"

"No idea!" replied Ferdie. "Capital fellow, Justin, but a bit odd, y'know. Popped up on my doorstep yesterday. Devilish glad to see him, too, I can tell you." He added, "Mean to say, you know what a regular gabble-monger my mother is. Drives me distracted, she does. But now she's got a marquis in the house, she'll do the polite right enough. Keeps her in tow, don't y'see."

"Oh Ferdie, you are wicked," she protested. "Your mama is a dear sweet soul, and you adore her, and well you know it." Mr. Brice only grinned. "How long will he be staying with you?"

"Lord! I don't know. Deuced mysterious fellow, Justin. Pops off at a moment's notice for God knows where. Pops up again where you never expect him. Hope we can get in some fishing this time before he's off again."

"And you will come and ride with me, won't you, Ferdie? It would be such fun."

"Well, I make no doubt you can still outride and outjump me. You always could show me up proper."

"Perhaps one or two fewer puddings would make you lighter in the saddle," she said archly, but her mouth twitched into an impish smile. "I promise I shan't show you up, Ferdie. Only say you'll come."

"Just see if I don't. We'll get up a little party. The first fine morning. How's that?"

Amy answered him with enthusiastic delight, then turned her attention to Sir Julian for the remainder of the meal, and soon the ladies had repaired to the drawing room, leaving the gentlemen to their port.

"What do you think of Lord Tyrone, Amy?" gushed Katie as soon as they were out of earshot of the dining room. "Is he not the handsomest man you ever saw?"

"Do you really think so?" asked Amy. "Of course he is very elegant, but he can absolutely freeze one with those eyes. What a cold fish!"

"Why, whatever can you mean, Amy? I found him extremely friendly and charming. His manners are perfect."

Amy looked surprised at her friend, and she wondered for a moment if they were speaking of the same gentleman.

Sukey fluttered up to them in a bustle of satin

ribbons. "However did you manage to catch the Marquis of Tyrone for your party, Katie?" she bubbled. She alighted upon a chair with a bounce, and a cloud of yellow muslin settled slowly around her.

Katie puffed up just a little. "He is rather special, is he not?"

Sukey answered with a heartfelt sigh. "Mama has seen him in town. He's all the crack, you know. Rich as Golden Ball, they say, and so unbearably handsome, don't you think?" She smiled a little shyly. "I did see him in the village yesterday, and when he nodded at Mama I nearly fainted away, such a picture as he makes on that Welsh black of his."

"Oh, do try not to be too terribly silly, Sukey. One would think you were still in the schoolroom," said Amy.

Sukey flounced her yellow curls and lifted her pert little chin. "Well, I suppose I may admire a handsome gentleman who happens to be single and very rich. Do you know he even keeps his own yacht at Lyme Regis? Is that not the most romantic thing? What luck to actually meet him here, Katie. I shall have a head start over all the other girls in London," she concluded in gushing schoolgirl accents.

"A yacht at Lyme Regis, you say?" asked Amy.

Sukey eyed her mournfully. "Oh Amy, it will be too bad of you if you decide to go after him yourself. I shan't have the least chance then, you know."

Before Amy could answer, the gentlemen reentered the room. Her eyes flew to Tyrone, who was regarding her with more coldness than ever. His narrowed eyes held a sardonic expression that stung her as though she had been slapped. Her own green eyes flashed him a quick challenge as he turned abruptly away.

Ferdie approached her directly as he entered the room. Carefully disposing his bulk on the delicate

pink damask settle where Amy was seated, he turned
to her an unwontedly serious expression.

"What's this I'm hearing about you and that Deventer fellow, Amy?"

"I've no idea what you're talking about, Ferdie.
What have you heard?" she asked in some surprise.

"Well, he didn't say it in so many words, you
understand, but the fellow made it pretty clear he ex-
pects to marry you."

"Did he indeed?"

"Don't do it, Amy. Curst rum touch, y'know.
Not at all the thing. Deuce take it, that fellow's not
for you."

Amy bristled at his comments. "I would have
thought, Ferdie, that that was for me to decide."

A little abashed, he looked down at her. "Damme,
Amy, I care about you. You're like my sister. Are you
going to have the fellow?"

"Oh, Ferdie, I know you are only trying to be
kind. And I do thank you for your concern. But you
really needn't worry about me, you know. I'm quite
grown up now." She could see that he was still
frowning. "If and when I decide to marry, Ferdie,
you will know it at once, I promise you." And with
that he had to be satisfied.

Lord Tyrone, who was well within earshot of
this conversation, took careful note of the fact that
Miss Clerville had not denied the report of her im-
pending marriage to Sir Julian. And observing that
gentleman's unctuous charm and the attention with
which she had favored him all the evening, he supposed that she must be pleased she could now afford,
with Standen's fortune, to buy herself an impecunious
rake of a husband. This impression, combined with his
information of some of Deventer's more treasonous
activities in the neighborhood, gave Tyrone an alarming picture of Amelia. A proud and beautiful care-
for-nobody, with plenty of money and no restraints,
dangling after a treacherous adventurer and in pos-

session of exceedingly dangerous information. His image of her was complete and accurate, he felt sure. And he decided that the haughty Lady Amelia Clerville would bear close watching.

Chapter Six

The dull rain returned the very next morning, and it was three days before the last vestiges of the heavy grey clouds were in retreat at last. A peacock sky shone down on a world washed shiny clean by the rain.

Amy was up with the birds and into what she called her "working clothes," an old and outgrown pair of her brother's buckskin riding breeches topped with a soft muslin shirt. With a grin at her own image in the glass, she knotted a Belcher handkerchief around her throat. She really looked remarkably like Ned, and the image pleased her.

As she pulled on her glossy black riding boots, she suddenly remembered the riding date with Ferdie and their friends. She glanced at the pretty little ormolu clock on the mantel. She would have just enough time to work the new colt for an hour or so. She tied back her shining curls at the nape of her neck with a velvet ribbon and skipped out the door and down the stairs.

After a quick but hearty breakfast, she stepped out and breathed deeply of the morning air. Starry drops of dew glistened on her boots as she strode across the still-wet grass. She thrust her hands into the pockets of her breeches, and, whistling a tuneless melody, headed toward the paddock.

The new chestnut colt was a beauty. Amy and Ned had chosen him together, very carefully, and they had named him Poseidon. As far as Amy could see, he was perfect. He was not yet broken to saddle, but he and Amy were already great friends. He nibbled happily at the lumps of sugar she pulled from her pocket. But as she hoisted herself up onto his bare glossy back, the young beauty tried to bolt. However, Amy was in firm control. She reached down for the bit and pulled slightly. The horse quieted almost at once, and she spoke softly and reassuringly into the smooth brown ear. "All right, my beauty. You will have a good run later. For now, my pet, let us see how well you can behave." The colt was already responding to her gentle commands, and she gave herself up entirely to the pleasure of the exercise. She felt very close to Neddie whenever she sat on Poseidon's back. As the young lady and the young horse got to know one another better, the sun climbed higher in the sky.

The chiming of the stable clock caused her to look up sharply. At that precise moment, she saw, with dismay, that several people were approaching. She realized with a start she had completely lost track of the time, and her friends had arrived for the projected ride to the old abbey. And here she was still in her breeches! Still and all, they were all her very old friends, just Ferdie and Tom and Katie. They knew her too well to be shocked by her unconventional attire. She could change in a trice, and they would be on their way.

She turned her ready smile toward them, only to notice with irritation that the Marquis of Tyrone was one of the party. For some reason she was loath to appear to disadvantage before him. His arrogance had put up her hackles, and the stubborn Clerville pride wished not to give him the edge in what she sensed was a coming battle of wills between them.

She slid from the chestnut's back to greet her guests. As she looked defensively up into the eyes of Tyrone, she was a little surprised to find no trace of shocked sensibilities there. Instead, his habitually sardonic expression was tinged with a trace of amusement as well as what might be grudging admiration.

With a bark of laughter, Ferdie broke in on her inspection of the unexpected guest. "Lord, Amy, one'd expect to call you Master Clerville in that rig. I was afraid you'd have turned into a proper priss of a young lady by now, but I can see that I needn't have worried. Devil a bit! The same old Amy." He ran his pudgy fingers through his furzy hair and laughed again. "What they'll think of you in town, though, I'd rather not imagine.

"Well, Ferdie, I think if I try *very* hard, I may be able to refrain from wearing breeches in Hyde Park, though I count on you to stand my friend if I should fail in my resolution."

Ferdie barked again. "Amy, love, for a girl, you are the most complete hand!"

She turned coolly to the Marquis. "Good morning, my lord. I did not expect to have the honor of your company on our ride."

"I hope you do not mind, ma'am." He bowed.

"Not at all, my lord. I should have expected you. You seem to have a reputation for turning up unannounced in the most unexpected places." Her eyes held a trace of mischief, and she wondered if he would take her bait. He did not.

"Do you often ride without a saddle, Miss Clerville?" he asked with genuine interest. He had never seen a young lady riding in such an unconventional manner.

"Only when I perceive the need, my lord," she returned. "Poseidon is not yet fully broken. My brother and I chose him together only a short time ago."

"He seems to be coming along nicely, though," said the Marquis, running a practiced hand appreciatively over the animal's glossy flanks. "A beautiful animal. Obviously Lord Standen had made good progress with him."

"On the contrary, my lord. My brother never had a chance to enjoy him. Poseidon arrived only a few days before his death. No one has been on his back but me."

"Indeed!" Tyrone exclaimed as his dark brows shot up. "I own I find that hard to believe, Miss Clerville. This animal is hardly a fitting mount for a lady."

"That's as may be, my lord," she answered with a toss of her curls, "but then, as you can see, I am perhaps not a lady," and she flashed him a totally charming smile, as unexpected as it was disarming. He was not to know what that smile had cost her, but she would not give him the satisfaction of getting the rise out of her that he was obviously trying for. Both contestants retired temporarily from the lists.

Turning to the others, Amy said, "I'm afraid I lost track of the time entirely."

"Lord, Amy," Tom pronounced affably as the group walked toward the house, "you don't imagine any of us are surprised at that, do you? Once get you on a prime piece of horseflesh and the world could fall down about your ears for all you'd notice. Just like Ned!"

Rightly perceiving this to be a high compliment, Amy beamed. "Well, I am sorry to keep you waiting. I don't believe my aunt will be down as yet, but Elinor has agreed to join us in our ride, if you've no objection. I'm sure she'll be pleased to entertain you while I change. She may even be able to produce some coffee and breakfast cakes," she added for Ferdie's benefit. "I shall not keep you waiting long. Come, Katie, and chat with me while I change."

The two young ladies disappeared up the stairs while the gentlemen were shown into the bright little breakfast room, beckoned there by the delicious smell of fresh coffee and by Elinor's light greeting.

It was no more than a quarter of an hour later that Amy and Katie reappeared. The breeches and the dust of the paddock had been left upstairs, and Amy now was quite ladylike in a simply cut riding habit of darkest Hunter green with black facings, her becoming black low-crowned beaver swathed in soft green veiling. Ferdie rose and crossed to her, wiping cinnamon and crumbs from his mouth.

"I say, Amy, that was quick. You're not one to keep a fellow waiting. Shall we be off, then?"

"You have proved yourself true to your word, Miss Clerville," said Tyrone smoothly. "For all that you now look quite like a lady, indeed you cannot be one. I've yet to meet a lady who could change her dress in under an hour."

Amelia laughed in spite of herself. "I would not wish to prove myself a liar, sir. Shall we ride? Cook has packed us a lovely nuncheon. I've sent it on ahead with John Groom. We can be at the abbey in less than two hours."

The three couples mounted and headed west along the River Axe. The veil of new green leaves that lightly dusted the trees shone in the bright sunshine of early spring. Fluffy white clouds floated across the sky like blossoms blown by the breeze, and the murmur of the river was a charming accompaniment to the light conversation of the party.

After a delightful ride, their path deposited them before the area's most charming ruins, a tumbledown pile of stone and moss that in the twelfth century had earned its long-standing reputation as one of the most beautiful abbeys in England.

Amelia rode beside Ferdie, and they laughed and chatted all the way to their destination. At one point, she looked back only to be surprised by the ease with which her cousin Elinor was conversing with the usually taciturn Marquis. He had a quite pleasant expression on his face, unlike the sardonic look that he nearly always turned to her.

They arrived at the ancient crenellated abbey and abandoned themselves to the joy of touring once again the well-known and well-loved ruins. This pile had played an important part in the childhood of nearly everyone who had grown up in the neighborhood. A perfect spot for games of hide and seek or rough-and-tumble rock climbing and stone throwing, it could not have helped but be a great attraction to the likes of Ned and Amy and their friends. Many were the times that the Princesses Amelia and Katherine had been rescued from this tower by their swains. Sieges had been held and pitched battles with mock cannon fought in and around the romantic old pile. And it had been in the shadow of the towers, with the benevolent ghosts of monks long dead all around them, that Katie and Tom had first held hands.

They walked and climbed, laughed and remembered, and the faithful groom had a beautiful lunch laid out for them before it even occurred to them how hungry they were.

"Famous!" rejoiced Ferdie at the sight of the elegant *al fresco* banquet. "I'm devilish sharp-set, I can tell you. C'mon, Amy." He began to load his plate at once.

They all laughingly joined him, and the group enjoyed an excellent repast that included paper-thin slices of baked ham, sirloin, and glazed tongue, good ripe cheese, cold poached asparagus, and the first rosy peaches of the year. They munched happily on a quantity of sweets chosen from sponge biscuits, carraway puffs, gingerbread, and a large sack full of barley sugar, and they washed the whole down with a great deal of champagne carried in raffia-covered bottles to keep it cool.

They sat on piles of rock under the beautiful old nodding oaks to eat the delicious meal, while the tethered horses, gleaming under a benevolent sun, feasted passively on the succulent young grass, their tails lazily flicking at the droning flies and buzzing bees. The young ladies scattered over the meadow gathering armloads of buttercups and wild violets, just as they had done in this very meadow for years. The gentlemen fashioned some very effective pea-shooters from the cow parsley that abounded around the stones and tried their luck at hitting dandelion heads. Lamentably, and laughingly, they discovered that the accuracy of their aim had degenerated with the years.

In mellow mood, the group finally remounted and headed back toward Standish.

Amy had managed to avoid having much conversation with Lord Tyrone, but she had often felt his eyes on her during the day. She could not help but notice the guarded look they always seemed to hold, even when he appeared to be in a happy mood. She found herself wondering about him and what had brought him to Somerset. Now, on the return trip, she was surprised to find him riding beside her. She complimented him on his truly magnificent horse, a blue-black stallion, obviously of Welsh blood. He stood nearly sixteen hands, with a perfectly balanced head and powerful quarters.

"Yes, I bred him myself, but he is of Welsh stock, of course. And he's sired a couple of promising colts for me. I may run one of them at Newmarket next year."

"If they are anything like this one, they must be very fine indeed, my lord. You may expect to do very well."

The conversation continued in this innocuous vein for some time. They spoke of inconsequential matters and exchanged commonplaces on the nature of the countryside through which they were riding. To Tyrone, it seemed that Amelia knew every stone and tree, and very nearly every cow and sheep. He was intrigued.

Wanting a bit of exercise, the group soon broke into a good run. The route had several good fences and a pair of streams, and by the time they were once again within the boundaries of Standish they were all flushed from the invigorating cross-country run. Tyrone was still beside Amelia, and he owned himself impressed by her horsemanship. Now that she was once again on her own property her conversation became even more animated. The run had put her in high good spirits, and she chatted happily about her estate. Tyrone could not help but notice what a pretty color the exercise had given her cheeks.

As they crossed a small stone bridge, Amelia explained to him that this small branch of the Axe broadened into a quite large lake a little farther on. By a peculiar layout of the land, this spot had caused them severe flood damage on several occasions, including the most recent storm.

"I've nearly decided to divert the river by means of a canal and to drain the lake and reclaim the land for crops. It will be so very much safer for the tenants on that part of the estate."

"That sounds very ambitious," answered the Marquis with a raised brow. "Rather a bold attempt at experimentation, is it now?" The tiniest note of sarcasm had crept into his voice, but Amy, warming to her topic, either did not hear it or chose to ignore it.

"You should see what they have been doing in Holland. The science of reclaiming land is far advanced there. I visited some of the polderlands as a child, and I remember being very much impressed by the ingenuity of the idea. I have been learning all I can about the process and have even sent to Amsterdam for more specific information. It would add a hundred arable acres to the estate, you know, but more importantly, it would protect those low-lying lands forever. Such a thing has never been tried on such a scale in this part of the country, but I see no reason it should not prove just as beneficial to us as it does to the Dutch."

"Surely the cost of draining such an area would also drain a great deal of capital from the estate." By now Amy found his tone patronizing in the extreme.

"That is true, my lord, but we are very healthy

right now. And it can only add to our value in the long run," she replied, her voice a shade colder.

The Marquis gave her an indulgent look, as though confronting a child. "Your trustees will no doubt think better of such a harebrained scheme."

Amy rose straighter in her saddle. "On the contrary, my lord. They have nothing to say to the matter." A look of astonished disbelief crossed his dark face.

"I cannot believe . . ." he began, but Amy interrupted him almost at once.

"While it is true that the bulk of my fortune is under the control of my trustees, my brother made it quite clear that in all matters of managing Standish I was to have complete freedom," she finished proudly.

"My God! Are you telling me that your brother was nodcock enough to leave a large and profitable estate in the hands of a chit of nineteen?"

She bristled with indignation at his ill-chosen words. "And why should he not, my lord?"

"Anyone with a brain should be able to see why not! One would have thought he'd be more concerned for the well-being of his tenants, if nothing else! And I always thought Standen a rather competent, clever fellow."

Amy's face flushed martial colors. "As it happens, my lord, that I am one of the principal reasons that Standish *is* profitable, I imagine my brother assumed it would remain so in my care. And I do not see what possible concern it can be of yours, sir, what I choose to do with my own land!" she finished indignantly.

Spurring Medusa into a brisk canter, she rode away in a huff, leaving Tyrone in a cloud of dust. Really! This man was abominable. If Ferdie meant to have him hanging about all the time, she would almost rather not see Ferdie, and so she would tell him. Thank goodness she would soon be leaving for town.

The party soon approached the Standish stables. Amy, still fuming, slid from Medusa's back before

Tyrone could come to her assistance. Tossing her curls in his direction and draping the heavy skirts of her habit over one arm, she slipped the other through Ferdie's crooked elbow and bore him off in the direction of the house.

As the group burst noisily into the drawing room, they were met by the sight of the Duchess trying, with ill-concealed annoyance, to entertain a somewhat taciturn Sir Julian Deventer. The look of relief on that gentleman's face at Amy's entrance was so patently obvious as to be almost laughable.

Greetings were made all round. Amy noticed a lack of warmth on the part of everyone present toward Sir Julian, but most particularly from Lord Tyrone. He was barely civil, and even that seemed to cost him an effort. He had learned many things about the impecunious Baronet during his few days in Somerset, and none of them good. He was still more curious to learn about some strange and unsavory French émigré friends with whom Sir Julian had been seen, albeit surreptitiously.

Amy herself was far from overjoyed by Sir Julian's visit, but she had decided to be insulted on his behalf by Tyrone's lack of civility. The Marquis had wounded her pride today and put her in what Ned would have recognized at once as a dangerous mood. Tyrone's obvious dislike of Sir Julian was sufficient recommendation to cause her to greet the latter much more warmly than she would otherwise have cared to do.

She gave him both her hands and her warmest smile. "How kind of you to call, Sir Julian. Did I know you were coming, I would have invited you to join our party. We have had the most delightful ride." She turned to her aunt, blithely ignoring the dagger looks that lady was giving her. "We've been over to the abbey, Aunt Louie. And Cook fixed us the loveliest lunch." Dropping Sir Julian's hands, she turned to her other guests. "Let's all be comfortable now, and I shall ring for refreshments."

But comfortable could scarcely describe the feelings of the other riders. The languidly mellow mood of the afternoon had suddenly evaporated, and none of them felt inclined to stay longer than was strictly necessary. As soon as civility would allow, they all rose to take their leave. Amy accompanied the group out to the great hall, where Ferdie at once pulled her aside.

"Now listen to me, my girl. I know you won't like to hear it, and I daresay you'll fly into a pelter, but I can't hold my tongue! That fellow Deventer's a here-and-thereian if ever I saw one! There's something devilish smoky in the way he's making up to you. Everyone knows he's under the hatches, and it's the Bank of England to a Charley's shelter that he hopes to get his hands on the Standen fortune!" Amy's eyes were beginning to flash martial lights. "Now, don't fly up into the boughs, Amy. I ain't saying you're not something special enough to attract any fellow in your own right, because you are. But if you've got some romantic maggot in your head about Deventer, you'd better know that he's a curst rum touch!" His eyes were pleading with her now, and her own face softened toward him. "He's not good enough for you, Amy!"

"Oh, give over, do, Ferdie!" she exclaimed, in her frustration borrowing one of her brother's pet cant phrases. "One would think I've been hanging on his coattails, which I'm sure I have not! Besides, I do not have 'romantic maggots'!" Ferdie's face still held a pathetic and worried look. Amy knew she must reassure her friend. "I quite realize the position I am in, Ferdie. There are bound to be many gentlemen more interested in my tidy fortune than in my more elusive charms. And I assure you they will find me an ill bird for plucking," she said briskly. "But I cannot refuse to see anyone simply because his notions might be the tiniest bit suspect. I should never have any callers else."

"The tiniest bit suspect!" exclaimed Ferdie. Before he could go on, Amy raised a lovely hand to cover his mouth.

"Come, let us not cavil over him anymore. I am not such a goosecap as to take seriously the compliments of a gentlemen of Sir Julian's stamp, for all they are very pretty ones. I shall promise not to marry him, and we shall cry friends again."

He smiled down at her with great relief and affection. Suddenly he barked out his old familiar laugh and ran his fingers through his bristling hair.

"Aye, but I'll wager you'll lead him a merry dance! I oughtn't to worry about you. It's just as I told Justin. Amy Clerville knows the time of day!"

She bristled again with indignation at mention of the name. "And speaking of that gentleman, Ferdie, I could wish you to leave your odious friend at home when next you come to call. He is the most abominably arrogant, pot-sure, consequential gentlemen I have ever had the misfortune to meet!"

"What, Tyrone? No, no, best of good fellows, Justin."

"All the same, I prefer not to be treated like a simpleton or a silly schoolgirl in my own home!"

"Well, it's true he don't have much truck with females," Ferdie conceded. "But now I've kept him waiting too long. I'll pop over later in the week." His eyes twinkled a smile. "Does your cook still make the best jelly pancakes in Somerset?"

"She does indeed." Amy laughed. "And when she hears you are coming, she'll likely bake some Bristol cakes as well. She does love an appreciative audience."

Having emptied the house of one set of guests, Amy found her delight in her other visitor seriously diminished. Sir Julian was obviously uncomfortable in the presence of the Duchess, and he at once invited Amy for a stroll in the shrubbery.

"It is such a lovely afternoon, my dear. To waste such a day indoors would be unforgivable."

"I fear my niece is wearied from her ride, sir. Perhaps she would be better served by a rest in her room," said the Duchess frostily. Amy felt a storm brewing. She did not feel up to dealing with her aunt just now, as she surely must do if Sir Julian were sent packing as the Duchess intended. Best to remove herself before the storm could break on her head, and give her aunt a chance to smooth her ruffled feathers.

"I should like a walk of all things, Sir Julian. If you will forgive me in all my dirt," she added with a gesture to the riding habit which she still wore.

"To me you are perfection in whatever you wear, my dear Amelia."

Ignoring the loud "humph" that issued from her aunt, and evading her disapproving stare, she said lightly, "We shall not be out long, Aunt Louie." And with that, she made good her escape, Sir Julian hard on her heels.

They soon reached the shrubbery, basking in the afternoon sun. For a moment they walked in silence, broken by the soft crunch of their feet on the gravel walk and the honk of a goose in the distance. The spring-scented air softly ruffled Amy's curls, for she had unconventionally discarded her hat. Sir Julian took her hand. Pulling it through his arm, he stroked it lightly as they walked. She felt an urge to pull it away, then told herself not to be silly.

"Ah, you are sure to be quite a hit in town. I own I am jealous already."

"What nonsense, sir," she laughed. "I am sure you can be no such thing."

"But only see how easily you have captivated Lord Tyrone." There was a hard and cynical edge in his oily voice as he spoke, but Amy was so astonished by his words that she did not hear it.

"Tyrone! Why, I vow I find him quite insufferable!"

Sir Julian's heavy black brows shot up in surprise, but he was distinctly pleased by this intelligence.

"So perceptive of you, my dear, to see at once what he is. I wonder he should try to push himself onto you so soon after your bereavement. Any normally thoughtful person would understand that you would wish to see only your very dearest friends." He gave her hand a proprietary squeeze. His tone of voice was offhand as he added, "I wonder whatever can have brought him into Somerset. A more fashionable area would seem to be more to his taste. But there, I hear he delights in being considered mysterious."

"Well, he is certainly abominably toplofty, is he not?" said Amy, still speaking with the heat of all her earlier anger at Tyrone.

"And so terribly affected, my dear. Do you know I heard him in the village yesterday speaking to Madame de Méreaux, that odious émigrée woman. And in French, my dear! He is quite fluent, I must admit. One might almost take him for a native." This was all said very casually and with the note of pettishness adopted by some of the more dandified members of the ton when discussing the latest *on dit*. But Sir Julian was watching Amy carefully for her reaction. "Yes, I do wonder what ever can have brought him to this neighborhood."

"He speaks quite good French, you say?" she asked speculatively. "Of course, many of us do so, but it hardly seems politic to flaunt it just now with Bonaparte at our very gates, so to speak."

"Precisely," he replied, looking closely at her face. He was well pleased with what he saw there.

They walked on another moment in silence, Amy trying hard to grasp at an idea that lay in the back of her mind. Sir Julian was giving her time for the full meaning of his seemingly meaningless conversation to sink in.

"Your aunt will be worrying about you, Amelia. I shall return you to her and wish you a good day."

At the house once again, he took his leave with punctilious correctness. He was being very careful not to scare off the wealthy Miss Clerville. He had come too far to give up the idea of marrying her, and her fortune, now. Amy, still thinking it wise to avoid her aunt, slipped upstairs to change her dress for dinner.

An hour passed, and still Amy had not been able to grasp that elusive thought. There was something she was trying to remember. She had sat in a steaming bath scented with rose oil, pondering. But still it would not come. As her luxuriant curls were being brushed till they gleamed, she had bent her mind to the phantom idea, but it refused to appear. Finally she was dressed in a pretty pale-grey muslin gown with violet ribbons, but she was not even now perfectly aware of what she had put on.

She descended the great staircase to meet her aunt and cousin for dinner. As her delicately shod feet reached the floor of the hall, with its tiles of large black and white marble squares, she stopped abruptly. She stood as if a statue, looking for all the world like the queen in a giant chess game. In her mind she distinctly heard Lord Tyrone's voice saying, "I always thought Standen a rather competent, clever fellow!" He had known Ned! But why had he said nothing to her before of their acquaintance? What had he to hide.

Suddenly all the afternoon's deliberations and revelations came into sharp focus in a rush. He had known Ned. He spoke French like a native. He kept a yacht at the "discreet little harbor" at Lyme Regis. He had appeared in Winsham unannounced shortly after her brother's death. He felt he had to hide his acquaintance with Ned. And he had obviously taken an immediate and violent dislike to her, Ned's sister. Everything seemed to fit.

"Oh!" she said aloud in frustration. "And just

when I must leave for London. But I must learn more about this odious Marquis!"

Ned's voice now joined the chorus of thoughts in her mind. "My comrades must not be jeopardized by you in any way, Amy. You have promised."

Yes, she had promised not to ask dangerous questions. And she had promised to go to London and act like every other silly girl there with no thought in her head but the next ball or new gown, she thought with a great sense of frustration and ill-usage.

But she had also promised to help if ever she could. She may not be able to do anything important just now, but she could watch and listen and learn everything possible about the Marquis of Tyrone. If he had been responsible for Ned's death, she would find it out. Of that she was determined.

Chapter Seven

Amy had no chance to advance her research into the actions and motives of the Marquis of Tyrone. The gentleman had seen enough for the present and had carried himself off, back to Lyme Regis. But he would spend rather more time in London this Season than he was used to do. He meant to keep a close eye on the hotheaded Miss Clerville and, if possible, find a way of defusing her potentially explosive information.

Within a fortnight, Amy herself was being carried away. With considerably mixed emotions, she bade goodbye to the home she adored but which, just at present, was too melancholy for her to abide. So she held to her promise to Ned and turned her face toward the bustle of the great metropolis.

On her arrival in town, Amy was immediately pitchforked into the hectic world of London during the Season. She found it invigorating. After the quiet of the country, the bustle and commotion of London was heady and exciting, and it was precisely the antidote she needed. She was surrounded by activity, and she threw herself into it with a vengeance in an attempt to assuage her own grief and live up to her promise to Ned.

The Season had as yet barely begun. Several of the great families had still not taken down the shutters or put the knockers back in place on the doors of the great mansions in Berkeley Square, Park Lane, and Mount Street.

Amy and her aunt were almost wholly occupied

with shopping. They spent each morning among a procession of fashionable ladies, making their way from milliner to mantua-maker, from the Pantheon Bazaar to Bond Street, from Grafton's to Mr. Wedgewood's showrooms in York Street.

The chief respite in the day's shopping would be a stop at Hookham's Library in Bond Street. Here they would see all the Ladies of the Ton pouring over the most recent issue of *The Lady's Magazine* or looking for the latest lurid marble-covered novel from the Minerva Press. Amy had herself chosen a new volume of Lord Byron's poems, but she never seemed to have the time to read them.

To add to the general hubbub, the Duchess had invited four ranking members from her large brood of grandchildren to spend a month or two with her in London. She was the fondest of grandmamas and somehow could always find the time to listen to a new story, caress a bandaged elbow, or administer a necessary but gentle scold.

The children had quite adopted Amy. Indeed, they thought of her as their private property. She was thankful for the excuse they provided for visits to Astley's Equestrian Exhibition and Circus or the menagerie at Exeter 'Change. They had dragged her, albeit quite willingly, to Madame Tussaud's Wax Museum and Mrs. Aberdeen's Papyruseum. Whenever Amy found her spirits sagging, she could count on the children to pick them up again. And she suspected that this was precisely the reason that her aunt had invited them to come to London at such a hectic time.

One bright morning shortly after her arrival Amy was, as usual, shopping in Bond Street with her aunt. She was in high good spirits as she stepped out of a shop, a small wicker basket on her arm. Tucked inside was a tiny Yorkshire puppy, as yet no more than a wriggling puff of white fur. It was to be a birthday present for her little cousin Letty. As she cooed to it prettily, she stepped forward only to run directly into Lord Tyrone.

She was so startled that it was a moment before she realized it was he. Then she saw his cool gaze travel maddeningly over her. His practiced eye took in her pretty amber piqué walking dress and villager hat.

"Good morning, Miss Clerville. I can see that your aunt has outfitted you in the first style of elegance. You are looking charmingly," he said with a suspicion of a shrug.

"My aunt has perfect taste, my lord," Amy parried.

The puppy peered over the edge of the basket. Tyrone bent to look at it and came up with a look almost of distaste. "I would not have thought you the lapdog type. Setters, perhaps, or at the very least a boxer, would seem to suit you better."

Amy gave her head a toss. She was on the verge of explaining that the puppy was a child's gift, but changed her mind. She owed him no explanations of her conduct. Before she could think of a suitable rejoinder, the Duchess stepped out of the shop.

"Why, Justin! We did not look to find you so soon back in town. Have you decided to grace the season with your august presence?"

Tyrone turned a warm smile on the Duchess. "I discovered things to be running so smoothly in Kent without me, Your Grace, that I found myself quite free to hurry back to the joys of town. Indeed, I sometimes fear that my agent at Harwood finds me a trifle *de trop*. And I own I had no wish to resist the enticements of town this Season."

"Hah! She must be quite an enticement indeed, to bring you to London." The Duchess eyed him closely. Tyrone was looking mischievously at her. It well suited his purpose to have her think what she was obviously thinking. He feared he had been spending too much time away from town lately and making

too many trips into France. People had begun to ask
questions. So far they had not been too awkward, but
he was endangering his cover.

He had decided to appear more conspicuously as
a leisured member of the ton for a while, appearing
at Almack's and the more select evening parties, occasionally gambling a bit at White's or one of the
discreet clubs in Pickering Place or St. James'
Square. He would squire some lovely lady around the
park and generally let himself be seen and commented
upon. At the same time, his residence in town would
afford him ample opportunity to further observe the
young lady who now stood before him, as well as her
paramour, Deventer. The Marquis was confident the
fellow would follow Miss Clerville to London.

"Well, whatever your reasons, we can all benefit
from them," continued the Duchess. "It will be lovely
to have you here, Justin." She smiled at him with true
warmth and admiration, a smile which he returned,
for he was genuinely fond of the Duchess. "And how
fares your mother? We have missed her sorely in
town."

"She is well, Your Grace, I promise you. She
finds the air of Kent agrees with her rather more than
that of London, but she's bid me send you her fondest regards. She hopes to see you at Bath for the
summer."

"And how is that fine strapping boy of yours? If
he's like his father, I'll wager he'll be riding to hounds
before the year is out."

A gleam came into the gentleman's eyes that
Amelia had never thought to see there, and he
chuckled. "He's a bit young as yet, ma'am, but he has
promised to race me across the meadow on his new
bay as soon as I return home again."

During this exchange, Amelia had been closely
watching the Marquis. She was amazed at the change
in his tone, indeed in his whole demeanor, as he spoke
to her aunt. He obviously afforded the lady great re-

spect, and his voice and eyes sparkled with a humor that gave him an almost boyish look. And when he spoke of his son, the pride in his voice was not to be denied.

The boyish look was certainly at variance with the rest of his appearance, for he was looking very top-of-the-trees, a definite man of the world. His Hessians gleamed with the unmistakable glow of a champagne polish. His powerful shoulders were encased in a beautiful coat of dark-blue Bath cloth that clearly announced Weston as his tailor. Biscuit-colored pantaloons fitted his well-muscled legs to perfection, and his snowy cravat was tied with a subtle elegance that was mimicked unsuccessfully by many of the younger bucks.

"What do you think of my granddaughter's birthday gift?" she asked, scooping the squirming puppy from the basket. "Silly-looking little thing, isn't it? But I believe she'll do well for the child's first dog."

Tyrone looked at Amelia with a rueful grin. His eyes retained a faint glimmer of warmth. With the tiniest nod of apology, he said, "My mistake, Miss Clerville." He took the squirming puppy in his strong hands, stroking the little ears with a surprising gentleness. Then he deposited it back in the basket, giving it a final pat, and turned to Amelia again. After a slight pause while he studied her face, he said, "You really should have setters, you know. Just the color of your hair." For one brief moment their eyes met clearly, then his became hooded again with their habitually guarded look, and he turned to the Duchess. "See that your granddaughter learns to care for it well, Your Grace. I bid you good day."

Amelia watched him go, then turned to her aunt. "Well! That is surely one of the strangest men I have ever met, Aunt Louie! He always talks to me as though he positively dislikes me, though I cannot think why he should. I'm sure I've done nothing to earn his displeasure. To me he is always insufferably rude and arrogant, then you walk out the door and he becomes a veritable Prince Charming."

"Ah yes, poor dear. I do remember when everyone found him so."

They entered their carriage and began their return to Berkeley Square. The Duchess related a little of the Marquis's history to her niece, including the story of the disastrous marriage. Amelia began to understand a bit more about this enigmatic nobleman.

"I can't imagine why he has come to town so early in the Season," continued the Duchess. "His invariable habit is to pop up every now and then for a few days, and then to infuriate a great many hostesses for the rest of the Season by hibernating in Kent or wherever it is he chooses to spend the rest of his time. He must have a very particular reason for being here."

Amy pondered the story and seemed to come to a conclusion. "Well, it is all very tragic, Aunt Louie. But you know, to my mind, his sad background cannot excuse his ill manners. I still find him insufferable."

"Well, yes, I suppose that's true. And you are right, of course, about his arrogance. The Saviles have always been terribly proud, and Justin is the worst. Perhaps that made his poor choice of a wife even harder to bear." She gave her niece a long look and added, "In fact, I know only one other person who can match the Marquis of Tyrone for pride." She raised an eyebrow slightly, then turned gracefully and peered out the window of the slowly moving carriage.

They rode some little way in silence, Amy cuddling the puppy in her lap. She was considering her aunt's view of Tyrone. The Duchess had always been a shrewd judge of character, and Amy instinctively trusted her opinions. Perhaps she herself had judged the Marquis a bit too harshly. She recalled that she had disliked him almost on sight, and she tried to remember why. She did know that whenever they chanced to meet he set her hackles up at once. And he seemed to react the same way toward her. And she still had an inexplicably strong feeling that he was somehow connected to her brother and his death. She was glad that he was in town, where she would have an opportunity to learn more about him and perhaps to subtly question him about Ned.

"By the by," said the Duchess presently. "I spoke to Maria Sefton while we were in Hookham's this morning. She has promised to send along our vouchers for the opening of Almack's. I've explained your situation to her, and she doesn't feel it's necessary for you to appear in black gloves. But your conduct must be particularly seemly, since you are technically in mourning. I cannot impress upon you too much, my dear, how important Almack's is. The most tedious place, of course, but there, who ever said London society made any sense at all? You must do well at Almack's, Amelia, or we may as well all pack up and go back to Somerset."

The Duchess proceeded to outline to Amy the importance of this shrine of the *beau monde* and its Lady Patronesses. These Rulers of Fashion and Arbiters of Taste could make or break the come-out of any young lady in London, and Amy had no desire to disgrace her aunt by a failure before them. Consequently, she tried to listen closely as her aunt outlined the unwritten but no less stringent rules of this most exclusive of clubs.

"And of course, you must not dance with any gentleman more than twice in one evening. You may not waltz until you have been given clearance by one of the Patronesses. Mrs. Drummond Burrell is the sourest old thing imaginable, but you must pass her inspection in particular if you hope to be a success. You must be sure that each of your partners returns you to me at the end of the dance. It's all very tedious, my dear, and a more boring place you'll not find in the whole of London. One cannot even get a glass of champagne! But a success at Almack's can go far in opening other doors to you." She patted her niece's hand. "There, I have no fears for you, my love. You'll take very well indeed."

Try as she might to pay close attention to these instructions, Amy's mind kept wandering to the memory of a pair of blue eyes so dark they were almost black and a face that had never really smiled at her. She had her own reasons for wanting to appear at the opening assembly at Almack's, and they had nothing to do with the dictates of a society she was not yet certain she wanted to be a part of.

Several days passed, and Amy began to grow accustomed to the pace of London. One morning that was particularly fine, showing promise of becoming one of the loveliest days of the Season, the Duchess was, as usual, breakfasting in her room. Amy had eaten some time earlier, for she could not adjust to the fashionable London practice of keeping to her bed till the morning was half gone. In fact, she had already enjoyed a brisk ride on Medusa, crossing the park at an extremely unfashionable hour which allowed her some of the real exercise that was impossible there later in the day, when the park was thronged with members of the ton, seeing and being seen.

She had enjoyed a hearty breakfast of ham, grilled kidneys, buttered eggs, muffins, and strong coffee. And now, also as usual, she climbed the stairs to her aunt's room to discuss their plans for the rest of the day. The pretty flounce around the soft muslin skirt of her sage-green morning dress brushed lightly against the dark wood of the railing, and the homey smell of lemon polish greeted her as she ascended.

"Good morning, Aunt Louie. Is it not a beautiful spring day?"

Her aunt gave her a withering glance. "Not being myself a country wench, I could not say. Like other civilized people, I have not yet ventured from my room."

"Oh, but you should, Aunt Louie. You really should. There's nothing like a good gallop across the park in the morning air to set one up for the rest of the day."

"That's as may be, but I do hope, my dear, that you will take care to confine such unladylike behavior to the extremely unfashionable hours you have heretofore chosen."

"Oh, give over, do, Aunt Louie. You know very well that you were used to race with the Duke across the park yourself, and in full view of the *beau monde*."

The Duchess's eyes twinkled. "Well, I fear I must admit that I was always fond of a good run on a solid piece of horseflesh," she admitted with a tiny smile. "But let me remind you, my love, that you are a young lady in her first season, not even yet presented at Almack's and technically in mourning. And you have not the protection of a title, as I had, to maintain your reputation. When you are well and solidly married, you may be as dashing as you like."

"Oh dear." Amy sighed. "Then I had as well return to Standish at once if I don't wish to bring ruin down on all our heads." She gave a gamine smile. "Come, Aunt Louie, let us not be so deadly serious. It is a lovely day. What plans have we for it?"

"If you recall, you are to have another fitting with Madame Fanchon this morning."

"Another fitting! Indeed, Aunt Louie! You have helped me to chose so very many pretty gowns already. I do adore them, but I cannot imagine how I shall wear the half of them."

"You will see, my dear. The season has but just begun, but soon you will have a calendar more crowded than you can imagine. How many gowns do you suppose you will need for a day that begins with a morning dance, followed by a Venetian breakfast, then an afternoon musicale, a drive in the park, a dinner party, a rout, and two balls?" Amy's soft eyes grew wide. "Such a day, I promise you, will not be so unusual."

"Oh my! I do not think I shall last a week at that pace."

"Nonsense. You shall do very well. As the invitations are sure to come tumbling down on us after the opening of Almack's tomorrow, I've not planned anything for this afternoon. It will be our last chance for a rest, and I wish to spend some time with the children."

"Oh, did I not tell you? I am engaged to ride in the park with Sir Julian Deventer this afternoon. Poseidon has never been among a crowd, and I think he is ready for a tryout."

The Duchess frowned heavily. "I cannot like your spending so much time with that 'gentleman,' dear. There is an oiliness in his manners that I find quite disgusting, and few members of the ton receive him. You know his reputation is quite shocking, and it can do you no good to be seen with him."

"I did not know that he is not accepted. He said he would be at Almack's tomorrow."

"That, I fancy, is Sally Jersey's idea of a joke," snorted her aunt.

"Still, Aunt Louie, while I may not be overfond of Sir Julian, he has been very kind to me, and I very much wish to ride Poseidon in the park this afternoon." She paused, and a mischievous light came into her eyes. "Would you rather I rode alone?"

"Amelia! You shall do no such thing!" Her aunt looked genuinely frightened that her niece might try such a stunt. "Oh, very well! Ride with the Deventer fellow. I do hope that after tomorrow evening you will be able to provide yourself with a more suitable escort."

Chapter Eight

The rest of the morning passed pleasantly for Amelia. She was still too new to the extravagances of London shopping to be bored by them. It seemed to her wondering eyes that each gown she tried on was lovelier than the last. The fitting progressed from a dusky-blue Scotch cambric walking dress with a slate velvet spencer to a redingote with double capes in brick merino to a sea-green tamboured muslin morning dress, then ended with several ball gowns in spider gauze, silver tissue, sarcenet, and crape.

The decision to restrain herself to the more subtle colors and styles as a sign of her mourning had indeed been a wise one. They suited her to perfection. In the smoky blues and greens, the mauves and russets, that she, together with her aunt, had chosen, she glowed with an almost ethereal loveliness.

Just as she was preparing to leave the shop of the most fashionable mantua-maker in London, Lady Waverly bounced in the door.

"Katie!" exclaimed Amy in delight.

"Oh, Amy, what luck to run into you here! Are you in a hurry? I'm off to find a truly devastating hat to go with the new jonquil mull walking dress that Madame is making for me. I've just come for a swatch of the fabric for matching."

She turned to a bright-eyed shop assistant and asked prettily for the sample. "Isn't London shopping fun? I don't know when I've enjoyed myself more. I daresay Tom will wilt when he gets the bills, so I plan

to discover the day they'll arrive and simply unman
him with my loveliness." She let out an engaging
giggle, and her friend smiled warmly. "Do come with
me to the Pantheon Bazaar. You must help me find a
crushingly divine creation to help turn the trick.
Maybe a high poke with a ruched lining. Feathers,
maybe? I'm so tired of having roses all over my head.
But then, maybe a bunch of grapes would be just the
thing."

Amy laughed as her friend's words tumbled out
over one another. She always found Katie such a delight, and her enthusiasm was contagious. "Of course
I'll come with you, Katie. But you must promise to
help me pick out a new parasol."

Katie clapped her hands together in delight. "My
dear, I've seen the very one! Pale salmon with brown
lace trimmings. It will be simply heavenly with your
new russet pelisse." She plucked the swatch of beautiful yellow muslin from the shopgirl with a ready
smile of thanks, and linking her arm through Amy's,
ushered her friend out the door.

By the time Amy had returned to Berkeley
Square, loaded with parcels full of trinkets that Katie
had insisted Amy could not live without, the day was
far advanced. The two young friends had dallied over
tea and cakes in a fashionable tearoom, and now Amy
had just enough time to change for her ride with Sir
Julian.

She was ready when he called. She was unable to
adopt the fashion among ladies of the ton to keep every gentleman cooling his heels in the parlor awhile
till they made their appearance.

Amy was smiling as she and Sir Julian stepped
out into the afternoon sun, and he tossed her lightly
up onto Poseidon's back.

"You will certainly turn heads today, my dear.
You are looking very elegant, and this is a most magnificent animal."

"I thank you, sir," replied Amy as she stroked the

chestnut's glossy neck. She did indeed look very fetching in a habit of dark-rust velvet with beige facings. Her rather masculine riding hat was softened by a beguilingly curled beige ostrich plume, and her embroidered gauntlet gloves held the reins lightly and comfortably.

"He is indeed a fine animal. I've been wanting to try him out among the throngs in the Park for a while now."

"Are you sure you can handle him, my dear? I know your fame as a horsewoman, but he is a strong-spirited animal, hardly a lady's horse."

Amy's eyes flashed. She was overproud where her horsemanship was concerned, and she rose very straight in her saddle. "If you do not wish to risk riding with me, sir, perhaps I had as well go alone!"

Sir Julian turned a languid look in her direction. "I see I shall have to learn not to rouse your ire, my dear." After a slight pause he added quietly, "But then perhaps the right man may know how to tame you."

Amy was once again in control of her temper. "I am sorry, Sir Julian. I'm behaving like the hoyden I'm often told I am." She showed him a dazzling smile full of repentance. "Shall we have our ride?"

They entered the Park through the Stanhope Gate. The famous Rotten Row was a mass of barouches, tilburies and phaetons, old-fashioned landaus and dashing curricles, old dowagers and shy young misses. And beautiful horses with splendid young men atop them, eyeing the whole show. Amy as yet knew few people in London. She saw very many heads turn her way, but, though Sir Julian Deventer doubtless had a large acquaintance in town, no one approached them for some time. Several heads were bowed vaguely, and coldly, in their direction, and Amy began to realize the strength of her aunt's words earlier that morning. Sir Julian Deventer was obviously no favorite among the ton.

As she pondered this thought, a gentleman approached and tipped his hat. "Afternoon, Deventer!" he said a bit too heartily. "I've come to be introduced to the loveliest lady in the Park." He turned a roguish smile on Amelia. As she acknowledged a brief introduction to Lord Phillimore with a nod, she quietly took stock of him. She saw a man in his early forties, a ruddy face lost to years of dissipation, and a glint in his eye that seemed to go well with his oily and over-familiar manners. In fact, he was remarkably like Sir Julian. Amy was much struck by the fact that only such as he would deign to notice them.

"How fortunate we all are to have the Season graced with a new star, both exceedingly beautiful and, I understand, obnoxiously rich. You should have a very full schedule almost at once, my dear."

Amy was shocked by the freedom he used in thus addressing her, and was relieved to see at that moment her cousin Elinor with her mother-in-law the Dowager Countess of Kendall, driving nearby.

"If you will excuse me, Sir Julian, I should like to speak to my cousin. I will rejoin you presently." With a nod she rode off. As she approached the barouche, Elinor's face flashed her a warm smile.

"Amelia, you are looking lovely. I hope you are enjoying your first taste of London."

"Oh, Nell, I've been in such a whirl ever since we arrived," She laughed as she said, "I never would have thought it possible that one could do so much shopping." She turned to the Dowager Countess. "How lovely to see you again, Lady Kendall. I do trust that you are well?"

"Quite well, my dear, I thank you. I was so sorry to hear about your dear brother. Such a tragedy. He was an exceedingly promising young man. We have all lost by his death."

A deep sadness came into Amy's eyes, and she fidgeted slightly on her horse. She was always an uneasy object of sympathy, and she had not yet schooled herself to accept the comfort of others. The pain was too deep and too fresh.

"I thank you, ma'am," was all she managed to say.

"I do applaud your decision to have your season anyway. You have waited too long already, my dear." She reached up for Amy's hand and gave it a little squeeze. "It is your turn, Amelia. Enjoy it. I'm sure it is just what your father and your brother would want." She gave Amy a warm smile. Amelia had always been fond of the Countess, and she returned the smile with affection.

Elinor, who knew well her cousin's aversion to sympathy, deftly changed the subject. "I trust that my lively young nieces and nephews aren't trying your patience too much. I was afraid they might prove to be too much for Mama just now, but she always seems ten years younger when any of her grandchildren are around."

"Indeed, they are a delight, Nell. You know how your mother dotes on them. And I must confess, I have come to do so as well. How else could I have such a charming excuse to visit Mr. Astley's fascinating equestrian show?"

The Dowager smiled. "I personally have always found my grandchildren wonderfully convenient when I tire of the strictures of being an 'elderly lady.' And as I recall the rules for a young lady in her first season, they are just as boring. Do allow yourself to have fun, dear."

"But do say you'll come for a drive with me tomorrow, Amelia," begged Elinor. "We haven't had a chance to chat since your arrival."

"I should be most pleased, Nell."

Just then, Sir Julian rode up to rejoin her, and she made the necessary introduction to Lady Kendall. The warmth of the previous moment evaporated abruptly.

"I believe Sir Julian and I have met," she replied coldly. "I trust you are well, sir."

"Very well, my lady, and the more so now for the sight of two more such charming ladies."

In answer, the Dowager turned to Amelia. "Do ask your aunt to bring you to call one morning soon, dear." Without another glance at Sir Julian she ordered her coachman to drive on.

Amy saw the gentleman beside her stiffen slightly, but all he said was, "Shall we continue our ride, Amelia?"

She was somewhat taken aback by the coldness of Lady Kendall toward him. She had always thought that the stories of his shocking reputation as a rake and gambler were somewhat exaggerated. Now she pondered her aunt's warning about him and began to wonder.

As she looked up from her thoughts, she saw another pair of riders across the Row that were turning not a few heads. There was Lord Tyrone riding with the most dashing and beautiful lady that Amelia had ever seen. She had hair the color of pale straw, a creamy complexion with cheeks like roses, and sparkling eyes of cornflower blue set deeply into a lovely heart-shaped face. The eyes were matched perfectly by the blue velvet habit she wore. It was cut in the new and fashionable Polish style with deeper-blue frogging and braid trim. Atop her pale curls was a dashing hat à la Hussar set at a jaunty angle. She rode gracefully on an exquisite mare of pure white, whose creaminess seemed to match her own complexion.

The lady was all the more striking as she rode beside Tyrone. The contrast was complete to a shade. He sat atop his black stallion, which glistened like onyx. He wore a finely cut coat of the darkest midnight-blue superfine that showed off his muscular and athletic body to perfection. His black curls shone under a perfectly set dark-blue beaver.

The picture they made was perfectly calculated

and altogether effective. Amy wondered idly if the creamy mare had been a gift from Tyrone, and she sighed audibly.

Sir Julian heard the sigh and followed the direction of her eyes. "Ah, I see we are graced with the presence of the fair Olivia. Beautiful, is she not? Quite the most dashing widow in town." He was watching Amy carefully as he added, "They present quite a striking picture, don't they? Such a suitable pair in every way. The whole of the ton is in daily expectation of seeing their betrothal notice in the *Gazette*."

Amy studied them another moment. "They are a quite remarkably handsome couple." She noticed the arrogance behind Lady Cole's lovely blue eyes. "They would seem to be quite well matched."

"They've been the primary *on dit* for weeks. I do believe my Lord Tyrone is truly snared at last."

By that time Tyrone had spotted them, and the beautiful pair turned their horses and made their way through the throng. Every eye in the park followed them.

Tipping his hat negligently to Amelia, Lord Tyrone said smoothly, "Good afternoon, Miss Clerville. I see you have brought the beautiful Poseidon to heel at last."

"Good day, my lord. Yes. I felt he was ready for a trial in the park traffic."

"I believe you have not met Lady Cole. Lady Amelia Clerville has just arrived from Somerset for the season."

"How do you do, Miss Clerville." The voice was musical but brittle, and Amy noticed more clearly the coldness in the lovely eyes that were turned on her. Lady Cole held out her hand to Amy, and the creamy mare fidgeted slightly. Just as Amy would have taken the proffered hand, Poseidon took exception to the fidgety mare and reared his head. With a great neigh, he took off across the gravel, jumped a low fence and galloped across the park.

As Sir Julian watched in amazement, unable to move, Lord Tyrone turned his own horse. flew over the fence, and thundered off after her. Poseidon had cleared a few low hedges and was now racing across the open lawn of the park, but Tyrone caught up quickly. He reached down for the young horse's bridle and with one swift pull brought him up short. Both horses came to a standstill.

As he looked up into Amy's face, he was astonished to see something rather different from the gratitude he had expected to find there. Her cheeks were red with anger, and there was fire in her eyes.

Amelia was so angry she could hardly speak. Her trembling fingers clutched at the reins, and through clenched teeth she managed to say, "Don't you ever do that again!"

Tyrone was amazed. And in no more than a moment he too was angry.

"You may be assured that I shall not, ma'am. If a silly chit of a girl who doesn't know better than to bring a young and inexperienced animal into such traffic before he is ready chooses to break her neck in such a fashion, who am I to interfere?"

Amy's whole body grew rigid with indignation, and her face was redder still. "Interference, my lord, is precisely the word I should have chosen myself," she shot out. "When I can no longer handle my horse, by myself, I shall walk!" She turned Poseidon, who was now perfectly controlled, and walked him back to where Sir Julian was waiting.

"I should like to return home now, Sir Julian, if you do not mind."

"Of course, my dear."

Amy could feel the attention of every promenader in the park on her as they rode once more toward the gate. Her anger had subsided, and now she was thoroughly humiliated, the more so because she knew that Tyrone had been right. She had misjudged

Poseidon and brought him into the park much too soon. She had made a silly error in judgment that might have cost her much more than wounded pride. Even more unforgivable, she had endangered her horse.

But she could never admit to the haughty and arrogant Marquis that she had made a mistake where a horse was concerned. And she would certainly never beg his pardon!

As they rode toward BerkeleySquire, Sir Julian's voice brought her back to her surroundings. "It's sure to be quite a glittering evening. The opening of Almack's is always one of the high points of the season."

"Oh, yes, I am quite looking forward to tomorrow evening," she replied, but her dispirited tone of voice belied her words.

"I hope you will grant me the opening dance, my dear."

"Yes, of course," she answered unenthusiastically. The rest of the ride home was completed in silence, Amelia deep in her own thoughts, and Sir Julian watching her with a dark and almost surly look.

As they parted at the door of the imposing Harcourt House, he took Amy's hand and kissed it gallantly. "Until tomorrow evening then, my dear."

Amy surprised herself when she recoiled from his kiss and involuntarily pulled back her hand. She tried to cover the moment with her charming smile. "I hope you will forgive me, sir, for being such very dull company today."

"Ah, but you could never be that, my dear. You might be many things, but never dull." It was true, thought Sir Julian in frustration. He never knew quite what to expect from Amelia Clerville, and it bothered him greatly. While marriage with such a beautiful and spirited girl might have its compensations, he would have been better pleased if her immense fortune had been paired with a more biddable disposition. He had no intention of leaving his more independent pursuits behind after he had brought Amelia's wealth under his control. But he knew he would have to learn to control her temper as well.

Chapter Nine

The morning of the opening of Almack's came in clear, warm, and promising. Wherever Amy went that day she encountered a buzz of excitement about the important event of the evening.

In the shops, ladies of the ton were searching for the perfect ribbon or feather to complete their evening's toilette. Driving in the park with her cousin Elinor, Amy noticed fewer promenaders than usual, and learned that many of the ladies were laid down upon their beds to rest so that they would be in looks that night.

Even Katie, the respectably married Lady Waverly, was excited about the opening of the famed Matrimonial Mart. Amy herself began to grow nervous about the decided probability that she would make a cake of herself and disgrace her aunt.

The Duchess sent Pitt, her own exacting dresser, to Amelia early in the evening to help her dress and to arrange her hair. She fussed and clucked and admonished Lady Amelia to please hold still, or she could not be responsible for the results. At last, that brisk and acerbic servant had done her best, and Amy turned to survey herself in the tall gilt pier glass. She could hardly believe her eyes.

She saw a graceful and delicate figure set off to perfection by one of Madame Fanchon's loveliest creations of the palest mauve gauze over white satin. Rosettes and ribbons of moss-green velvet caught and trimmed the front, and long green gloves of the softest French kid covered her arms. Her mother's delicate amethysts set off her long smooth neck.

Her usual red mop had been brushed till the curls shone like burnished copper; they were caught by a simple gold fillet. Green rosettes peeped out from the curls, echoing the velvety green of her eyes. Those lovely eyes seemed to be shining with a special radiance tonight. Amy had disappeared, and Lady Amelia Clerville had taken her place, ready to go to the ball.

She lowered her eyes from the vision. In a very small voice, she whispered, "Do you like it, Neddie?" As if in answer, the efficient Pitt actually managed a half-smile of pride in her creation. Placing a gossamer shawl of Norwich silk shot with gold around her young charge's shoulders, she ushered her out the door.

Downstairs Amy relaxed a bit. Her aunt seemed pleased with her.

"Why, you look positively radiant, my love. I'm sure I shall be the envy of all the fond mamas."

"Such fustian, Aunt Louie." She laughed. "But you look like heaven! That gown!"

She gazed upon the Duchess, resplendent in a gown of the softest and finest crimson crape, cut *à l'antique*. It was caught up into gracefully classic folds, and a drapery of silver net hung from one shoulder. The hem was embroidered with delicate silver spiderwebs, and her magnificent hair was accented with an aigrette of gently curled crimson feathers caught with diamonds.

"It is rather nice, isn't it?" she said with an elfin smile. "Cost the earth, of course. But my name is Harcourt. Can't disgrace it with a tawdry gown. Come, my love. Let us go and do our worst." The young lady and the older woman, arm in arm, stepped out to the waiting carriage.

Amy looked around her at the glittering company as they entered the Assembly Rooms. All the young ladies on display seemed to be hanging onto their mamas and looking as if they were on their way to the gallows. Strangely enough, their terror served to calm Amelia. She was unconcerned with the success of her own season, wishing merely to refrain from disgracing herself in front of her aunt, and so she was soon able to relax and be completely herself. And, of course, for that very reason, she was the biggest hit of them all.

"So refreshingly natural, is she not?" commented one dowager. Another, with an unmarried daughter of her own, said less kindly, "Well, she is different." Comments like "an Original," and "quite out of the common way," flitted about the room. Amy became one of the season's Incomparables almost at once.

It was true that Mrs. Drummond Burrell, that most supercilious of the Lady Patronesses, was quizzing her with a decided frown. Leaning to Lady Jersey, she harumphed, "I cannot like that young lady's ease of manner. And with her brother scarce a month in his grave."

Sally Jersey bobbed her feathers. "Oh, don't be sillier than you can help, Clementina. The poor thing has been in blacks a year already for her father. And you must know that it was her poor brother's very command that has kept her out of mourning again. I find her manners just as they ought to be, and only what I should expect from a Clerville. Louisa will do well with that one, I promise you."

Amy was going down the first set of country dances with Sir Julian Deventer. He was quite properly dressed in the formal evening attire that was de rigueur at Almack's. She was relieved not to have been left on the sidelines, and as he was an accomplished dancer, she began to enjoy herself.

"I have seldom seen you lovelier, Amelia. I can see that I shall have to look sharp to maintain my advantage with you."

"Oh, Sir Julian, you do talk such nonsense. You

know that you will ever be one of my first friends in London."

"I shall often remind you of it, my dear, for I can see by all the heads turning your way that there will be many to vie with me for the pleasure of your company."

His words were easy and his tone was bantering, but when Amy looked up into his face there was something disquieting in the intensity of his gaze. Luckily at that moment the movements of the dance separated them, and there was no chance for further converse. As the music ended, Amy found herself relieved to be returned to her aunt.

"Oh bother!" declared that noble lady. "There is the Countess Lieven beckoning to me. Odious woman, but I suppose I had better go and see what she wants." Turning to Lady Sefton at her side, she said, "Maria, be a dear and look after Amelia while I deal with the creature." She sailed away in a cloud of silver net and egret plumes.

As Amy sat down next to the agreeable Lady Sefton she perused the assemblage with interest. Across the room a gentleman was seen to be surveying her through an elaborate quizzing glass. Good breeding prevented her returning the stare, but she was hard pressed not to let her curiosity show. She had never seen quite such a creature. His coat was so pinched in he could scarce breathe; his dancing pumps were varnished to a high gloss and festooned with elaborate buckles with gold and diamonds. Silk knee breeches that seemed painted to his spidery legs topped a pair of rather alarming yellow-striped stockings. His neckcloth was folded into the dangerous Oriental, its points so high he could scarce see where he was going and so rigid he could not turn his head. She inquired of Lady Sefton his identity.

"He is quite simply, my dear, the most consummate coxcomb in existence and, *entre nous*, as flighty as a schoolroom miss. Have a care, my dear. Sir Francis Stepworth is on the lookout for a rich wife."

At this the said Sir Francis began his approach. His progress was slow, for he walked as if on stilts, and when at last he bowed gravely over the hand of Lady Sefton, it was with great deliberation. The elaborate stays at his waist precluded impulsive moments.

"Good evening, my very dear Lady Sefton. You look more charmingly at every assembly."

"Humph!" snorted the lady. "Don't know that Louisa will approve, but since you are here I'd best introduce you. Lady Amelia Clerville, Sir Francis Stepworth," she said with a negligent wave of her hand.

Suppressing a giggle, Amelia made her very best curtsy, which, as she had feared, set him off into another of his creaking bows.

"Charmed, my dear Miss Clerville. Ah, I believe they are forming for a country dance. May I beg the very august pleasure and honor of leading Miss Clerville into the set?"

Such gravity of address! Amelia's "Thank you" was equally grave, but the laughter in her eyes could not be suppressed.

Anyone less wrapped up in his own image of himself would have wondered at the twitch of her lips as she offered her hand, but Sir Francis saw only the slight flush of suppressed laughter. He took it for maidenly confusion and gratification at the honor bestowed upon her by his attention, and the couple glided onto the floor.

Sir Francis's dancing could, at best, be described as determined. During the few moments when the movements of the dance brought the pair together, he did not speak but turned a smile upon her overwhelming in the number of very large teeth it showed.

Unfortunately, the brilliant smile would break his concentration and invariably cause him a misstep. But he could not but believe Miss Clerville so dazzled by his charm that she did not notice. The set came at last to an end.

"May I make so bold as to request the exalted pleasure of your exquisite company for a ride in the park this week, Miss Clerville? I may assure you I am accounted a fair whip, and that you need have no fear for your safety in my hands."

"I am very sure that is true, sir," she replied with a twinkle. What fun it would be to set the ton by the ears by letting this silly creature be her escort in the park.

"I should be quite pleased to accept your kind invitation, sir, and am aware of the honor you do me."

Sir Francis beamed. The buckram wadding inside his fitted coat expanded slightly as he puffed up even more. Amy would not have thought it possible, and she struggled to keep her countenance.

"Shall we say Sunday, then?" Amy, afraid to risk speaking, could only nod her agreement.

How very fortunate, mused Sir Francis, that such an eligible heiress should come along this Season. The dandy had no doubt his suit would prosper. Already Miss Clerville was obviously suitably dazzled by his magnificence. A very little time only, he was sure, and he could be quite comfortable again. The couple made their way back to Lady Sefton.

It was with a start that Amy saw that lady talking to Lord Tyrone.

"Ah, here she is now, Justin. My dear, Lord Tyrone has asked my permission for you to waltz. I would not deprive the company of so beautiful a sight, so off you go."

Tyrone bowed over her hand. "I hoped you would not mind, Miss Clerville." His dark eyes glittered down into her own. "I doubt not that you will prove to be the most graceful dancer in the room," he added in a tone both mocking and begrudgingly admiring.

"I am not at all sure, my lord, that I am a match for your own talents, but I should like above all things to try," she answered, a challenge in her eye.

The corners of his mouth twitched momentarily; his eyes warmed by one or two degrees. His arm slid neatly about her waist, and she felt herself being propelled onto the floor.

Despite Tyrone's mocking compliment, she was unsure of her own abilities in the elegant new dance. She had only ever waltzed in her own drawing room with Ned for her partner. Had her first partner at Almack's been Ferdie or Tom she would have felt more at ease. Both she and Tyrone felt the sense of competition between them. She would not let herself be shown the fool to this overbearing man!

As they swept toward the center of the floor, Amelia's nervousness began to fade, to be replaced by an emotion totally new and confusing to her. Her feet scarce touched the floor, and she seemed to glide across the room with no effort at all. She felt her heartbeat quicken. She was aware of Tyrone's arm about her waist as if it had been a red hot poker. In this man's arms she felt as if she had sprouted wings. No wonder so many of the tabbies frowned on the waltz, she thought, when it made you feel like this. She was suddenly very glad that her partner was not Tom.

Amelia was instinctively aware that every pair of eyes in the room was upon them as they spun and dipped. And she could not but admit that they must make a very striking picture indeed. Whatever else Lord Tyrone might be he was certainly handsome. She looked up into his face to see him gazing down at her with a sardonic smile.

"You dance well, Miss Clerville," he said.

"If that is true, my lord, I'm afraid you must credit yourself. It would be impossible to do otherwise with such an accomplished partner," she answered with only the slightest touch of sarcasm.

"Ah, then, I perceive that Sir Julian Deventer must be an effective partner as well. You seemed to so enjoy your dance with him earlier in the evening." He felt Amelia stiffen in his arms. "When may I wish you happy, Miss Clerville?"

"I cannot conceive, my lord, how you should think that any of your affair!"

"I stand rebuked, ma'am."

Her expression softened a very little. Perhaps she would do well to scotch some of the rumors that were apparently running rampant about her and Sir Julian. "I think you need not wait in breathless anticipation for such an announcement, sir." Suddenly she could not bear the scrutiny of those blue eyes, and she began to stare concentratedly at his black-clad shoulder.

They danced silently for some moments. As the music began building to a conclusion, Amy raised her eyes once again to see him surveying her closely. Her face was glowing from the exertion of the dance. It struck Tyrone that she was looking especially lovely.

"You are very much like your brother, Miss Clerville."

"That, sir, is the very finest compliment you could pay me," she answered heatedly. Her eyes flashed in anger, and Tyrone's own dark brows rose perceptibly.

"I agree, ma'am." It was more and more apparent that the sister had some of Clerville's spirit. The thing still worrying Tyrone was how she would use it. After some hesitation he added, almost to himself, "I wonder just how like him you are."

Her gaze lifted quickly to meet his own; an aura of some confusion spread across her pretty features. She saw, with some surprise, that his habitual look of sardonic amusement had been replaced by one of concern.

The music ended, and Tyrone led a bewildered Amelia back toward Lady Sefton. The Marquis's thoughts were also racing as he crossed the floor with

Amelia on his arm. He was trying to decide whether or not he should drop a discreet warning in her ear concerning Sir Julian Deventer.

A warning of what? he asked himself. That Deventer may just possibly have had her brother killed, and then again he may well have had nothing to do with it at all? She would think me a fool indeed, he thought. No, better to wait until there was more proof of the gentleman's treachery, as well as a bit more certainty concerning the young lady's feelings toward him.

"May I get you a glass of orgeat, Miss Clerville?"

A voice from behind him answered sharply, "That won't be necessary, my lord. As you can see, I have just procured Miss Clerville's refreshments myself."

Tyrone wheeled sharply to see Sir Julian Deventer standing just beyond him. He looked back at Amelia, regarding her for a long moment with his old accustomed icy stare.

"Your servant, ma'am," he said. Sketching the briefest of bows, he turned sharply and strode across the room without another word. Amelia was left to ponder his odd changes of mood and that obscure reference to her brother.

"You waltz beautifully, my dear. May I hope to be honored with one before the evening is out?" asked Sir Julian.

"What?" She shook out her mind and tried to turn her attention to him. "Oh yes, of course, Sir Julian. I would be most honored." She found she did not wish to speak to him further just now and was relieved to see Ferdie Brice approaching. "Oh, here is Ferdie come to claim his quadrille. Do forgive me, sir." The two young friends took their places in the dance.

Sir Julian scowled heavily after them. He could see that his carefully laid plans were being threatened now that Amelia was in London. He had been so sure that the "fortuitous" event of her brother's death would keep her in the country, where he was more certain his suit would prosper. It had been a rude awakening when he learned that she intended coming to London anyway.

Things were now at a desperate pass with him. Only this morning, he had barely missed one of his creditors by the expedient of slipping out through the garden of his lodgings. The last payment he had gotten from the Bonapartists had served to discharge only the more pressing of his gambling debts. If Miss Clerville did not agree to marry him, and soon, he would be forced to flee to the Continent to avoid a debtor's cell. Obviously he would have to set things in motion, and at once.

The assembly drew at last to an end. Amy had not missed a dance, and her head was in a whirl. Her future as a full-fledged member of the ton was a certainty. She had even been seen entertaining the demanding Mr. Brummell. The Beau was known to be exceedingly particular about where he lent his countenance and had a known aversion to chits fresh from the schoolroom. But he had sat with Miss Clerville through a whole quadrille. At one point, he was even heard to laugh! Amy's place in society was assured.

Now she was thankful for the chance to review the events of the evening as she rode back to Berkeley Square in her aunt's town carriage. She leaned back against the inviting squabs and mused on the puzzling words of Tyrone. Her aunt's chatter washed over her.

"Well, I think we brushed through that rather well, don't you? Of course, I knew you'd take. Not sure I'm up to having an Incomparable on my hands, but then I was one myself, of course, so I expect we'll manage."

"Oh come, Aunt Louie. I'm hardly what Ferdie would call a diamond of the first water."

"Actually I think 'slap up to the echo' were Mr. Brice's exact words. Now don't try to flummery me,

Amelia. You could not but know that every eye in the room was following your progress from the moment you entered the place," said the Duchess with more than a trace of pride. "Particularly all the young bucks. You should have seen the black looks that fellow Deventer was shooting your way when you were dancing with Tyrone." She gave her niece a scrutinizing glance. "Even I must admit that the two of you were quite a picture. The prettiest girl in the room waltzing with the most eligible bachelor in all of London. I doubt not that it will be the primary *on dit* of the week."

Amy laughed. "I collect that you would be pleased by such a match, Aunt Louie. A marquis, no less, and tolerably well up in the stirrups, I hear."

"My dear! He is rich enough to buy an abbey!" she exclaimed. "A very good boy, Justin. You could do a lot worse. However, you know very well that there is not the slightest need for you to marry money, Amelia. In case you didn't know it, you are nearly as rich as Golden Ball yourself."

"I do know it," Amy replied lightly. "And so I collect there is not the slightest need for me to marry at all," she said with some finality.

The Duchess gave her a sharp look but said nothing, and Amy perceived a need to change the subject.

"I am engaged to ride in the park this week with Sir Francis Stepworth."

"My dear! He is the veriest mushroom!" She snorted.

"Oh, I know, Aunt Louie. But he is so unlike anyone I've ever seen. He quite amuses me. I can scarce wait to see the faces of the tabbies in the park when we appear." She giggled. "And he has most particularly assured me that you need have no fear for my safety."

"Hah!" the Duchess guffawed. "Well, I am persuaded that such arrogance combined with his incredible stupidity will be no match for you, my love. And

I must admit that I would as lief see you there with him as with that scowling encroacher Deventer," she said. "Still, I hope you will not encourage Sir Francis, dear. I've no wish to see such a coxcomb hanging about my drawing room."

With that they arrived at Harcourt House, and it was with something like relief that Amy took herself and her aching feet up to her room. She was both glowing and exhausted. She had had a great success, been showered with compliments and invitations, and made many new friends. She had also had her curiosity piqued by Lord Tyrone's enigmatic manner. Yes, she had much to consider as a result of this evening's success, she thought.

But no sooner had the sea-green damask hangings been pulled close around her bed and her head touched the cool satin of her pillow than she was fast asleep.

Chapter Ten

Amy slept soundly, and she was up and dressed long before any of her newly acquired fashionable friends, as was her wont. Surprisingly, after last night's success she was not in spirits this morning. Donning an old cambric morning dress of faded green, she went down to breakfast for a solitary cup of chocolate. She moped about the house, wandered into the garden, and strolled about aimlessly for a while. She had not even the pleasure of wondering what had put her down in the hips. She knew only too well. There were too many unanswered questions and conflicting emotions warring in her mind, and they all centered about the same noble lord. Her suspicions of him were still present, but she could not forget the feeling of waltzing in his arms.

She needed a respite, an easing of the turbulence, a short breathing space. The children! They were always able to restore her innate ability to laugh at herself and her troubles.

Running lightly up the stairs to the nursery, she thought how lovely it would be to become a child again, even for a while.

"I shall, then," she told herself with determination.

The children were not only awake and dressed but were high-spirited and restive. "Good morning, troops," she cried with a smile.

"Amy! Amy!" they screeched, clustering about her.

Six-year-old Robin took hold of her hand and looked up adoringly with his big pansy-brown eyes. A little white ball of fur with two big black eyes was bouncing around her ankles, attempting to chew on her toes, and little Miss Letty somersaulted up to her with a giggle.

"We're going to the Park, Amy, and Cat says I may sail my new boat on the pond," cried Robin. "Won't you come too?"

"Oh do, Amy. Please do! Please come," came a chorus of cries.

"Now, you mustn't trouble Lady Amelia. I'm sure she has better things to do than to chase after an unruly bunch of children in a public park," scolded their nurse.

"But, indeed, I do not, Miss Catterson, and I would dearly love to go. In fact, why don't you stay here and rest a bit, and I will take them myself? You are only just over your own bad cold, you know. They will be perfectly all right with me, I do assure you."

"Oh, but I couldn't, Miss," said the nurse from a strong sense of the respect due such a lady.

"Please, Miss Catterson," said Amy. The green eyes she turned to the nurse held a silent plea. "I should really like it very much."

"Please, Cat, please! Amy will see to us. We'll be so very good! Please, Cat, dear Cat," chanted the chorus.

"Well, if you are quite certain, Miss. I wouldn't want them to tire you. You know what they can be."

"Indeed I do, but I never tire, Miss Catterson, and their high spirits are precisely what I need this morning. I promise to have them back by ten."

"I should count it as a great favor, Miss. I am a little tired still, and I shall be glad of another hour on my bed."

"Can we take Paisley with us?" cried Letty, scooping up the puppy. "Please, Amy."

"I'm afraid Paisley is still too little, Letty. She might get lost or stepped on in such a big park." The little girl's face fell. "But I'll tell you what. We'll take her out into the garden later and give her a romp. Come along now."

Before a sense of duty could overcome Miss Catterson and detain them longer, Amy ushered her charges out the door, grabbing an old straw bonnet for herself as she passed her own room.

The children entered the park with a whoop of high spirits suddenly released. Amy was soon laughing gaily as she joined in a hearty game of tag with Lizzy and Letty. Her bonnet soon became untied and fell to the grass. She looked around quickly, a brief worried frown between her brows. It was definitely unseemly for a young lady to be seen bonnetless in the park. But at this unfashionable hour, the only other people in the park were other small children and their nursemaids, along with one or two young housemaids taking their mistress's overfed dogs for morning exercise. No one here would care a fig about a rather too old hobbledehoy schoolgirl without a bonnet.

Robin was calmly sailing his new boat on the nearby pond, and Richard had joined another boy his own age in chasing a squirrel. It felt so good to laugh like a child again. Amy could almost imagine herself back in the country, with none of the problems that had accompanied her to London. She giggled and took off after Letty, who had just ducked behind a bush.

"Amy! My boat, my boat!" came a plaintive cry from Robin. Amy ran to the side of the pond to see the little white sailboat floating out into the middle of the glassy sheet of water, Robin having inadvertently dropped the lead. The little boy was sobbing. "M-my new b-b-boat! It's gone, Amy."

"Hush, my love. Don't cry. We'll get it back," she soothed. She held her hand to her chin a moment, pondering this new problem. "You know what it is,

Robin? The captain of that boat seems to have a desire for distant seas and shores. We'll just have to get him turned around and sail him right home again."

She smoothed the little boy's hair and wiped his tears with the end of her sash. A pair of very big, very brown eyes looked up at her trustingly. She could not bear to disappoint him.

Returning her attention to the pond, she noticed that despite the presence of several large and slithery goldfish, the water was less than a foot in depth. A quick look around reconfirmed her earlier observation that there was no one but small children and nannies about.

"Very well, Robin. The great mermaid of Hyde Park is about to retrieve the endangered craft."

Off came the kid half boots and the white silk stockings. The hem of the old cambric gown was hitched up nearly to her knees—how fortunate, she thought, that it was not her newest sprig muslin. Into the water she plunged. To her surprise and dismay, she discovered the bottom to be quite slimy with moss, and she nearly lost her balance. "Yecch!" she exclaimed involuntarily with a comical frown.

By the time she had advanced a few feet into the pond, she had gained quite an audience of screaming and laughing children along with a gaggle of nurse-maids, some horrified, others amused.

"Oh, be careful, Amy, do!" came Lizzy's frightened voice.

"Oh, don't be such a widgeon, Lizzy," replied Richard from the wisdom of his superior twelve years. "Amy's up to every rig!"

Soon the imperiled craft was reached. Amy bent slowly over to pick it up, gingerly holding her skirts in one hand and grabbing the boat with the other, meanwhile trying to maintain her precarious balance on the slippery bottom. A grimace twisted her face as one of the slithery goldfish slid past her ankles.

"Got it!" she cried at last, with a note of triumph, and she turned around with the little boat held over her head like a trophy. And there, behind the screaming children, a wry smile playing about the corners of his mouth, stood the Marquis of Tyrone.

Amy's face immediately flushed as red as the cardinals' robes which she had seen as a child in Rome. She instinctively dropped her skirts, forgetting that she was still standing in ten inches of water, and brought the little boat to her chest. She slowly lowered her astonished gaze and, concentrating with difficulty on her feet, carefully picked her way back to the edge of the pond. She could not bear to look up at his handsome face. She knew well the cynical smile she would see there. After last night's waltz, she could not bear the thought of having him laugh at her.

At the edge of the pond, as she struggled with her now thoroughly wet skirts, she suddenly felt a strong hand under her elbow, helping her from the water.

"Pray let me assist you, Miss Clerville."

The retort that she had been rapidly trying to formulate in her mind died on her lips as she realized that his voice held a note of gentleness that she had never heard in it before.

She nodded to him without looking up, stepped from the pond, and, having handed over the wayward craft to its young captain, tried to regain a little of her lost dignity by smoothing out her hopelessly ruined dress.

"Your shoes, I believe, ma'am."

She raised an eye to his face and was undone by the genuine smile she saw lurking there. Suddenly the situation struck her as hopelessly funny, and she began to chuckle. Despite her best efforts, the chuckle quickly built to a full-throated gale of laughter. Tyrone was laughing as well, and she was surprised to hear how deep and pleasant was the sound.

"Oh dear," she said at length, wiping her streaming eyes with his gallantly proffered handkerchief. "I certainly had not thought to find you, or indeed any-one I know, abroad so early, my lord."

"I find the hour a convenient time for exercising my horses."

"I say, sir!" came a voice from behind him as young Richard stepped forward. "Is that Welsh black yours? He is a beauty, sir!"

"Forgive me, my lord," said Amy. "I am being unforgivably rag-mannered. I believe introductions are in order. Master Richard Thornhill, Master Robin Thornhill, Miss Elizabeth Thornhill, and Miss Letitia Thornhill," she pronounced with great civility, as each of them made a bow or curtsy, more than one accompanied by a giggle. "This is his lordship the Marquis of Tyrone."

The gentleman made a very elegant bow in re-turn and kissed the elder Miss Thornhill's hand pret-tily, to which Lizzy responded with a furious blush. He shook Richard's hand. "Yes, that is Northwind," he said in answer to that young man's earlier question. "You've a good eye to see that he is of Welsh stock. He was foaled on my estate in Kent. He carries me well."

"I should rather think he would, sir!" gasped Richard. "I've never sat on anything half so fine, I can tell you."

"Perhaps you would like to try him sometime?" said Tyrone with a grin.

Richard's eyes grew so wide that Amy feared they would pop from their sockets. "Really, sir? I've been told I have a very good seat, sir, and light hands. I'd be ever so careful with him, I promise!"

"I should take very good care that you were, I assure you. Very well. I shall arrange it with your grandmother."

Richard's face looked as though he'd gone to sleep only to awaken and find himself in heaven. Amy was looking at Tyrone intently. "That is very kind in you, my lord. As you can see, the boy is horse-mad."

Tyrone laughed. "So is my own son. It will be no trouble at all, I assure you. I am in the Park nearly every morning at this time, in any case. And I should welcome the boy's company. And you, Master Robin," he continued, turning to the younger boy. "You'd best learn how to hold onto your boat, for I fear Miss Clerville may not always be around to bail you out. I can see I'll have to show you my favorite loop knot." He was on his knees beside the awestruck little boy. "You see, if you slip this loop over your wrist, there, like that, then it can't get away again." He grinned up at Amy over his shoulder.

Tiny Letty had been hiding behind her sister during this interlude. Tyrone spotted her peering shyly around Lizzy's skirt and let out a warm chuckle. Picking a daffodil that was growing nearby, he presented it to her with great pomp and a truly grand bow. She giggled and buried her face in her sister's skirts, but not before she took the flower.

He rose to be greeted again by Amy's wondering smile. This was a side of the man she would never have thought existed. He was smiling back at her. "What has brought you out at such an early hour, Miss Clerville?"

"Oh, I have ever been an early riser. I know it is not at all fashionable, but I fear my country habits die hard. And I find this the perfect spot to imagine myself back in Somerset for a while."

"Are you so soon bored with London, then, Miss Clerville?" he asked on a note of surprise.

"Oh no, indeed," she said quickly. "I love the bustle of town life, and am quite in a whirl." Her tone changed, and she said more quietly, "And I really could not bear to remain longer at Standish just now, in any case."

"Yes, I can understand that." There was a quiet moment. For the first time, she felt that Lord Tyrone was not mocking her.

She looked down once again at her dripping

gown, her still-bare muddy toes, and her bonnet lying on the fresh grass a few feet away, where a robin was testing it for signs of life. "Oh dear." She laughed ruefully as she pushed back a tumbling curl. "I fear you must think me a sad hoyden indeed, my lord. I am a pitiful mess. I beg that you will not judge me too harshly."

He did not speak for a moment but walked slowly instead to retrieve her bonnet. He handed it to her gravely, the laughter now gone from his face. But the habitual coldness had not returned. "On the contrary, Miss Clerville. I begin to think I may have done so already."

Her eyes flew to his face with a look of curiosity and caught a brief pensive expression there. After a moment, he nodded politely to the children, reassuring Richard that he would not forget the promised ride. Setting his curly beaver on his head at the perfect angle, he turned and strode off toward his horse.

What an odiously confusing gentlemen! thought Amy. One simply never knows where one is with him.

Turning to Robin, whose eyes had followed the Marquis with a look of severe hero worship, she said, "Well, captain, the ship is now safely ashore, even if the first mate nearly drowned in the attempt. Shall we see it safely into the dry dock?" The merry party turned toward home.

During that afternoon the previous evening's pageant at Almack's was a quite natural subject of lively discussion wherever the members of the haut ton gathered. For the ladies, these meetings took the form of visits in each other's elegant drawing rooms, carefully casual encounters in Hookham's library or the more modish shops along Bond Street, or comfortable cozes over cups of tea and dainty cakes in a very proper ladies teashop.

The gentlemen headed inevitably for St. James's

Street and the distinctly masculine comforts of their clubs. The most tonnish of the ton gentlemen were, of course, to be found in White's.

At such an hour of the early afternoon, the reading rooms of this preeminent home of the London dandies were filled with swells, bucks, and exquisites, poring over the pages of the *Racing Chronicle* or the *Weekly Dispatch* or swapping the latest crim. con. stories. In the opulently furnished cardroom a pair of elderly gentlemen in wide-skirted coats were engaged in a rubber of picquet.

"That point should have been mine, you old nip-farthing, and well you know it! You'd no right to hold on to that spade guard," said one of them. By way of emphasis, he shook his head so hard that a cloud of white powder rose from his old-fashioned hair.

His smug-looking partner shrugged complacently and glinted his eyes over a ruddy, bulbous nose. "At five-shilling points, you can afford to lose a damn sight more than I can, guinea pig!" The powdered gentleman harumphed his strong sense of ill usage at this last animadversion. It referred to the one-guinea tax on the hair powder of which he was so fond. The tax had driven powder quickly out of fashion with the younger set, but many of the older gents, from lords to clerks, refused to abandon it.

The two old cronies continued their grumbling and their picquet, exactly as they had been doing for the past twenty years and more.

In the center room, Mr. George Ragget, the eagle-eyed manager of the establishment, carefully surveyed his domain. His sharp scrutiny never missed a thing, and it was said that he had managed to amass a tidy fortune by personally sweeping the floor of the gaming rooms every evening at the end of the play. The dropped counters thus retrieved had added up very quickly.

At the moment, he was smiling rather indulgently

on some of the new members of the aristocratic world of which White's was the pinnacle. The young men were endeavoring, a little too casually for belief, to inch their way closer to the famous Bow Window, anxious to overhear the pronouncements of the oracles of their day.

Here the older dandies and wits held court with the aloofness of the gods, while Beau Brummell preached his gospel of fastidious elegance. Just now they were letting fly with some of their more barbed observations on the unfortunate mortals who chanced to pass the window before their censorious eyes.

Their current victim was Sir Julian Deventer, who had just strolled past. A scowl that was quickly becoming habitual had removed the last vestiges of charm from his gloomy face.

The portly Lord Alvanley took a noisy gulp of the brandy that had been sitting at his elbow. He rose an elaborately chased quizzing glass to a protuberant eye and followed Sir Julian's progress a moment.

"Good God! In the very middle of St. James's Street! You may meet the fellow anywhere!"

"I daresay he feels somewhat safer here than in the area of Bow Street or the Fleet," said "Poodle" Byng with a nod of his curly head. "I hear he's about to get a clap on the shoulder for debt."

"Loath as I am to say it," replied Alvanley with a false note of sympathy and a genuine look of distaste, "the fellow's a bit of a commoner."

"Well, I mean to say," Byng answered. "Stands to reason. I mean, we must have had some reason for blackballing him from the club. After all, the fellow ties a decent enough knot in his cravat."

"My good fellow!" said Brummell with a slow lift of one exquisitely plucked brow. "Do you call that a knot?"

Alvanley very nearly smiled but covered it with a small shrug. "I daresay he thinks it's high-water with him again. He's been dangling after Clerville's daughter. Fifty thousand pounds a year at least, I hear. The old Duchess is puffing her off this season."

"He'd do better to head for Calais. She'll not have him, not that one," replied Byng. "She needs a bit of town bronze, to be sure, but she's as bright as she can stare. She'll not be taken by a clod like Deventer. Rather a taking little thing, don't you think?"

Alvanley pulled his supercilious gaze from the street show being performed beyond the beveled glass and cast a laconic eye at Brummell.

"Saw you condescending to speak with her last night, Beau. What do you make of her?"

The Beau slowly drew an exquisite Sèvres snuffbox from the pocket of his elegant waistcoat, flicking it open with one graceful and practiced movement of his left hand. With his right he extracted a delicate pinch of Fribourg's best Martinique, laid it lightly on the back of his left hand, and inhaled deeply. With a snowy linen handkerchief he flicked an imaginary speck from his exquisitely fitted blue coat before he finally deigned to answer.

"I have very nearly decided to bring her into fashion."

The attention of the dandies was drawn back to the street by the person of the Marquis of Tyrone, who was at that moment approaching the club. His turnout was perfect, from his rakishly set curly beaver and his ivory-headed ebony stick to his buff-colored gloves and gleaming Hessians. He drew a look of approval from the Beau himself, who signaled to him as he entered the club.

Tyrone merely nodded a greeting and crossed into the subscription room, his eyes scanning the group there assembled for a sign of Ferdinand Brice. He had some rather particular questions he wished to put to his Somerset acquaintance.

He espied Ferdie among a group of aspiring Tulips of the Ton at the other end of the room. Ignoring two very young gentlemen at his right who were trading wagers on which of three lumps of sugar the next fly would land on, he turned to a lackey and ordered a glass of madeira before joining his friends.

They were deep in a discussion of the newest Incomparable in town. "I shall write an ode to her heavenly green eyes," a young baronet with a decidedly romantic cast was proclaiming.

"Do, and she's like to laugh you right out of the door," said Ferdie with a chuckle. "A reg'lar right'un, Amy. No bam-laughing her."

"Do you no good anyway, Jack," said a rather bored-looking young viscount. "She's promised to Deventer."

"The devil you say! That ramshackle fellow!"

"Very bad ton, Deventer," replied another. "Bit of a bounder, you know. Hear he's a Captain Sharp if there ever was one."

"Girls!" exclaimed another young fellow with shirtpoints like blinkers. "Plaguey nuisances, the lot of 'em! Can't see why any fellow would let himself get caught in parson's mousetrap."

"You should have a pretty good idea why, Gil, with your pockets always to let. Thing is, Deventer's all to pieces, rolled up. Hasn't got sixpence to scratch himself with. He's even had to sell out of the Funds. He needs a rich wife, and as soon as may be."

"Precisely," yawned the Viscount. "And Miss Clerville is rich beyond the dreams of avarice. Deventer is not without a certain charm, and she can well afford to have him."

Ferdie's face had been slowly turning pinker, and now he truly glowed with indignation. He rose ponderously from his chair. "Damme, that's enough! Only tell me who's been spreading such rubbish about Amy. He'll deal with me, sure as check!"

"My dear fellow," answered the Viscount in his customary bored tone, "I had it from Deventer himself. They've not announced it as yet because of Standen's recent death, but it's an understood thing. Lady

Amelia Clerville is certainly going to marry Sir Julian Deventer."

It was during this last speech that Tyrone reached the group. This final statement stopped him short, and there was thunder in his face. The eyes of the group turned to encounter a frightening glitter in the cold blue eyes that were turned on the Viscount. The power of the black look diminished them all to silence for a moment, a silence broken by the crash of the Marquis's glass coming with sudden force to the table beside him. After a minute pause, he glanced down at the table, the wine now spilling over its edge onto the red Turkey carpet. With great deliberation, he took a spotless handkerchief from his pocket and slowly wiped the spill from the polished wood. Anyone who knew him well could see that he was expending a great deal of effort to bring himself once more under control. When he raised his face again, his expression was calm, but the blue eyes glittered more than ever.

"I should not lay any money on that eventuality if I were you." Forgetting his reason for coming, he turned on his heel and strode from the room.

Five astonished faces watched him go. Shortly thereafter there were two new wagers recorded in the club's famous betting book.

"Ten guineas to receive twenty if Miss Clerville marries Sir Julian Deventer."

"Ten guineas to receive one hundred if Miss Clerville marries the Marquis of Tyrone."

Chapter Eleven

Amelia had spent the rest of that day in some bewilderment as to what to make of the behavior of Lord Tyrone. In the park that morning, he had seemed quite a different gentleman from the haughty cynical lord she was used to seeing. She thought through all her encounters with him, her dislike, her suspicions, and the sudden warmth of his dazzling smile. She also clearly remembered the feeling of his arm around her waist as they floated together through the waltz. She knew no more of her feelings when she retired very late that night after a glittering ball at Holland House.

As Lady Holland was still the London hostess par excellence, the affair had proved a great crush. Under glittering chandeliers, their hundreds of wax tapers reflected in the huge gilt mirrors that lined the room. Amelia danced with a royal duke, curtsied to several duchesses and marchionesses, and was generally praised and petted as a lovely and pretty-behaved young lady. She had dazzled the Spanish ambassador with her perfect command of his language, then teased a Prussian general in fluent German. She had laughed with gaiety and danced with sprightliness. Nonetheless, the evening had proved hollow to her.

She was in the dismals, and she could not well account for it. She laid it down to her increasing longing to share her thoughts with her much-missed brother. She badly needed the confidant that Ned had always been to her.

She would certainly have been amazed, not to say indignant, at any suggestion that she might also be missing that night the presence of the dark Marquis. She had noticed at once on her arrival that Tyrone was not present in the ballroom.

At one point she had remarked casually to her aunt, "I do not see Lord Tyrone in attendance this evening."

"I understand he sent his regrets," answered the Duchess. "Provoking boy, one never knows when to expect him."

"Oh," was all that Amelia had replied before another of her lovesick suitors came to claim her.

She was being swept around the room in the arms of an exceedingly handsome young officer, striking for his scarlet regimentals, his adeptness at the waltz, and his very pretty partner, when Olivia Cole made a fashionably late and very grand entrance. Amy felt herself go unaccountably cold at sight of her.

The lady was looking stunning, as usual, in a Grecian half robe of dull-gold crape over a pale and very sheer gauze gown. Her petticoats had obviously been dampened, for they clung to her elegant figure, displaying it to perfection. Her pale curls were caught up into Grecian knots which had an enchanting tendency to fall softly about her face.

Amy could scarce tear her eyes from the vision, when she was reluctantly returned to her aunt by the young officer. She thanked him quite civilly, but her entire attention was still on Lady Cole. Amy studied her for a long time without being perfectly aware that she did so. When she noticed her aunt watching her, she had said offhandedly, "Lady Cole is exceedingly beautiful, is she not?"

"Oh, exceedingly," replied her aunt without taking her penetrating gaze from Amelia's face.

"I suppose we shall soon read the notice of her engagement to Lord Tyrone," she said with a false brightness. "I understand it is expected daily. I hear they are betting heavily on it in all the clubs."

"Do you?" Still the Duchess's gaze did not waver.

"Why yes, Aunt Louie. Everyone talks of it. Even you must admit they are a strikingly handsome couple."

"Strikingly so."

A tiny sigh escaped Amy. Another moment passed. Then, with a toss of her head, she said, "She seems to me to be of rather a cold disposition. I imagine they will suit very well, do not you?"

"No doubt," said her aunt oddly. After another moment, apparently satisfied with what she read in her niece's face, the Duchess deftly changed the subject, and the Marquis of Tyrone was not spoken of again that night.

Amy was still blue-deviled when she arose the next morning. She had taken Medusa out quite early for a hearty gallop in the Park. She was unable to explain, even to herself, why her spirits had not revived as they invariably did after a good hard ride. The fact that she had seen no one of the remotest interest to her who might also be exercising his horse in the Park was a thought she did not allow space in her ruminations.

So passed the rest of that day and the next. Her calendar was already very crowded, and she raced from one engagement to the next. She was the delight of all she met, full of bright conversation, always lovely, always interested. There was more than one young man who hung about her wherever she went, sent her baskets and bouquets of flowers every morning and watched the door of every ballroom for her entrance. But still she did not see Tyrone. And still she was depressed.

On Sunday morning she had accompanied her aunt to morning service at St. George's Hanover Square. Her eyes automatically scanned the congregation for familiar faces. She saw several, smiling pleasant greetings to them all. But the one face she was not even aware she was looking for was not there.

To make a bad day worse, Amy, having thought up a convenient headache as a means of crying off from an invitation to accompany her aunt to an afternoon musicale, was sitting quite alone in the green drawing room at the back of the house when Sir Julian Deventer was announced. She was momentarily too nonplussed to order herself denied to him, and the gentlemen was very shortly ushered in.

"How very convenient, my dear, that I should find you alone. I shall take it as an omen that the luck is with me today." This was said with a dash and a glinting eye, both of which struck Amy forcibly and with more than a note of falsity.

"I have heard it said, sir, that you have not always the best of luck," she said, trying for a bantering tone.

His eyes seemed to flash a warning that Amy could not read, but his light tone did not change. He continued urbanely, "Ah, but I believe my luck has lately taken a turn for the better. And I do hope, my dear Amelia, that you do not believe everything you hear."

"Oh, be assured that I never do that, sir." She laughed. "I should have to be a great gudgeon indeed if I were to believe half of the nonsense that members of the ton delight in spreading about."

"Then you persuade me to hope, my dear." He crossed to the delicate green-and-gold-striped chaise longue where she was seated. The afternoon sun laid warm stripes of light on the floor and glinted on her copper curls. As he positioned himself next to her and took her hand in his, his voice became more serious. A small involuntary shudder went through Amy at his touch. As she looked up to see if he had noticed, she saw that his smile did not reach his eyes, which were cold, hard, and black.

"You can have no doubt why I am here, my dear. I made up my mind the first time I saw your lovely face that it was Amelia Clerville that I must wed." Amy's eyes grew wide, but he continued, "I have been overjoyed by the many small encouragements you have given me. So today I have come to claim the consent of my chosen bride," he finished with a flourish.

Amy tried to draw her hand gently away, but he held it fast. She thought quickly and decided that the situation called for her best Aunt Louie tone, softened with a liberal dose of Amelia.

"I am afraid, sir, that I do not perfectly understand you. I am sure that I have never given you any such encouragements." Ignoring the kindling light in his eyes, she continued, "Indeed, I can never have given you reason to think that I wished to marry you, Sir Julian, for I am quite decided not to marry at all." He still held her hand fast, and now he stroked it possessively. Amy was forcibly reminded of the stroke of a cat's paw that has temporarily pulled in its claws.

"Ah, I see I have been too forward with the business," he said mournfully. "I should have understood that. It is far too soon after the death of your brother for you to be thinking of marrying." He stroked her hand again, and his hold on it tightened. "It is only my overwhelming regard for you that has brought me here so soon. You are now being squired about town by so many other more worthy gentlemen. Don't think that I am unaware of how ineligible my suit must be from a worldly standpoint next to theirs. But I think they cannot love you as I do, Amelia. If I am not to be driven to distraction by jealousy, I must have your promise now, my love."

With a great wrench, Amy at last succeeded in pulling free her hand. She rose quickly before he could seize it again, and crossed to the green marble fireplace. She took a short space of time to gather her disordered thoughts, then turned to face him once

121

more. Her voice was still gentle, but there was more than a touch of her aunt's steel in it.

"I think you cannot have heard me properly, Sir Julian. I said that I shall not marry. I am fully aware of the honour you do me in making this offer, but in truth, sir, I will not marry you. I beg you will believe what I say."

The gentleman had not wanted to make his declaration so soon. He knew she was not ready, and he had been brought here today only out of desperation. He saw the result of his carefully nurtured plans slipping further and further away, and he could not and would not allow it to happen. Damn the girl! Why could she not have kept herself buried away in the country?

Sir Julian Deventer had never been known for the sweetness of his temper, but he had been at very great pains during the last months to keep Amelia from seeing so much as a glimpse of it. The carefully constructed facade had stood him in good stead until now. But desperation, frustration, and anger now caused this smooth facade to crack. Amy was amazed when he spoke again. His tone was ugly and heavy with sarcasm. The claws had come out with a vengeance.

"Believe you?" he sneered. "Believe you will never marry?" The black look now dominated his face. The smile had become a hideous leer, and Amy feared that he was fast losing control. "You surely cannot believe, my dear Amelia, that such a thing will be allowed! The beautiful, wealthy, and oh so eligible Lady Amelia Clerville left on the shelf? Your family will not suffer the magnificent Standen fortune to go to some insignificant cousin or other. No, no, my dear. You will certainly marry. Your family will see to it."

Amy felt as though she had been slapped in the face by his words and manner, and she turned quickly away, her head still held high. She stared fiercely at the little silvergilt mantel clock in an attempt to keep the tears of indignation that she could feel welling up and stinging her eyelids from overflowing.

Sir Julian continued ruthlessly, snapping the words out with vicious pleasure. "I know, of course, who it is you are hoping to wed. But it will not do, my dear. Lord Tyrone is not likely to take such a green girl to wife. You see, he has no need of your fortune." She gave up her mental hold on the clock and spun around, her face a study in astonishment. "Particularly not when Olivia Cole has been at such very great pains to bring him up to scratch. And she very nearly has him there, you know. We have discussed the situation at some length, she and I, and the lady is very certain of victory. I am sure, lovely as you are, you have no wish to pit yourself against the beautiful and exceedingly cunning Lady Cole. You are not up to it, my dear, I promise you."

"Tyrone!" exclaimed Amy, grasping at this one word from his diatribe. "Sir! If I did not perfectly understand you before, I must own myself completely dumbfounded now. Whatever can you be talking about?"

"Oh, really, my dear. Whatever you may have heard of me, I am sure stupidity was not one of the vices put down to my credit. Anyone with eyes in his head can see that you have tumbled top over tail in love with him," he mocked. "I just think you should know that it will not do. You had much better have me and be done with it."

She could not speak at all for a moment. But she soon gathered her shattered wits, and, in a dignified tone, she said, "I think you must be mad as Bedlam, sir, and I can only hope that your crazed condition may be temporary. Indeed, I am sorry to grieve you, but I shall marry neither Lord Tyrone nor yourself."

His lip curled into a contemptuous smile. He had played the hand badly, he knew, but the game was not yet lost. Not while Amelia was still at large, so to speak. He must and would have the magnificent Standen fortune for his own. He looked at her piercingly and said, in accents both caressing and threatening, "Are you quite, quite sure, my love?"

Before she could reply, the door to the drawing room opened to admit Trundle, her aunt's formidable butler. "A messenger has just arrived from Dorset, Miss. I would have speedily dispatched him, but he is quite adamant. He will leave no message and speak to no one but yourself." It was clear from the butler's unrelenting tone and his more than usually forbidding face that he had tried unsuccessfully to eject the intruder and now felt that he had singularly failed in his duties. "What would you have me do with him, Miss?"

Only by a strong effort of will did Amelia refrain from throwing herself on the unsuspecting servant and embracing him as a deliverer. "Thank you, Trundle. Tell him I shall be with him immediately, and show him into the library."

As soon as the door closed, she turned again to Sir Julian, great relief in her eyes now that this most uncomfortable interview must end. "I fear I must take my leave of you, sir. In any case, I believe we have nothing further to say to one another. I thank you again for your kind offer and bid you good day."

The gentleman was looking at her with a very odd expression. She thought she read anger, resolution, and curiosity all mixed into a quite unpalatable brew. His eyes were piercing, but she only lifted her chin defiantly and did not lower her gaze.

Sensing defeat, at least temporarily, he finally took his leave with as good a grace as was left to him. With a very small nod, he crossed to the door, which with mock gallantry he held open for her to precede him out. Without turning to look at him further, she crossed immediately to the library and out of his sight. He watched her go, the gleam of curiosity in his eyes growing more pronounced. What could the fellow from Dorset want with her? Standish lay in Somerset, and to Sir Julian's own personal knowledge, Standen's dealings on the Dorset coast had been of a type not to involve his sister.

The fact that the mysterious messenger refused to speak to anyone but Amy piqued even further his strong desire to know everything about Lady Amelia Clerville.

He looked quickly about him. Seeing that there was momentarily no one in the hall, he slipped back into the drawing room. The French doors leading onto the garden opened easily to his touch. He slipped silently through them and out onto the terrace that ran the length of the house. A few short steps took him to an identical set of doors at the other end of the terrace.

He let a sneering smile escape his face. How very obliging, he thought, that the efficient Trundle had felt it necessary to air the room for Miss Clerville. The French doors to the library stood open to the soft afternoon air. From where he stood beside them, he could easily hear the two voices from within, one uneducated and weary, the other light and anxious.

"Yes, mum, Mr. Parker woulda come hisself, on'y the doc didn't want him to ride so far yet, mum. Not with his leg an' all."

"Yes, of course, I understand," said Amelia. Her voice was pleasant, but she was giving her unexpected visitor a thorough study. She must be sure that this man had indeed come to her from Ned's valet. "And you have brought me some word from Mr. Parker. How may I help him?" she asked in a noncommital tone and with a carefully scrutinizing eye.

The messenger was a bright young fellow, and he at once understood her measuring look and tone. In spite of his awe of the glamorous surroundings in which he found himself, he gave her a small smile and a nod.

"Aye, an' Mr. Parker said as how you was a

downy one, mum. I can see no one's like to get past you unawares. But I got proof right enough that I come from Mr. P hisself, and glad I am you'll be wantin' ta see it, mum."

He searched a moment in the capacious pockets of his baggy serge trousers. When he pulled his hand out again, it held a small mountain of lint, sand, bits of straw, and the crumbling remains of his supper. In the center of his pile of debris lay Ned's ring, the ring Amy had given to Parker with her own hand as a token of her eagerness to help if ever she could do so. She lifted it gingerly from his outstretched palm and dusted it off. Putting it tenderly on her middle finger, she looked up again with moist and glowing eyes.

"An' I got a paper for ya too, mum, from Mr. P hisself." He fumbled once more in a pocket, this time inside his worn corduroy jacket. At length he pulled out a badly crumpled letter. Amy carefully smoothed the page and read:

Dear Lady Amy,
   I once promised the master that I'd not quit our work, and so I'll not do till it be no longer necessary. But I'll always be here if you should ever need my help. You may always find me at the White Hart, Weymouth.
   If you can be of any help at all to Mimms, who will present this to you, we would all account it a great favor.

Your humble servant,
A. Parker

Amy looked up, now thoroughly reassured.
"We gotta be mighty careful in our line o' work, so he sent me along to explain."
"How can I help you, Mr. Mimms?" she asked in a voice scarce above a whisper.
He flushed at hearing such a fine lady address him thus. "Well, mum, Mr. P said as how I could be

open wi' ya, an' so I'll tell ya. When we had that there trouble with yer brother a while back—and sad I was ta see it, mum, a right fine gentleman was Master Ned. We all of us thought so—we had ta leave off workin' that part o' the coast. 'Twere too dangerous, ya see," he explained carefully. "But some of our best information had been comin' from that very spot, mum. Pity ta lose it, so ta speak." Amy was listening closely. "So the boss, he's made up his mind to give it another try there, real careful-like. But we gotta know who our people over there are, if ya get my meanin'. Didn't no one know but Master Ned. Not even his lordship hisself."

Amy was sitting on the very edge of her chair. The young messenger's voice dropped to a conspiratorial whisper, and Sir Julian, just beyond the window, was having to strain to catch his words.

"Now Mr. P knows as how yer brother had a list of 'em all, and he hid it in his house here in London. I were sent ta look for it, mum. But if I knows Master Ned, he woulda put it someplace where the likes o' me won't never find it. Mighty clever cove was Master Ned, mum." Amy smiled her agreement. "Now here's where you could mebbe help us, mum. Mr. P says as how you and Master Ned was as close as peas in a pod. Now you might just know where he'd put it, mum, you knowin' how he was thinkin' an' all."

A slight frown of concentration had replaced Amy's smile. She was thinking hard. "Yes, I see. If anyone would know, I suppose it would be I." She rose abruptly from her chair and began to pace, mentally going through the rooms of the mansion in Grosvenor Square and muttering slightly. She crossed briskly to the French doors and stood looking out at the garden in all its spring finery. Sir Julian only just managed to jump back in time to escape detection, throwing himself flat against the wall and pricking himself severely on the thorns of the roses growing

127

there. He swallowed an oath, sucking at his bleeding hand.

"No, not belowstairs, I think," Amy was muttering. "Too many servants about. The nursery? The furniture's all been moved out from there." She continued her pacing and thinking. Mimms stood patiently, hat in hand, watching her progress.

"Not in the drawing room, I think, and not the back parlor, no. And there is no place in the dining room. The library has . . ." She stopped short. "The library! Of course." She swung around to face the young man. "I had nearly forgotten. There is a smallish secret alcove behind the paneling, just near the fireplace. My father kept cash and jewelry and other valuables there from time to time." She laughed as a long-forgotten memory came to mind. "Neddie and I found it the perfect spot to hide from our nurse when we were quite young. It's just big enough for two small children if they don't wiggle too much." A little pause and a smile. "Neddie always wiggled."

"Aye, mum. That'd be the spot, I'm thinkin'."

"I'm sure of it. It is very well hidden, and no one would even suspect it was there unless they had been told. It is the perfect spot."

"If you could tell me how ta find it, Mum, I'll be on my way there straightaway."

"Yes, of course. Let's see." Casting her mind back to a time when she had been small enough to fit into the tiny cupboard, she searched the room for the little handle that unlocked a section of the paneling and sent it swinging open. Her mind alighted briefly on the marble fireplace, pushed aside a few of the sporting prints hanging on the dark wooden walls, and swept back the heavy damask draperies. The fingers of her memory flitted over the leather-bound books and even flipped up a corner of the Aubusson carpet.

"Oh dear. I can't seem to remember where it opened. Maybe if I was there. It has been so long."

Sir Julian was clenching and unclenching his fist.

Stupid chit! he thought fiercely. Remember, damn you!

Amy suddenly looked to the messenger with a look of decision. "When do you return to Weymouth, Mr. Mimms?"

"Why, tomorrow mornin' early, to be sure, mum. Why do you ask?"

"I must go to Standen House myself. I'm sure when I am there it will all come back to me, and I shall remember. Can you return here this evening to collect the paper?"

"Aye, mum. But I'm thinkin' it's best I should come along wi' ya."

"Yes, perhaps. But I think I cannot simply walk up to the door, you know. The house is closed, with only a pair of old servants in residence. I shall have to sneak in the back way. I can very easily do it alone, but it would be much more difficult with you along." Her voice dropped to an even quieter level. "Also, I have suspected that those responsible for my brother's death may be watching me. If they were to see me with you, you would be in danger. But I'm quite sure I can slip into the house alone, unobserved either by them or by the servants. It is quite the safest way."

She was nearly whispering now. But to Sir Julian it no longer mattered. He had heard all he needed to hear. He was already stealing across the garden, to slip out unseen through the stable entrance.

It was clear he must go to Standen House at once. That paper could bring him a tidy sum, together with the other quite valuable bits of information he had managed to gather on this trip to London. And if he managed to pull off the quite dazzling coup that he had in the works, he would be well kept until Amelia could be brought to heel.

But how to delay her just now? He had no desire for yet another confrontation with her today, particularly not in the guise of a housebreaker in her own home. It might take him some time to discover the secret cupboard, since the stupid girl could not recall it for him. He must think of some way to keep her from rushing straight to Grosvenor Square. He began to make his way back toward the front of the house, raking through his mind for a plan.

Amy was still making her own plans. She had persuaded Mimms to return that evening to retrieve the missing paper, though he did so with great reluctance and misgiving.

"I am sure I can get away from here unremarked. I can take a hackney to Grosvenor Square, get the paper, and be back in a trice. I am sure no one will suspect me of anything at all untoward if I am careful, and I mean to be that. Do you return here at—let's see—seven o'clock. My aunt will be dressing for dinner then. Come to the stables. I shall meet you there."

The messenger seemed uncertain. "If you be sure, mum. Mr. P did say as how I was to trust you."

"Be assured you may do so. I shall not fail you. Go you now to the kitchens and tell Mrs. Woodin to feed you. You have had a long ride. I shall see you at seven."

Amy was out the door and up the stairs almost as she spoke. Her heart was pounding with excitement as she shrugged herself into a wrap and went for her bonnet. At last here was her chance to do something for Neddie. She would go at once, before her aunt returned.

Just as Sir Julian rounded the corner of the square, a perch-phaeton swept around the garden headed toward Harcourt House. At sight of him, the horses were pulled up short. Sir Francis Stepworth smiled his ghastly smile and tipped his hat to Sir Julian.

"Ah, worthy sir. I perceive you are on your way to pay a call on the so very beautiful Miss Clerville." He puffed up till his gilt buttons, the size of crown pieces, threatened to pop off of his buckram-padded puce coat. "How very sad for you, worthy sir, to be disappointed in your journey. The lady, you see, is engaged to drive with me in the park this afternoon."

Sir Julian's eyes lighted with triumph, and he smiled broadly.

"Now do not look so crestfallen, sir," continued Sir Francis. "I daresay Miss Clerville may spare you a dance at the assembly at Almack's next week. She cannot as yet save every dance for me."

Sir Julian nearly laughed his most derisive laugh in the gentleman's face, but he was too well pleased by the intelligence that Amelia was engaged to drive with him. He said nothing but tipped his hat and strode off into the garden of the Square. Sir Francis tooled his carriage on its way.

Sir Julian carefully but casually secreted himself behind a tree, from which vantage point he had a clear view of the front of Harcourt House. He must be quite certain that the clever Miss Clerville did not manage to rid herself of this pompous swain. She must drive with him!

Amelia was down the stairs again in only a moment. She stood pulling on her gloves in the front hall when the knocker sounded. Too late did she dive for the door of the drawing room. Trundle had already opened the heavy front door to admit Sir Francis Stepworth.

"Ah, my very dear Miss Clerville," he said with a surprised smile and a creaking bow. He was indeed surprised. He had expected to be left waiting the standard twenty minutes, as was the fashion. He frowned a little to think Miss Clerville was so very unfashionable as to be ready on time for their drive. But then, he thought indulgently, she was but fresh from the country and obviously eager for the treat of being seen driving in the Park with such a dashing gentleman as himself. Any young lady would be overjoyed by such marks of favor and condescension from a gentleman in the first stare of fashion, such as himself. And she did look quite presentable, he thought, pleased that he need not be seen with a dowd or a country mouse, however wealthy she might be.

It was true that Amy looked lovely and quite the young lady of fashion, in a bronze-green pelerine cut high to the throat, and a chip hat with green ruchings set jauntily on her tumble of curls.

"Sir Francis! I had not . . . I cannot . . . I mean . . . how very nice to see you!" sputtered Amy.

Ah, thought the gentleman, as he bowed once more, very slowly and carefully. How very gratifying. She is overwhelmed. On his entrance he removed a yellow plush hat with an absurdly high crown that revealed his thin yellow locks pouffed and pomaded into a quite elaborate coif. Now he very carefully replaced it, being certain not to disarrange a hair, and offered Amy his arm.

"Shall we have our drive, Miss Clerville? I declare I have been in alt these three days in expectation of an hour in your so charming company."

Amy slumped perceptibly. She had completely forgotten her ill-advised acceptance of the pompous dandy's invitation to drive in the Park today. Now she heartily repented her folly. There was no possibility of escape. The trip to Standen House would simply have to wait.

"Why, thank you, sir. I too have been looking forward to it," she said feebly. She gave him her arm, and the two of them made their stately progress out the door.

Amy's eyes flew wide at sight of Sir Francis's perch-phaeton. It was the most shocking shade of pink imaginable. The wheels were picked out in red to match the satin of its cusions, which were heavily fringed with gold. The groom, now holding the horses' heads, but soon to be perched up behind them, wore a long-tailed wig of flaming red tied back with a pink ribbon and was in livery of canary-coloured satin, laced with black.

Poled up to the carriage were two short-legged

greys. Their colour was very pretty and they were well-matched, but Amy's experienced eye saw at once that they were plodders and had been run into the ground besides. They were harnessed in yellow leather. Huge plumes of red coq feathers bobbed on their heads, and their tails and manes were braided with red and yellow ribbons. It all combined to complete a picture the most hideous and outrageous that Amy had ever seen.

Sir Francis noted her wide-eyed astonishment with evident pleasure. He was inordinately proud of the new turnout he had designed himself. Now Miss Clerville would know that he was a man of taste as well as address.

"How very . . . different!" she managed to choke out at last.

"Yes, I flatter myself that there are very few setouts in town to compare. I fancy we shall turn not a few heads today, Miss Clerville."

"I am very sure we shall, sir," she replied meekly as they headed for the Park.

Chapter Twelve

It was not to be hoped that Amelia would be able to cut short their ride. Sir Francis was a most complete slave at the feet of fashion, with no will in the world to deviate from its dictates. In London during the season, a Man of Fashion could simply not exist if he did not show himself in the Park of a Sunday afternoon. The grand promenade of the haut ton now taking place on Rotten Row was a veritable river of fashionable equipages, prime horses, and smartly dressed strollers.

Sir Francis slowly and with great concentration poured his phaeton into the crawling stream of vehicles. He at once began a series of grave and stately nods and bows to dowagers in barouches and young misses in landaulets. His salutes were, of course, restricted to the lucky promenaders who found themselves directly in front of him. His neck was today swatched in yards of muslin of the same unfortunate shade of pink as his carriage. The intricate Osbaldeston knot in which it was tied forced him to maintain a rigidly forward expression. In his eagerness not to miss anything of importance, his eyes were rolling in their sockets, left to right. A veritable jig seemed to be taking place on his powdered and roughed countenance. Amy was forced to forget her own anxieties for a moment. It took all her mental energy to school her expression into a semblance of sobriety. A whoop of laughter escaped, and she only just manged to cover it with a great show of coughing.

Sir Francis's upper torso shifted in her direction. He looked at her with a face of pale concern. "I do trust you are not ill, Miss Clerville?" He nearly creased his cravat as he fumbled quickly in a pocket. "The air, you know, so full of noxious humors." He withdrew a dainty handkerchief soaked in lavender water. "Ah, so efficacious, lavender water. So purifying."

"No, no, I am quite well, I do assure you, sir," she answered quickly, raising a hand to fend off the obnoxious handkerchief. " 'Twas but a momentary indisposition. I beg you will take no notice of it."

"Ah, I am so glad," he said with relief as he applied the small square of linen and lace to his nose. "I fear I am dreadfully susceptible to fevers and inflammations. I should have been grieved beyond belief to have been forced to forsake your company, but one of my delicate constitution can never be too careful. I am so pleased I need not deprive myself of your so charming companionship."

Amy sank a little. Bother! she thought. Too late! I could well have convinced him to take me home. Now I have prevented my own escape.

Sir Francis kept up a stream of inane chatter as they made their slow progress down the Row. Occasionally he lifted the enormous quizzing-glass that hung from a yellow ribbon about his neck to study a passing bonnet or neckcloth. He had been right. Many heads indeed were turning to watch this ill-matched pair.

Amy found she could not bear to listen to him longer, and she turned her attention to the crowd around her. She was more than a little embarrassed to be seen with Sir Francis, and her spirits were so depressed that nothing could really catch her interest. Not the proud and beautiful horses, from the choicest studs in the kingdom, prancing beneath some of the choicest gentlemen. Not the crested carriages with crested dowagers enfolded in their velvet lined interiors. Not even the gay Cyprians, wrapped in bright colors and tinkling laughter, perhaps on the lookout for a new gentleman to take them under his protection.

The day seemed to have wrapped itself around her like a grey fog. The ugly interview with Sir Julian was preying on her mind. Had she really given him so much encouragement? Had he truly expected her to accept his offer? She could not believe it. And what on earth had he meant about Lord Tyrone? How could he think her in love with the man? He must be mad! She would not think of it. She would put the odious Sir Julian out of her mind.

But there was another trouble preying heavily on her thoughts as well. She was thinking about her second visitor of the afternoon. To be forced to sit here tamely in this silly carriage, listening with complacency to this simpering outrageous fop and smiling at all the insipid ladies and gentlemen of the ton, was truly painful when she should be at Standen House trying to retrieve Ned's paper. She was out of all charity with the silliness and shallowness of the society around her when there was important work to be done. She must get away from here. If only she could light upon a scheme to get away from this prosy bore of a gentleman.

Perhaps she had queered her chances with the illness ploy. But perhaps not. She looked at Sir Francis tentatively.

"'I fear perhaps I do have a slight chill coming on, Sir Francis. Could you perhaps . . .''

She broke off abruptly. Her attention had now been well and truly captured. Approaching just across the Row was a dashing pony-phaeton of celestial blue. Between the shafts was a pair of lovely smoke-grey ponies, harnessed in silver.

Lady Cole was cutting a dash indeed. She perched proudly in the phaeton, the reins held lightly in her delicate hands. Everything about her seemed to sparkle, as though sprinkled with silver dust, from the blue-tipped ostrich plumes curling in her poke bonnet to the silver buttons down the front of her deep-blue Circassian dress, to the delicate silk embroidery of her kid gauntlet gloves.

Perched up behind her was a diminutive Tiger, not more than six or seven years of age. The boy was dressed in blue-and-silver livery, an elaborate oriental turban atop his dark woolly little head.

The smoky ponies were dwarfed by the silky blackness of Nightwind walking beside the little carriage. Lord Tyrone was seated like a king atop his powerful back. At intervals he leaned to address a few words to Lady Cole.

Amy's heart turned over at sight of him. A sharp pang pierced through her at the smile Tyrone was bestowing on her ladyship. The fog around her seemed to deepen, and Sir Julian's words came back to her in a rush. My God! she thought. Could it possibly be true? Of course not, she told herself sternly. How could she possibly be in love with a man she wasn't even sure she liked and knew she did not trust?

She was studying his features and expression with such concentration that it was a shock when his dark-blue eyes flicked up to meet her own. They held hers a moment. Amy felt a slow blush creeping up her face.

To cover her confusion she turned to Sir Francis with a gay laugh. From the corner of her eyes, she saw Tyrone lean once again to Lady Cole, and that same pang shot through her again. Then he moved out of her field of vision. When next she looked up, she saw with a start that he was beside her.

"Good afternoon, Miss Clerville." All of a sudden the sun seemed to come out.

With great vexation, she felt her blush deepen. "My lord," she said with what dignity she could muster. Turning to her escort, she said coolly, "Have you met my lord, the Marquis of Tyrone, sir?"

Sir Francis colored with indignation. "Well, of course, Miss Clerville!" he whispered harshly in a loud aside. "I am pleased to think myself *au fait* on all matters of ton." He raised his quizzing-glass to survey Tyrone. "My lord," he said with a sour little smile. He plumped the satin cushions beside him and adjusted his neckcloth slightly to better display a grotesquely oversized diamond stickpin.

Oh dear! thought Amy. I do believe he's preening—and to my Lord Tyrone of all people." She turned a droll glance to the Marquis. His face held a look of wry amusement, and with an effort she stifled a giggle. Their eyes caught. The two of them shared a private moment of merriment. Laughter spoke in his eyes. It occurred to Amy that she had never seen them so warm and full of life.

At length he spoke. "I have come to claim my due, Miss Clerville."

"I do not perfectly understand you, my lord."

"I believe I was able to render you some small service the last time we met, in this very Park, in fact." His mouth curved up in a wickedly devastating smile. The Marquis of Tyrone was finding himself becoming a Prince Charming once again whenever he chanced to be in Miss Clerville's company.

Amy flushed at the memory of their encounter by the pond, but she did not look away. Why, his eyes were positively twinkling, she saw. "That you did, my lord. I fear I have not thanked you properly."

"But you may easily do so, ma'am," he said smoothly. "You need only promise me the first waltz at Lady Waverly's ball tomorrow evening, and I shall count myself amply recompensed."

A little thrill of pleasure ran up Amy's spine at the words. She was beginning to realize, with a mingling of unspeakable joy and immense chagrin, that Sir Julian's reading of her emotions had not been amiss. Alas, she was hopelessly in love with the handsome gentleman now before her. She could not tell how it had happened, or when, but that it was true struck her like a blinding light. Now what in the world was she going to do about it? She lowered her eyes from the flashing power of his, and she said, "I should be most honored, my lord."

Sir Francis sat up a little straighter in something closely akin to indignation. His torso turned even more to face her. "Ah, Miss Clerville," he oozed in chiding accents. "I see I have let Lord Tyrone steal a march on me. You must grant me also the happy honor of sharing with you a delightful interlude upon the dance floor." His fatuous smile was so absurd Amy had to look away to preserve her own gravity. She looked at Tyrone, but the growing laughter in his face forced her into another of her coughing fits.

"Oh dear, ma'am," said Tyrone in mocking seriousness. "I do hope you took no permanent harm from your dampened feet of the other morning."

"Dampened feet!" exclaimed Sir Francis. "Miss Clerville, you should have informed me of this earlier! You are sure to be coming down with a putrid sore throat or worse." He thrust his lavender-scented handkerchief to his nose again. "I must return you to your home at once!"

Before she could even take her leave of Tyrone the phaeton was being turned and driven toward the gates. She only had time to look over her shoulder at the Marquis. He was now laughing heartily. He tipped his hat to her as he watched her being carried ruthlessly away.

As Sir Francis tooled the pink carriage purposefully toward Berkeley Square, Amy's mind was a muddle of conflicting images and emotions. But she resolutely pushed them all aside.

Not now, she told herself briskly. The important thing now is to see to getting those papers.

Quick as thought, Amy found herself delivered to the door of her aunt's house once more. Sir Francis made a timely and, he hoped, uncontaminated retreat as soon as the great door was opened to her.

"Trundle, has my aunt returned yet?" she asked the butler.

"Yes, Miss. She has been resting upon her bed this half hour. She asked me to remind you, Miss, that you are bespoke for dinner to Lord and Lady Kendall. She has ordered the carriage to be brought around at eight."

"Yes, thank you, Trundle," she said absently. She was calculating how long it would take her to get to Standen House and back. She was sure she could do it before her aunt could remark her absence. In any case, if she was to meet Mimms at seven, she must go at once. "I have an errand I must run, Trundle. I shall not be gone above three quarters of an hour. You need not trouble my aunt with my absence."

"Yes, Miss. I shall summon the carriage and call for your abigail to accompany you."

But Amy had already opened the door. "That won't be necessary, Trundle. I shall call a hackney." Without turning to see the look of shocked disbelief on his face, she was down the steps and on her way.

Deciding it was silly to summon a hack for so short a distance, she set out on foot toward Mount Street. Turning into Audley Street, she saw a pair of young bucks eyeing her curiously. She wondered a moment if they had perhaps been sent to watch her. But they did not have the look of spies somehow. They must be just two young men on their own way somewhere. Really, she was being needlessly anxious about this escapade, she scolded herself. She ignored them and hurried on.

But she could not help but see the smirking smiles on their faces. Only one kind of "lady," she knew, was to be seen completely unchaperoned or escorted on the streets of London, and she was well aware of what they were thinking of her. Thank heaven she did not know them. She turned her head sharply away and hurried on, hoping fervently that they would not follow.

She was heading for the mews that backed up to the great mansions on the west side of Grosvenor Square. As she turned into the little alley, a figure ahead of her darted swiftly out of sight, but she was looking back over her shoulder, fearful that she had in fact been followed, and she did not see it.

The voices of the two young bucks floated down the mews to where she stood, terrified that they would follow her into the dark alley. She looked around her in alarm, realizing how vulnerable she had made herself, and threw herself against the wall, silently praying that they would move on. The voices moved closer.

"I tell you, she was a prime little bit. Why should I let her get away? C'mon, Bo. Let's catch her up. She'll give us a rare evening's sport, I'll wager."

"Can't. Lady B's party. Promised my mother. There'll be other fancy birds."

"Not like that one, I'll swear. Did you see her? The devil with Lady B. I'm going after her."

"Not the thing, Tony. Betrothed an' all. Miss Windham wouldn't like it. Can't leave her stranded at that damned party. C'mon. We're late."

"Damme, you are a one to remind a fellow of responsibility! S'pose you're right, though. Caro won't like it if I don't turn up. C'mon, then."

The voices faded away down the street at last. Amy, frozen with fear and mortification, let out a slow sigh of relief and continued down the mews. She soon came to a small, weathered door in the back wall of the garden of Standen House. Only a few feet from her stood a shadow, still as death The air of the mews was permeated with the strong smell of horses, stale sweat, dark ale and new leather. The familiar scent had always been a comforting one to Amy, but this evening it struck her as sinister. A horse whinied nearby, and she jumped with a start. Pulling herself together with a strong admonition to stop being a silly, missish female, she looked to left and right.

Seeing nothing, she removed a rusty key from behind a loose brick next to the gate. As she reached to unlock the splintering door, she saw that the rusty lock was broken loose, hanging limply by one nail. At her touch the oaken door swung back with a resounding creak. She froze a moment, fearing she had announced her presence to some unknown evil nearby. She looked about her quickly again. Nothing moved. She silently took off her slippers, slid through the door and closed it again with a little thud.

Once safely inside the garden, she realized her heart was pounding a veritable military tattoo against her breast. She stopped a moment, leaning against the rough, damp wall, trying to still the wild beating of that unruly organ and scolding herself for this show of nerves. Like most young girls, she supposed, she had often longed for adventures. Now she felt like a character in a novel, and she was finding it somewhat less to her taste than she had fancied. Reading about spy rings and sinister dark alleyways was one thing. Actually creeping about London and breaking into a house, even if it was one's own, was quite something else again.

But here was her chance to pay back a small part of Ned's account to the French. He had never failed her when she had needed him. She could not fail him now.

No sooner had she disappeared into the garden than the shadow on the other side of the wall peeled itself from the niche where it stood. Looking very pleased with himself, Sir Julian Deventer walked quickly and silently away.

Knowing that old Simpson, the caretaker, and his wife were somewhere in the house, and not wishing to encounter them in such an awkward situation, Amy made stealthily for the windows of the library. The room was, unfortunately, one floor up, but Amy was quite familiar with the intricacies of a certain elm tree that grew just outside the window she sought. Dropping her slippers and expertly hitching up her skirts, she was up the tree quick as a squirrel. To her confusion, she saw that the window was ajar. Swinging it wide, she eased herself into the room. It had grown quite dark now, and she dared not light a candle. She slid back the heavy gold draperies to let in such light as there might be. As she turned into the room again, with what astonishment did she see the sight that greeted her there.

The furniture near the fireplace had been pushed all anyhow. The large and beautiful portrait of her mother by Reynolds that had hung over the mantel had been taken down and flung onto a sofa. All the drawers of her brother's desk stood open, papers scattered everywhere. Books had been pulled from their shelves and dropped onto the floor and the hearth. And worst of all, Amy saw almost at once, the secret cupboard beside the fireplace stood wide. It was empty.

She stood for a long while rooted to the floor. Who else could possibly know the paper was there? Or did they know at all? Perhaps it was just a common housebreaker with a prime bit of luck. Perhaps he would have no idea of the importance of what he had stumbled upon. Amy tried to comfort herself with this thought awhile. But the idea did not stand up to her intensive thinking.

She remembered now where the latch was hidden. If one removed a certain book, it was plain to see; but no common housebreaker, however lucky, would come upon it by accident. Obviously, it had been found by someone who had known what he was looking for.

If only she could know when the break-in had occurred. It could have been days ago. Or weeks. Or it could have been this very afternoon. She considered that further. It must have been today. Old Simpson might not trouble himself to tour each room of the vast house every day, but Amy was certain he would make sure that every door and window was secure for the night. He would surely have noticed the open window.

She could make no sense out of the situation. The only person she had told about the secret cupboard had been Mimms. And since he knew she intended to give him the paper, he could have no possible reason for breaking in after it. She trusted him, and felt tolerably sure that he had trusted her. It simply did not make sense for him to have come here.

Could their conversation have been overheard by one of the servants? If the enemies of her brother's operation had been intent on keeping a watch on her, perhaps the most efficient means of doing that would be to introduce an unsuspicious-looking servant into her very home. That would be clever, indeed. But the more she thought about the possibility, the more she saw that it was no solution. As she catalogued her aunt's staff in her mind, she realized that not one of them had been in the Duchess's employ for less than ten years, unless you counted the groom's nine-year-old assistant, who was the son of the head footman. Not a very likely possibility.

Perhaps someone, she dared not think who, had accosted Mimms and forced the information from him. It seemed hopelessly likely. So many questions were warring in Amy's mind, all demanding their right to an answer. She gave herself a shake. She could not stand about here any longer. She might be discovered by the Simpsons, and that would be very uncomfortable indeed.

She slipped through the window, carefully shutting it behind her, scampered lightly down the tree, and made her way across the now completely night-darkened garden and out the little door. Slipping on her shoes again and smoothing out her sadly rumpled skirt, she turned toward Berkeley Square.

It was nearly seven when she reached Harcourt House, and she headed directly for the stables. Mimms was waiting for her, a little gloomily. He had been having second thoughts about the wisdom of having allowed Amy to go off by herself to Standen House. His face swelled with relief as he saw her striding across the cobblestones of the stableyard, looking a bit the worse for her excursion, as he could see by the flickering light of the stable lanterns. But his expression clouded over again when he saw her worried frown. It rapidly changed to a look of great relief at sight of him, and she beckoned him to follow her into the garden. He did so at once, and both were silent until they were well out of earshot of anyone. They sat on a stone bench hidden by a little bunch of trees. Amy turned to him and took a deep breath.

"The paper was gone," she said baldly. "Someone was there before me." She recounted the story of what she had found, and could see immediately from his face that he was not responsible for the disappearance of the paper. He was looking at her very hard. She knew that he was trying to decide whether or not to believe her story. It did seem quite incredible, even to her. So far from being indignant at his lack of trust in her, she felt a wave of remorse break over her.

"I've no notion at all who might have done such a thing," she said untruthfully. She had what she was certain was a very good notion. Though she still had no idea how he came to know about the cupboard, all her supposed "evidence" against Lord Tyrone had come flooding back to her in a rush as she stood in that darkening room. But she could not tell them it was Tyrone. She just could not! Not yet! She loved him, and she could no longer deny it to herself. Somehow she must find out the truth before she told anyone else of her suspicions. She prayed that her fears were groundless, though she had little hope. But she determined to set out to prove them so.

"This is bad, mum, very bad, an' I don't mind tellin' ya," said Mimms, shaking his head. "If that paper gets back to the Frenchies, we'll lose a lot more good fellas 'sides yer brother."

He continued to study her face. He read the great sadness there and was reassured. "Now, mum, yer not to fret yerself. 'Tweren't yer fault and no one ta say it were." He found himself patting her hand. "The boss'll haveta know straightaway, that's sure. He won't like it, I can tell ya," he added with a frown. "But he'll not be blamin' you, mum. Nor no one else will neither. You done yer best, an' now you'll leave it fer the boss ta settle. He'll know what's best ta be done. I'll take him the news myself, mum, that I will."

Mimms was on his feet and off to the stables before Amy could rise. She sat on the cold stone bench a long time, her fingers running idly over the rough surface, thinking. She must find a way to prove once and for all whether Tyrone was involved in this unhappy business. If she found such proof, she knew she must and would tell Parker at once, for then Tyrone would be an enemy of England and a very dangerous man. She prayed she would not find that proof. She must also see what she could do to retrieve the missing paper. She felt very responsible for its loss, though she could not explain it. She had no idea how to go about the task of its discovery and return, but with her inborn optimism she felt sure she would contrive somehow.

She shivered and realized with a start how late it had become. She must run upstairs and change for Elinor's dinner party. She could not deal with the very difficult questions that were sure to arise if she was late.

The "boss" was at that moment sitting in his own luxurious library in his house in St. James's Square.

Tyrone sat with his long booted legs stretched out to the grate, where a merry little fire crackled, for the fine day had turned into a surprisingly chilly evening. His face was not merry. It held a deep troubled frown as he stared into the dancing flames. He had only just returned to town that morning from Lyme Regis and Weymouth. He had brought with him the evidence he needed against Sir Julian Deventer, Bonapartist spy. He felt certain that the group of which Deventer was a part was not a large one, but Tyrone did not want any of them to slip through his fingers. And, as the situation in the Peninsula worsened for the French, their spies in England had been getting bolder. Desperation could cause carelessness, and Deventer was the perfect sort of pawn of whom they would make use. He just might lead them to a really big fish if only they played him awhile on the line. That he was firmly hooked was beyond doubt. This one would not get away, but for the present Sir Julian would remain at large. The Marquis had this very hour sent two of his men to keep a constant watch on the Baronet.

A doleful smile played about his lips as he pulled a quill absentmindedly through his long strong fingers. If he was to be completely honest with himself, he had to admit to a solid sense of relief that he need not arrest Sir Julian just yet. He was very much afraid for Amelia Clerville.

After six long years of bitterness and cynicism, the Marquis of Tyrone had been captivated at last, and well he knew it. When he had seen Amelia in the Park this afternoon, it was as though a cold hand that had gripped his heart for years had melted away, to leave that poor organ vulnerable to her smile and the sparkle of her green velvet eyes.

He could not bear the thought that his beautiful girl might be involved with a rotter like Deventer. He knew that her name had been strongly linked to Sir Julian's ever since she had come to town. The betting on their engagement was running high at the clubs. However ignorant she might be of the fellow's "profession"—and Tyrone prayed that she was—there would be talk when he was finally arrested. Amelia was bound to be scorched by it, if not badly burnt. Tyrone felt an overpowering drive to shelter her from it for as long as possible

And what if she was not ignorant? He had no doubt that she would hesitate at very little where she truly loved. The question now was whether or not she loved Deventer enough to protect him or even to spy for him. The thought made Tyrone's heart ache, and he could not believe it could be true. But he knew that if it was proved, he would have no compunction in arresting her for treason as well. It would be like cutting off one of his own limbs, he knew, but he could not hesitate.

A brisk tattoo tapped out on the window behind him brought him out of his reverie. He rose from his chair and crossed to the window. Opening it wide, he saw in the shadows the face of Mimms, one of his agents from Weymouth, flushed and breathless from running. What the devil was the fellow doing here?

"It's bad news I'm bringin' yer lordship, sir. Mebbe real bad."

Chapter Thirteen

Music floated out through the brilliantly lighted windows of Waverly House in Piccadilly. It mingled with the sound of hundreds of carriage wheels on paving stones, the soughing of wind through the plane trees in the Green Park, the whinny of crowded horses, and the bubbling tinkle of excited voices.

Amy made her slow progress up the great staircase toward the ballroom, carefully holding up the train of her white velvet cloak to protect it from the feet of the horde of people around her. Katie's parties were always a crush. Lord and Lady Waverly were very fashionable, of course, but more importantly, Katie's parties were fun, a quality not always to be found at ton affairs. There was always something a little different happening, a little surprise, and no one wanted to be left out.

The ballroom of Waverly House had been cunningly designed so that one needs must appear in the great double doors, then descend into the magnificent room, in view of all who were there assembled. It was perfectly calculated for the "grand entrance." Amy stood on the threshold, drinking in the scene. Katie had redone the entire room for this evening. It looked like some fairy princess's snow palace, all white and silver and blue.

What seemed like miles of white silk chiffon, shot with silver, was draped and swathed from the ceiling and around the French doors in great swags and fanciful shapes, caught up with bright-blue silken cords.

The pretty chairs and settees beside dainty side tables that were set around the edges of the room were painted white, their tracery of scrollwork picked out in silver, and were upholstered in blue-and-silver damask.

Huge glistening mirrors lining one wall had been surrounded with camellias, snowdrops, orange blossoms, and white roses. Their heady fragrance floated around the room, mingling indiscriminately with the perfumes of the gaily clad ladies.

Light seemed to blaze from everywhere. The great chandeliers glowed warmly; the tiny crystal sconces dotted around the room each held a pair of blue candles; hundreds of tiny lights winked in the trees beyond the wall of the French doors, which stood open wide. The terrace that ran the length of the room had been turned into a veritable bower with masses of fragrant white spring blossoms bunched along the entire length, and pretty marble benches set out for those who wished to cool off from the rigors of the dance floor, which had itself been polished till it glowed.

The musicians in the gallery had begun to play, and the melody seemed to float and dance about the room on a silvery cloud. Everything was light, shimmer, movement, and fragrance, and all pronounced themselves enchanted.

Amy was standing quite still at the top of the stairs, gazing down at the fantasy, as Lord Tyrone looked up from the floor below. He nearly gasped at sight of her. My God! he thought. She looks like an empress! His heart turned over as he gazed upon her. He wished so much to believe her as innocent as she now appeared, standing there in a glow of light. He had been very worried by the news Mimms had brought him last night. Had Ned's paper indeed been stolen, he wondered, or had Miss Clerville cleverly secreted it herself to deliver it to Deventer? It was true that she had not seen Deventer since at least yesterday afternoon, as his agents had been able to assure him. They had been watching Sir Julian carefully ever since he had returned to his home yesterday at about six o'clock. Perhaps she meant to pass the paper on to him this very evening.

Tyrone knew he must watch her closely. What a pleasure it would be, he thought to himself with a wry smile. He must try to draw her out on the subject of Sir Julian if he could. He could not much longer stand this uncertainty.

But for the present he wanted only to give himself up to the pleasure of looking at her and waltzing with her for what he feared might be the last time.

Amelia had taken great pains over her toilette this evening. Her eyes held a special brilliance. Her softly draped gown of spider gauze floated down over a petticoat of deep-blue silk. Silver ribbons edged its hem and the low neckline, which showed off a pair of perfect white shoulders. Her thick curls had been caught up atop her head with a silver ribbon, one only set loose to fall over her shoulder. Crystals winked in her ears and at her neck. Deep-blue gloves climbed high up her arms, and blue silk slippers with silver rosettes peeked out from under her gown. She carried a posy of white roses and blue violets in a silver filigree holder, a gift from Ferdie.

Tyrone stood motionless, watching her descend the gracefully curved staircase. She reached the bottom and paused. She had not yet seen him, and turned with a start when she heard his deep voice beside her.

"Miss Clerville, I do hope your friendship with Lady Waverly is quite sound. She may not like to be so far outshone at her own ball."

The smile that wreathed her face was the crowning effect of her beauty. "Small chance of that, my lord. Have you not seen her? She is all white velvet, orange blossoms, and diamonds, and quite exquisite," said Amy. "Never fear for our friendship, my lord. Katie has been outshining me for years, as I am sure she will continue to do, yet, perverse creature that I am, I continue to love her." She surveyed him from top to toe. "And you, my lord! I'll wager Prince Charming was just such a one," she said, smiling at her own private joke.

It was true, of course. In his long-tailed coat of midnight-blue velvet and blue silk knee breeches, white satin waistcoat, and snowy cravat, with just a touch of lace at his throat and wrists, he was magnificent. A sapphire glowed subtly among the folds of his neckcloth, another on his finger. The fob and single seal at his waist were in perfect taste. Amelia could scarce tear her eyes from him.

He gave her a crooked grin. It struck her that it made him look very like an endearing little boy. "I find it impossible to believe, ma'am, that any lady in the room could look lovelier, or more perfectly suited to the setting, than you."

She found herself blushing, and, an even more unusual condition for her, speechless. While she rummaged in her mind for a response, he continued, "I pray you have not forgotten your promise of the first waltz to me, ma'am."

"Of course not, my lord," she replied. She caught sight of the Duchess descending the stairs. A mischievous twinkle came into her eyes, and she dimpled merrily. "At least, I have a very great favor to ask your lordship."

She had promised Katie that she would get the Duchess of Harcourt to dance at her ball. The idea had occurred to them weeks ago, in Somerset, after she had teased her aunt about it and dared her to stand up for the waltz. It was just the sort of lively touch that Katie had become famous for. It would liven up her party, and possibly set the ton by the ears.

"You see, my lord, my aunt adores to dance, and I know it must gall her that she always needs must sit on the sidelines with the other dowagers when the waltz is played. I have dared her to dance it tonight, for I know she would love to, but she swears she will not." She gave him a most persuasive smile. "Would you mind very much, my lord, asking her to stand up with you for the first waltz?"

Tyrone laughed warmly. "Why, you little minx!" He looked down at her with a look that made her blush again. "Of course, I should be honored to dance with the Duchess. But if I must give up my dance with you, Miss Clerville, I fear the cost be too high. Only if you promise me the second waltz will I go along with your wicked scheme."

With a pretty curtsy and an "I thank you, my lord," the bargain was concluded just as the Duchess arrived. The first strains of a waltz were heard.

"Your Grace," said Tyrone with his deepest and most elegant bow. "I believe they are beginning a waltz. As it is my invariable practice to begin the evening by dancing with the most elegant and beautiful woman in the room, I beg to solicit your hand for the waltz."

The Duchess looked surprised, then turned an arch expression to her niece. "This is your doing, I fancy, Miss."

"I, Aunt Louisa? Why, whatever can you mean?" she answered with feigned astonishment.

The Duchess looked back at Tyrone with a face that held both displeasure and gratification, tinged with what Amy was sure was disappointment. "You must know, my lord, that I no longer dance. I have not done so in years."

"Then it is high time you did so, Your Grace. You are depriving us all cruelly."

"My lord, it would be quite unseemly at my age, I assure you." He still twinkled his smile at her. "Oh, go away with you, Justin. You are being a naughty boy! I am sure Amelia would be quite pleased to substitute for me."

"Oh, I am sorry, Aunt Louie, but I am already

promised to . . . to . . ." She looked frantically around her. "To Mr. Brice!" she exclaimed as she perceived Ferdie nearby. He was bearing down on a poor dab of a girl not likely to have many partners that night. With a quick pang of guilt, Amy raced off in his direction before he could reach her and virtually pushed him onto the floor

"Well, Your Grace?" said Tyrone, holding out his hand. "I assure you I shall not go away, for I have every intention of dancing with you." His eyes had an old look of deviltry that she knew well but had not seen in them for many years. The Duchess knew when she was beaten, and, in truth, she had not the heart to put out that spark of fun, rekindled after so many years. And she did so love to dance.

"Oh, very well, my lord. I do not wish to make a scene," she said, hoping her voice was sufficiently icy. And with that she was swept into the lilting dance.

Although the waltz had been only recently introduced into England, the Duchess was not unfamiliar with the steps. She had appointed herself to watch over the dancing lessons of various daughters, nieces, and grandchildren. And if the furniture could speak, it might tell of a lovely old lady, humming to herself and waltzing quite alone around the room.

Lord Tyrone was an excellent partner, and she easily followed his smooth steps. Despite her sixty-odd years and her tall elegance, she was remarkably light on her feet. After the first few moments of hauteur, she gave herself up to the pleasure of dancing with such an accomplished partner.

"How well I recall dancing with your father, Justin." She sighed. "Now there was a man!"

"And I believe, Your Grace, that he never forgave the Duke for snapping you up from under his very nose. How often did I hear him say, 'Louisa Clerville'—for he always called you that, you know—'now there's a woman!' "

Her Grace of Harcourt dimpled deeply and very

nearly blushed. The pair circled on in silence. Slowly the floor began to clear. Such a sight was not often seen. And soon the noble pair was alone on the gleaming parquet surface, sweeping in great arcs and circles as the bemused bystanders watched in admiration. As the music drew to a close, Tyrone swept the Duchess a stately bow, which she answered with a slow, deep, and majestic curtsy that was still the envy of every woman in the room. With regal tread, the pair left the floor to a flutter of applause.

"Oh, Aunt Louie!" breathed Amy, running up to her aunt. "You were beautiful! I knew you would be!"

The Duchess cast a stern look at her niece. "I shall have words for you later, Miss!" But her mouth twitched into a tiny smile and her eyes sparkled. "But perhaps not," she grinned.

Tyrone bowed to Amy. "I shall return soon for my reward, Miss Clerville, though I warn you, I am now thoroughly spoiled for younger women."

"Gammon!" exclaimed the Duchess, well pleased. "Be off with you, silly boy, and stop making a cake of yourself, and me into the bargain."

"Your wish is my command, Your Grace." With another magnificent bow, he walked away.

"Such a famous sight, Aunt Louie! I knew you would enjoy it," said Amy, clapping her hands.

"Well, and so I did, my love," she admitted. "But you are not to do such a thing again. To be dancing at my age is not at all the thing."

"Oh, stuff!" scoffed Amy. "I'll wager every dowager in the room will be dancing before the evening's out, now that you have broken the ice. They all want to, you know, so why should they not?" She gave her aunt a sly glance. "I think I'll ask Ferdie to stand up with you next."

"Amelia! You will do no such thing! I flatter myself that if I wish to dance again I may still be able to procure my own partner," she said as she patted an errant crystal curl back into place.

"That I doubt not at all!" said Amy brightly as she was carried off on the arm of a young captain for the country dance then forming.

Throughout the next two country dances and the quadrille, Amy's eyes kept straying to Lord Tyrone. He did not dance, but wandered about the room speaking to various gentlemen of his acquaintance, and receiving compliments from dowagers on his skill at the waltz. Amy laughed to see them. They were angling to be asked to dance themselves, she felt sure.

At last the waltz was heard once again. Tyrone took a very civil departure of Lady Bessborough, to that lady's evident disappointment, and turned his steps toward Amelia. She suddenly grew nervous. She had given up neither her resolve to find out what she could about him nor even the last of her suspicions about him, but she knew that this might well be the last time she could ever hope to waltz with him, to feel his arm around her. The thought cut through her like a knife. She pushed it aside, extended her hand and her prettiest smile, and gave herself up entirely to the heavenly feeling of floating in his arms.

They spoke in commonplaces and compliments. Her aunt gave a knowing grin when she heard Amy's light laugh and saw Tyrone's very human smile as the pair floated past. I do believe my Lord Tryone is well and truly catched at last, she said happily to herself.

Amy heard her partner chuckle softly. "I hope you are well pleased with yourself, ma'am. If you will but look around you, you will see no fewer than four dowagers, none of whom has been seen to dance these five years or more, in the arms of various and sundry gentlemen. From their faces, I fear some of the gentlemen may never forgive you, or me."

Amy looked around her and laughed again. When she looked back at Tyrone, his blue eyes were peering at her as though they would see into her very soul, and she fell silent. After a moment, he said, "Yes, indeed, Miss Clerville, you are remarkably like your brother."

She went cold, all her suspicions returning in a rush as she remembered the first time he had spoken those words to her. Why had he to remind her at such a lovely moment? "It is a fact, my lord, of which I am exceedingly proud," she answered, the pride flashing in her deep-green eyes.

He raised a brow in surprise at the brittleness of her tone. "As well you should be, ma'am. Edward Clerville was one of the finest men it has ever been my privilege to know. He will be much missed."

Her green eyes widened. A faint hope dawned there, for she had heard sincerity in his tone. She studied him a long time before she said quietly, "And so he is, my lord."

Almost under his breath, she heard him say, once again, "I wonder just how like him you are." His smile had gone, and Amy saw a serious and questioning look in his face, but one that held none of his old cynicism. She regarded him quizzically, but he did not speak again. Soon the dance was over, and she was returned to her aunt. Still he did not leave her side.

"Your niece dances almost as charmingly as you do yourself, Your Grace," he said to the Duchess. Turning to Amelia, he added, "May I hope, Miss Clerville, for the honor of escorting you in to supper later in the evening?"

Her bright smile broke through again. "I should be very honored, my lord."

"Good. I shall fetch you at midnight then. I do hope you enjoy the dancing until then." He turned his smile to the Duchess. "Your Grace, your servant." And he strode across the room.

Watching him go, Amy caught sight of Olivia Cole standing by one of the French doors. In this fairy fantasy of white and silver, her low-cut crimson crape gown covered with gold lace seemed heavy and out of place, almost garish. Amy fancied that Katie might have hinted ever so slightly to Lady Cole that she rather thought she might do her ball in pink and gold this year, though of course she was not perfectly decided. Tyrone seemed not to see the lady at all as he walked past her and crossed into the cardroom. Lady Cole fumed, and Amelia grinned broadly.

"Lord Tyrone has not yet danced with Lady Cole," she said to her aunt. "Is not that odd?"

"Distinctly odd," said the Duchess with a very self-satisfied smile. Before she could say more, Amy was borne off on the arm of yet another lovesick young fool. The rest of the evening seemed interminable to her as she anxiously awaited the supper hour. When finally it approached, she found herself standing near Lady Cole. Lord Tyrone was crossing toward them to take Amy down to supper as planned.

"Why, Justin, here you are!" gushed the widow, reaching her hands out to him. "You have not been near me all the evening," she said with a little pout. "I declare I am quite out of charity with you. But now you are here, I shall allow you to take me in to supper."

"I am honored you should wish to bear me company, Lady Cole," he said civilly "However, I am afraid I have already engaged Miss Clerville to dine with me." The lady pulled herself up very straight, taut with indignation. Her eyes flashed fire, but Tyrone had already turned to Amy. "Ma'am?" He offered his arm, and Amy, inordinately pleased with what had just happened but anxious to avoid a scene, quickly took it, and they strolled away. Lady Cole watched them go, a dangerous glitter still burning in her bright-blue eyes.

When Amy was seated at one of the little white tables topped with blossoms and candles in crystal holders, and had had a plate filled with lobster patties, oysters, fresh pineapple, and sweetmeats set before her, she turned with an ingenuous smile to Tyrone and said, "I do not think Lady Cole is very pleased with you, sir. You have not danced with her the whole evening."

"Have I not?" he replied in his best Brummell tone. "I had not noticed." A telltale muscle quivered in his cheek, destroying his *sang froid*. She nearly choked on a sugared walnut as she swallowed a laugh. "As to that, Miss Clerville, I doubt not that Sir Julian Deventer is also displeased. You have yet to dance with him tonight"

A scowl crossed her face. "And how should I, sir, for he has not asked me." Tyrone imagined he read disappointment in her words, and he slumped a little in his chair. Her own scowl deepened. "And, in truth, I hope he does not do so, for, though I've no wish to cause a scene, I shall not dance with him. A more odious gentlemen I have yet to meet."

Hope now rekindled in the Marquis's heart. "Can that be true, ma'am? One has heard that he was in hopes of winning your favor and perhaps even your hand."

"My fortune, I collect you mean, my lord," she said drily. "I am aware of what has been said about me. Indeed, I was a great fool to let those stories grow to such proportions. Sir Julian can never have seriously believed that I meant to marry him. And I shall take care to add no more fuel to that gossip, I assure you." She flushed to realize how freely she had been speaking to him, and made a mental note to say no more about it.

Tyrone's spirits rose so high during her speech that he looked at her tenderly, seeing her beauty and her spirit. "Indeed, Amelia, your brother would be pleased to hear you speak so."

She looked searchingly into his deep eyes. She felt a glow of warmth at hearing her name on his lips. "Tell me, my lord, what do you know of my brother? I must know."

"And I should very much like to tell you, but a

crowded supper room or ballroom is not the place. Unfortunately, I must leave London early tomorrow. I may be gone for some days. But if you will permit, I shall call on you as soon as I return."

"Thank you, my lord. I should be very pleased to hear whatever you can tell me about him." It was with dismay that she heard that he was leaving town. Could it mean that he had the paper that was stolen from Standen House, and must now arrange for its delivery to the French? Oh, how she hoped it was not so. She was sure she had heard real admiration in his voice when he had spoken of Ned. He could not be responsible for the death of a man he had admired. She was more confused now than ever, for she knew no more of his part in this business than she had before. But she so wanted to trust him.

Just for tonight, she would put the whole matter from her mind. Mimms had seemed very sure that his superior would be able to handle the situation of the missing paper. She would leave it in their hands and enjoy what was left to her of this one magical evening.

The conversation of the two undeclared lovers soon drifted into less dangerous channels. Each was too bemused by the other to remember later what they had discussed. Their absorption in each other had even kept them from noticing that Sir Julian Deventer and Olivia Cole had seated themselves at the next table. These two had been able to overhear, each with his own sense of horror, most of the conversation of their neighbors. They soon left the room together. Anyone who had cared to look, though no one did, might have noticed them later, out on the flower-bedecked terrace, consulting, or perhaps one would say debating, in fierce undertones.

A bit later in the evening, Tyrone, upon passing through the cardroom, felt himself roughly jostled. Making a punctilious bow, Sir Julian said, "I do beg

your pardon, my lord. How very clumsy of me."
Tyrone merely bowed and passed out of the room.

The evening wound to an end at last. The Marquis escorted the Duchess of Harcourt and her beautiful niece to their carriage.

"I do hope you two are satisfied with the results of your trickery," smiled the Duchess. "I've never seen so many silly old tabbies trying to dance in my life." She twinkled up at Tyrone. "But I did love my waltz, Justin. And I must thank you for forcing my hand. I'll wager the ton will not give up talking about this party for a while to come. Good night, you young scamp."

The spark of deviltry danced in his eyes at her words. "The two Clerville ladies were the only ones worth dancing with tonight." He kissed her hand lightly. "Goodnight, Your Grace. I shall take the very first opportunity of calling on you when I return to town." He bowed to Amelia and bid her also a reluctant goodnight. A rather star-struck young lady entered her carriage and was driven home. As Tyrone stepped to his own vehicle, he still had not noticed that his seal, with its formal curving T, was missing from its usual spot at his waist.

To the Marquis of Tyrone the evening had been a complete success. His Amelia did not love Deventer. And there could be no other reason for suspecting her of complicity in the French operations. As soon as he could manage to return from Lyme Regis, he would present himself to her aunt and make a formal offer for her hand. He felt confident from the look in her amazing eyes this evening that she would not refuse him.

Sir Julian had slipped away from the ball a bit earlier in the evening, as had Lady Cole. The outwardly ill-matched pair were now seated in that lady's comfortable drawing room. They were, in fact, very much alike at this moment. Both were afraid, as they saw the goals toward which each had worked so long slipping away. Olivia Cole would not sit by and see the prize she had so long coveted go to a silly little chit like Amelia Clerville. And Sir Julian had been too intoxicated by the smell of Amelia's fortune to let her go to another so easily. Both of these adversaries were cunning and both could be very dangerous. The candles had burned low in their sockets before Sir Julian at last took his leave, a completely formed plan in his mind, a fat purse for carrying it out in his pocket, and a smug smile on his sinister face.

Chapter Fourteen

The agents that Tyrone had set to follow Sir Julian were thorough. The night man had seen him leave Lady Cole's house at a very unseemly hour of the morning. He'd also seen the self-satisfied smile on that gentleman's face. The agent grinned to himself and looked at his watch. Pulling a rather grubby little notebook and a stub of pencil from a baggy pocket in his moleskin waistcoat, he jotted a quick note, then took off once again in stealthy pursuit.

Sir Julian strolled leisurely down Piccadilly, heading for his own lodgings in Ryder Street. The agent, just as leisurely, walked along on the other side of the road, carefully keeping under the dark-purple shadows of the trees in the Green Park. When at last his prey was safely tucked into bed and the light in the bedroom window had been extinguished, he arranged himself more or less comfortably in a nearby shop doorway and settled in for the long wait. Relief, in the guise of his partner, would arrive somewhat after dawn.

As the principal figures in the drama soon to unfold slept, the sun peeked over the soot-blackened buildings of the City. The rippling water of the Thames glowed orange and yellow in the early-morning light, and London began to come alive again.

The last linkboy, having fulfilled his mission in lighting the way for a tipsy late-night reveler, extinguished his torch and headed wearily home, jingling in his threadbare pocket the few pennies he had earned that night. The bells of St. Paul's, St. Mary-le-Strand, and other churches spread their chiming of the hour through the town. The last note died away on the air. A full quarter of an hour later, a Charley tardily shook himself awake and left his box in the Haymarket. "Five o' the clock and a fair night!" he announced as he strode off in the direction of Piccadilly on the last of his night's rounds.

The flower and vegetable sellers in Covent Garden were already doing a brisk business. Burrows were piled high with carrots and potatoes; a little girl with bare feet was tying up bunches of violets amid the clattering, rumbling, and shouting of "Turnips, four fer a penny, fine, nice turnips, 'ere."

Outside the grand houses to the west, a milk cart rumbled along the stones, its heavy-footed mare stopping now and then while the cool frothy milk was sloshed into a bucket and handed back to a waiting kitchen maid. The smell of fresh bread was followed at once by a wicker baker's cart pushed by a boy wearing a wool cap and a toothy smile. An herb seller, savory bunches of knotted marjoram, basil, and London thyme overflowing her basket, went from kitchen door to kitchen door, the high pattens on her feet clattering on the steps.

In Berkeley Square, Amelia dreamed. She had a smile on her lips, and the image of a laughing handsome face in her mind.

In St. James's Square, Lord Tyrone's valet was already having his breakfast belowstairs. In less than an hour he must wake his master, and soon thereafter they would be on their way south. The master would drive himself today. His famous greys would be harnessed to the light curricle. They could make sixteen miles an hour and were good for at least two stages. With the help of Tyrone's own horses stabled along the oft-traveled route, they would be in Lyme Regis in time for a very late supper and a good night's sleep.

And in Ryder Street, Sir Julian Deventer slept deep and dreamlessly. He knew what he must do. It did not worry him.

The man in the moleskin waistcoat waited, eyes open, sometimes humming softly to keep himself awake. The sky grew steadily brighter, and he turned his eyes to the east. Aye, it looked to be turning into a right fine day. And he'd have been just as well pleased to spend a goodly portion of it in his bed.

The second of Tyrone's agents soon came whistling softly down the street toward the doorway that sheltered his mate. "So, Tom. An' what's the cove been up to, then?" he asked as the other unfolded himself and gave a mighty stretch.

"Spent a good part of the night with the boss's pretty widow lady, that he did. Belike his lordship won't be pleased to hear that the gent's been messin' with his woman," said Tom.

"Like as not, he won't care a fig," replied the other. "I never seen the boss give more'n a snap of his fingers for any female. An' this one ain't worth even that, if he'd be wantin' my opinion, which I'm sure he ain't." The new man glanced up at Sir Julian's curtained window, then seated himself in the shelter Tom had just vacated. He could sit here comfortably for a couple of hours at least before the shopkeeper would open up and shoo him off. "Be away with you then to your sleep. And mind you be back here by ten It'll be needin' us both to stay with this cove, or I miss my guess."

"I'll not be sorry to see my bed, that's sure. Keep your winkers open, Matt. He's a sharp cull, that one." Tom carried his sleepy head and his moleskin waistcoat off down the street, and Matt settled down to await Sir Julian's pleasure.

To poor old Matt's surprise and dismay, Sir Julian was up betimes this day. "And here Tom ain't back yet," grunted Matt. "What's the fellow about then, I'd like to know, to be going out so early, when

I'd lay my last groat he don't usually stir hisself till noon?" Scowling at the gentleman's lack of consideration, Matt began to follow him down Ryder Street. It was near to ten as they turned the corner into Bury Street, and agent Tom fell into step behind them. Matt gave a sigh of relief, and the cavalcade continued on into the melée of a London morning.

It took most of the day for Sir Julian to complete his share of the arrangements. To the casual eye, his routine was not so very different from that of many another young man on the town. He had taken great care that it should not appear so. But Tom's and Matt's eyes were far from casual, and they had to admit to a deal of confusion this day.

Upon leaving his lodgings, Sir Julian had headed for the fashionable shops in Bond Street. His first stop in this exclusive stomping ground of the ton was a very chic florist. He ordered a large bunch of white roses and violets to be delivered to Lady Amelia Clerville, Harcourt House, Berkeley Square. He handed the clerk a small folded and sealed paper to tuck among the leaves. Inside was one of Lord Tyrone's visiting cards, conveniently supplied by Olivia Cole.

He walked on to the most elegant stationer in this most elegant street. Here he purchased a small box of the finest hot-pressed notepaper, unadorned with gilt or embossing of any kind.

Emerging from the shop and pocketing the small parcel, he strolled jauntily on until he reached a chemist's shop on the corner. He stood a moment perusing the display of beakers, inhalers, and bottles of Russia Oil, Cheltenham Salts, and Dr. James's Analeptic Pills in the crowded little bow window. He entered and purchased an unremarkable quantity of laudanum.

His last intended stop was at Hatchard's, where he bought a small French grammar and dictionary. His command of the language had grown rusty, and he would soon have much greater need of it than heretofore.

His shopping complete, he headed for Arthur's, the only club in St. James's that still admitted him, for a bit of lunch. His steps carried him past the windows of a well-known ton dealer in men's furnishings. On a whim, he entered the shop and purchased some exquisite linen handkerchiefs and an extravagantly embroidered silk nightshirt in which he was sure to be irresistible. He ordered the parcels delivered to his lodgings and betook himself off to his club.

This little comedy didn't seem to be yielding up much in the way of useful information to Lord Tyrone's agents, but Tom dutifully recorded each stop in his notebook. When Sir Julian entered Arthur's at last, Tom and Matt fell into discussing their progress.

"I can't make nothin' at all of this mornin'," complained Matt in irritation. "He's been shoppin' an' nothin' else."

"What'd he buy in all them shops, do ya suppose?"

"How the devil should I know? Let's see that notebook, then." Tom laboriously fished it out, and Matt squinted over the nearly indecipherable scribblings. "A flower shop, a stationer, a chemist, a bookshop, and a fancy men's goods dealer. That mean anything to you?"

Tom rubbed the stubble on his chin. "Don't seem to add up to much, but it sits queer with me all the same. The cove's up to some rig, I'll wager." He struggled in thought a bit longer. "We oughta find out what he bought. Might lead somewheres."

"You'll stay right here with me, Tom Twilley! I ain't anxious to lose this one. And I don't want him sendin' off no secret messages like, neither, with them goin' one direction and me goin' t'other."

Presently, the gentleman in question emerged once more from his club. In the doorway he paused, pulling a gold repeater from his waistcoat and nonchalantly checking the time. Just as he reached the bottom of the steps, Lord Halverley, of the War Office, happened by. Sir Julian saluted with his walking stick, and Halverley pulled up.

"I say, Deventer! Have to thank you for that little tip last week on Shooting Star. Pretty little mare. Nosed in a first, she did, and won me a monkey," he crowed loudly.

"Pleased to have been of service, my lord," answered Sir Julian agreeably.

"Who do you like for next week, Deventer? Damme if I haven't learned to trust your nose. Seems you can smell out a winner every time."

"I may have one or two ideas, my lord. Is that the *Chronicle* you've got there? I'd have to look over the lists."

"Take it, my boy, take it," called out Halverley jovially. "If you get a good feeling about any of 'em, look me up tomorrow, won't you? I'd be much obliged."

Sir Julian took the folded newspaper, politely saluted his acquaintance, and turned away down the street.

One look from Matt was all Tom needed. They both knew that Lord Halverley's position at the War Office was an important one. Matt headed up St. James's after Sir Julian, while Tom took the other direction after his lordship.

By evening Matt was frankly mystified. The only other stop made by Sir Julian that afternoon had been to the bishop's residence, where he remained for just under half an hour. He reappeared in the doorway, where he stood some minutes in polite conversation with a young clerk, then took a hackney back to Ryder Street. Matt certainly didn't take Deventer for a religious man, and his curiosity was more than a little piqued by this odd start.

When Tom rejoined him, the two partners compared notes and came up with a big zero. The trailing of Lord Halverley had yielded nothing more of any value. After a couple of hours' idling in White's, he had returned to his office at the Horse Guards. As evening drew nearer, he emerged only to carry himself off home to his dinner.

Well, all the pair of them could do was to turn in their report and keep their eyes open wide. It would have to rest with better heads than theirs to make any sense out of it all.

It wasn't until nearly dinnertime that Sir Julian knew for certain that he was being watched. He stood looking out of the window of his bedroom. He was not at all surprised to see the little man in the moleskin waistcoat, trying unsuccessfully to blend with the stonework across the way. He could not see the other, curled up in an uncomfortable sleep behind his partner, but he guessed that the man was there. He remembered seeing the two of them earlier in St. James's Street, and his natural suspicions had been roused. The knowledge of their surveillance did not please him, but neither did it worry him unduly.

He quickly reviewed the day's activities for any clues to his plan. No, he was certain he had done nothing that could cause suspicion or comment. He was sure the encounter with Halverley would have been remarked, but there was nothing unusual or in any way odd about it. And Halverley was much too clever a fellow to give himself away. Sir Julian could sleep untroubled tonight, the last night in his own bed for a while.

He turned to the wiry little servant behind him, who was busily packing trunks and valises. "Is everything arranged for the morning?" he asked.

The little man's smile was almost as sinister as his employer's. "Aye, guv'nor. All's in order." He stood up as if to begin a recitation learned from memory. "Me big brother Jem goes in the big coach hisself. He knows what to do, an' he can handle any trouble, can

Jem. The fast coach pulls up here after you're gone in the mornin'. I puts up the bags and takes off. You step out early, real casual-like, and walk along to me sister's pie shop in Greek Street. Sissy'll show you the way out through the yard an' down the alley. When you comes out in Bateman Street, you gets in a hack as'll be standin' there for you. You tells the jehu to take you 'cross Westminster Bridge, where I'll be awaitin' for you, pretty as you please, an' we're on our way south. And no one'll be the wiser, guv'nor, you can lay your last megg on it."

"And is your sister to be trusted? How do I know she'll send no one after me?"

The little man looked hurt. "Ah, guv'nor, she's me sister!" Then a little smile curled his lip. " 'Sides, she cost you a pony, an' that buys a lot of trust on Greek Street."

Sir Julian looked out the window again at his companions in the street below. Everything was arranged, and he felt secure and confident. A malignant smile covered his face. He was intending to have a bit of London fun this night. The Lord knew when he might have another chance for it. He would lead these rogues a merry chase indeed, from one end of the town to the other, from Vauxhall to the Rookery, and with nothing to show for their trouble but their tired feet.

But tomorrow he would have to take special care to lose his hounds. He must be quite certain that no one followed him out of town or even suspected his direction. His vast experience and dexterity in avoiding his more persistent creditors should stand him in good stead on the morrow. Before they even began to guess where to look for him, he would be quite safely out of reach. And he would not be alone.

He turned back to the evil little servant, who had resumed his packing. "Put in the new silk nightshirt on top of the small valise," he said with a hideous grin and a lascivious light in his eye.

Across town, Amelia had been sharing a cup of chocolate with Katie in the morning room when the flowers arrived. The two young ladies had been talking over the great success of last night's ball and laughing together over the triumph of their scheme to get the dowagers onto the dance floor, when a footman entered, nearly staggering under the huge bouquet.

Amy had grown used to having flowers rained upon her by romantic young gentlemen, but this mass of roses with the little blue violets peeking delicately through their petals was something special. Breaking the seal on the note, she drew out Tyrone's card. At sight of the name, she breathed a tiny gasp, and her face went warm with pleasure. She turned over the elegant little card. "With thanks for a very enjoyable waltz, and in hopes that my business may not long delay our next meeting." The name Tyrone was signed with a flourish.

"Oh, Amy! How very lovely they are," exclaimed Katie. She inhaled deeply the scent of the roses and tried to peer over her friend's shoulder at the card. But Amy had tucked it into her reticule. "Amelia Clerville! If you don't tell me who sent them, I shall never speak to you again!" When Amy turned her face to Katie, the latter was astonished. "Why, you're blushing! I do swear I have never seen you do so before, not for any man."

"Yes, it is an odious habit, is it not? Yet I seem to be doing quite a lot of it lately."

Katie's face grew mulish. "Amelia?" Her tone held a stubborn warning.

"Well, if you must know, love, they are from the Marquis of Tyrone," she admitted, trying unsuccessfully to make her voice sound light and unconcerned.

"Tyrone!" Now Katie's mouth was well and truly open. "But you hate him! And you said he hated you, too."

"Well, it's true I did hate him," said Amy with a little twinkle. It was all Katie needed to see. She was out of her chair with a bounce and hugging Amy affectionately.

"Oh, Amy! I'm so glad. So very glad." She held her friend at arm's length, and her tone became confidential. "One could see, of course, by the way he looked at you last night, that he was besotted. Why, he looked like a schoolboy when he was waltzing with you. But I'd no idea you returned his regard. Oh my love, what a lark! You'll set the whole town by the ears. What fun it will be to see their faces. Oh, Amy, you will be so good for each other. I know you will. And I'm sure your aunt will be so very pleased."

Amy took hold of Katie's shoulders and firmly sat her down again, stopping her flow of chatter. "Katie, you will say nothing of this to my aunt, or to anyone else, as you are my friend! I shall take the flowers now where she will not see them." Katie was looking puzzled, and Amy softened her brisk manner. "It is true, Katie, that I love Lord Tyrone. It may also be true that he returns my regard, though of that I am far from certain. But there may be serious obstacles in the way of such a match."

"But Amy, whatever can you mean? Lord Tyrone is perfectly free to marry where he will, as are you. It is an eligible match in every way." A light dawned in her eyes. "Are you afraid that his feelings for Lady Cole are . . ."

Amy silenced her at once. "No, my love. I do not think I need fear Lady Cole." She could not contain a tiny smile of satisfaction as she remembered the lady's black looks of the evening before.

"Then why?"

Amelia sighed. "I hope I can tell you one day soon. Indeed, I certainly feel a strong need to confide in someone. It may be that my fears of and for his lordship are groundless." She almost whispered now. "And, oh, how I pray that they may be so!" Then, gathering her strength once more, she said, "But until I can know for certain, we shall speak no more of the Marquis of Tyrone."

This last was said in an obstinate tone with which Katie was only too familiar. She knew it was useless to press further. Not one more word on the subject would she get from Amelia.

Tyrone had spent the entire day bowling along the King's Highway at an exhilarating clip. The wind whipped his dark locks and brought a ruddy glow to his tanned face. The valet beside him, who had been with him these dozen years and more, recognized at once that his master was in irrepressible spirits. He'd not seen him so in years. With a boyish light in his eyes, his lordship was driving to an inch, feather-edging the curricle around sharp corners at full tilt.

They made several changes of horses and stopped once for a quick nuncheon, but Tyrone was in a hurry. He had sent word ahead about Ned's missing paper. It must not be allowed out of England, and his men were all on the alert for it. If Deventer had it, and Tyrone was quite certain he did, then he was safely covered in London. If he bolted, Matt and Tom would follow, Tyrone would be warned, and Deventer would be arrested before he could board a ship for France.

But with Wellington's campaign in the Peninsula heating up, there was even more important business to attend to. Tyrone must gather the latest information about troop movements in France and naval activity in and around the channel, and send off his regular report to the Commander-in-Chief.

He wanted to get the business over with as quickly as may be so that he could get back to town. His desire for London was no longer simply a ruse to avert suspicions from his real vocation. Even though he was worried about the outcome, he was anxious to put his fate to the touch and ask Amelia Clerville to become his wife.

At the rate he traveled, the cliffs of Lyme Regis came into view while the last lights were still winking in the windows of the snug little houses. They headed straight for the harbor.

He was soon aboard his own *Lady Faire*, sitting behind a littered desk in his cabin. Several men were waiting for him when he arrived. He barked out his orders; the men scurried off in various directions to carry them out.

He devoured a hearty supper of fresh grilled haddock and shrimp, an omelette with broiled mushrooms, and a crisp cold apple, washed down with a tankard of cool ale, then sat at his desk until well into the small hours of the morning pouring over the litter of reports, communiqués, and documents that had piled up in his absence. He made some notes and sent a few dispatches of his own, then blew out his candle for a well-deserved sleep.

As he lay there in the quiet darkened cabin, he gave himself over to the visions in his mind. There was a pathetic vulnerability that showed in his face whenever he thought of Amelia. He must be a great coxcomb indeed to think that she would have him. She had shown quite clearly at their first meeting, and on various occasions thereafter, exactly what she thought of him, and none of it was good. And now she was being besieged by eligible suitors, all of them with position and address to recommend them. She had no need of his wealth, and she could marry where she wished.

Still, her manner had seemed softer toward him of late. And there had been something in her look last night that led him to hope that he might in the end win the prize. He must just take the plunge and trust to fate to bring him to the surface.

Olivia Cole would not be pleased, he knew, and he would have to deal with her very soon. She had been a convenient means of establishing the very desirable image of a gentleman on the town, and he must admit that he had not despised her company. But she could never compare to Amelia in his mind.

That she had been using him as well he had not the least doubt. She was very fond of cutting a dash, and her strongest ambition was to become one of the leaders of London society. To be seen with the Marquis of Tyrone could only add to her consequence and could be quite useful in consolidating her position within the ton. They understood each other very well, he thought, and had served each other's purposes admirably. She had certainly known from the start that his feelings had not been seriously engaged.

But he had felt a subtle change in her lately. She had acquired a new sense of determination, for she had decided to exchange her respectable but lowly status as widow to a mere baronet for that of a marchioness. Tyrone was just as determined not to be entrapped by the likes of the cunning Lady Cole. Even before he had been certain of his feelings for Amelia, he had decided to allow the public flirtation to dwindle. Now he would end the association altogether.

No, the fair Olivia, who liked to get her own way in all things, would not be at all pleased. She would suffer no real anguish of heart at his defection, but she would be humiliated and angry. And anger could make her dangerous. He must protect Amelia from her lashing tongue. She would soon enough acquire a husband by some other means. Whatever hapless noble she finally snared was welcome to her.

Tyrone had no idea just how far Lady Cole's anger could take her, or quite how dangerous she could be. He snuggled under the down comforter and let the gentle rocking of the ship and the sounds of the gulls lull him into a deep and rejuvenating sleep.

Chapter Fifteen

"And who goes with you to Richmond this afternoon, my love?" the Duchess asked Amelia next morning.

"Oh, it will be quite like a family party, you know. There will be Tom and Katie, Ferdie and Sukey, Captain Havesham and myself." She paused and tilted her little head to one side, looking for all the world like a thoughtful bird. "It seems that Ferdie's attentions to Sukey are becoming very particular. Do you not think so, Aunt Louie?"

"So I have observed. As are those of Lord Marchness to her pretty mother. We shall end the season with a double wedding, or I miss my guess," offered her aunt with a nod of satisfaction. "And a pair of finer matches I could not imagine. Susanna is as senseless as Ferdinand is jolly. And Lord Marchness and Lady Thornton are two of the most charmingly silly people I know. They will all deal extremely well in glorious laughing chaos," she concluded with a laugh of her own.

"I do hope Sukey asks me to stand up for her at the wedding," said Amy. "It is bound to be one of the gayest occasions of the Season. And they are both of them such very particular friends of mine."

"Are you so fond then of being a bridesmaid?" asked the Duchess archly.

"Well, of course I enjoy sharing with my dearest friends in an event so likely to bring happiness to both."

"But marriage does not always do so, you know."

"Well, of course I know that, Aunt Louie. Lord knows I have seen enough disastrous marriages among the ton. But it will be happy for Sukey and Ferdie, you know." She sat thinking a moment, and her aunt did not interrupt her meditations. "Do you know, Aunt Louie," she said at length, "I think we have been very lucky in our family. We have always been free to marry for love. You know how very well suited my own parents were, and only look at Elinor. You may laugh about her John, but only see how she glows whenever he enters the room." She gave the Duchess a sly look. "And I think you will not deny that you yourself found great happiness with the Duke."

The elegantly beautiful old face took on the warmth of remembrance that made her look like a young girl in love. "No, I will not deny it," the musical voice said softly.

"And I vow I should never marry for any other reason," concluded Amelia.

Her aunt could not keep a tiny smile of triumph from stealing across her face as she said, "Oh, I thought you were quite decided never to marry at all, my love."

Amy flushed and looked quickly away, but her voice was still light. "Oh, as to that, quite likely I never shall." A long pause, then she added, "It would have to be a very special man that I could love."

"Of that I am quite sure, my love. Very special, indeed." With a glance at the little clock that stood to one side of her dressing table, she deftly turned the subject. "Oh, dear. I shall be late to the Countess Lieven's levée. And then she will be even more insufferable, I am sure. I suppose I had best call out the lozenge coach and wear my new embroidered levantine ensemble and my haughtiest duchess smile. She worships consequence, you know, so I had best give it to her. It will dazzle her into complaisance," she concluded, favoring her niece with a blinding smile quite different from the one she would later bestow on the odious Countess. "Now you run along, my pet, and let Pitt finish dressing me. I shall not return before you leave on your own excursion, so I will adjure you now to enjoy yourself. I shall see you later this evening. We are promised to Lady Carteret, if you recall."

Amy sighed. "I shall not forget, Aunt Louie. I declare I grow quite weary of so very many engagements. To tell the truth, I would rather eat my dinner in the nursery with the children." She made a visible effort at enthusiasm that was not quite successful. "But Lady Carteret has been very kind. I shall sparkle and laugh and chatter the evening away, saying absolutely nothing of any consequence. I shall not disappoint her." She took her leave and headed downstairs to the quiet and seclusion of the library.

It would be two hours at least before she must go to her room and change for the driving party to Richmond. She asked Trundle to deny her to any visitors who might call and resolved to spend the time quite pleasantly and quite alone with a book. Consequently, she settled herself into a comfortable padded chair, her stockinged feet tucked up under her, and tried to concentrate on the last, and most exciting, volume of one of Mrs. Radcliffe's more lurid attempts at literature.

But not even the lady's blood-chilling style could hold Amelia's attention for long. After half an hour and four or more pages, she realized she had taken in not one word, and she flung the book onto a side table in disgust. The French doors to the garden stood open; the call of a thrush drew her outside. She wandered onto the terrace and filled her head with the vibrant colors and rustling sounds of the spring garden. The pungent aroma of roses brought a smile to her mind as she thought of Tyrone's beautiful bouquet sitting up in her room.

Surely it showed that he felt some little regard for her. Ruefully, she had to admit that she could not imagine why he should. As she recounted their several meetings, she was ashamed of her own remembered actions. On nearly every occasion she had acted like a hoyden, an overbearingly arrogant matron, or a silly schoolgirl. He had good reason to dislike her.

And yet at Katie's ball the other night there had been real warmth in his smile and admiration in his eyes. She had felt it quite pointedly. If only she could know for certain what his relationship to her brother had been, then she would know her own fate and her chance for happiness.

Her ruminations were broken by Trundle, who, coughing discreetly just inside the French doors, pulled her from her reverie. He held a small silver salver with a letter.

"This has just arrived for you, miss."

Pulling herself up with a start, she took the letter and nodded her thanks to the butler, who departed as silently as he had come.

The letter was written on the simplest and finest of papers. As she began to break the large red seal, she noticed its scrolling T surrounded by wheat ears. Her heart began to beat faster. She tore open the letter with eager fingers. Before she even began to read the contents, she looked for the signature. "Tyrone" was written with a flourish, exactly as it had been on the card with yesterday's flowers.

"My dear Amelia," it began, and she flushed to see her name written by his hand.

Circumstances have allowed of my great fortune in being able to return to town much sooner than I had expected. I would speedily redeem my promise given to you the other evening to speak with you further of your brother and of my acquaintance with him. And as it offers the chance of furthering my acquaintance with his lovely sister, I am anxious to do so at once.

For reasons which I am sure will be understood, absolute discretion must prevail in any such discussion. Therefore I should prefer someplace away from Harcourt House, someplace where we may not be overheard or observed.

Can you come to the park at once and alone? I shall be awaiting you in one of the small arbors to the northwest of Grosvenor Gate. Do not be put off by my unconventional request, I beg you. You shall be reassured as to my motives when you arrive. In anticipation, I am, believe me,

Your obedient servant,
Tyrone.

P.S. You should always carry white roses and violets.

Her fingers were trembling as she refolded the letter and placed it in the pocket of her skirt. She glanced at her little lapel watch. Her friends would be arriving before long for their excursion. She would leave a note for Katie with some plausible excuse. Her friend would make her excuses to the others. Amy did not really want to go to Richmond anyway.

Stabbing a pen into the inkpot, she scribbled a few quick lines, sprinkled them with sand, folded the paper, and hurriedly wrote Lady Waverly's name across the front. Then she dashed upstairs for her most fetching bonnet of straw lace and a becoming shawl of soft green challis with a Persian border.

Descending almost at once, she handed Trundle the note she had written. "I have been called away rather unexpectedly, Trundle, on urgent family business," she improvised. "If I have not yet returned by the time my friends arrive, pray give this note to Lady Waverly."

Before he could answer, she had disappeared out the door, ignoring yet again his shocked sensibilities at her indecorous conduct in going out unescorted. Not far from her door she hailed a hackney and bade the driver take her to the Grosvenor Gate of Hyde Park.

Riding bumpily along, she had a few moments of

leisure to reflect upon the wisdom, or lack of it, in her reaction to Tyrone's note. Now she considered, it did seem an odd, not to say peremptory, summons. She was but slightly acquainted with the shaded arbors near the road to which he had bid her come. They were in a very secluded area, she knew.

But she also felt she knew what he wished to discuss. And oh, how she prayed that he would be able to set her remaining doubts of him completely at rest. She understood the need for absolute discretion. Her reputation might be sadly tarnished if she were seen there alone with him, but so eager was she to learn what he had to say that she felt the trip worth the risk. Just this once, she must trust him.

As the hired cab entered the gate, she felt her heartbeat quicken; her fingers trembled as she counted out the change for the driver. Then she plunged into the thickest part of the park, her footsteps unheard on the soft, lush grass.

The day was fine; the sun was sparkling brightly. In the near distance she could hear a dog bark and the high-pitched laugh of a child. But the day grew darker as she went deeper into the trees. At first the light was prettily dappled, forcing its way here and there through the spring leaves. Then evening seemed to close around her as she reached the deepest shadows. All sounds were muffled, and she felt very alone.

The little forest was dotted with rustic arbors, set with stone benches and climbing hedge roses. The first of these into which she peeked yielded nothing. The same with the second and third. The landscape became even wilder and more remote as she neared the North Ride. Her nerves were very much on edge as she crossed into a last thick clump of trees. She looked around her in bewilderment. She was certain that this was the spot to which Tyrone had bid her come. There was no one here.

As she stood there puzzling, a twig cracked

directly behind her; she sensed the presence of someone looking at her. With relief and a big smile for the Marquis, she turned to face him. But before she could turn completely, a bag of rough sacking was thrown over her head. She gasped, and the sharp mixture of salt and jute in her nostrils made her choke. She felt herself being lifted from the ground and carried away. With her head in the sack, she could scarce breathe, much less scream, but she kicked and wriggled so violently that her abductor dropped her. She tore at the hideous sacking, but her arms were immediately pinned to her sides again. She heard a muffled oath and was carried off.

A moment later she heard the fidgeting of horses and an unintelligible command and was thrown harshly into a carriage. The door slammed with a crack, and the coach lurched forward, the horses breaking into a trot. Amy lay a moment on the floor of the coach, afraid to move. But she soon sensed that she was alone. Slowly she pulled the rough sack from her head. For a moment she could see nothing at all. It was very dark in the coach. When her eyes had adjusted to the gloom, she realized that all the windows had been covered with heavy black shades, hung outside the glass. She could see nothing of the road they were taking. And, what was more worrisome, no one would be able to see her.

She pulled herself up onto the greasy seat and sank back against the squabs. Anger washed over her, overcoming for the moment her fear.

Well, you can curse yourself for a fool, Amelia Clerville! she told herself hotly. Whatever disaster you're bound for, it'll be no worse than your own stupidity's earned you. You were bird-witted enough to trust a man you've always had good reason to mistrust! Well, now you're in a devil of a fix, and no mistake.

She sat there raging in the dark, until her first burst of anger had spent itself and she could survey her position more dispassionately. She had always been proud of the fact that she kept her head in a crisis. She was not one to suffer a fit of the vapors or give in to despair, and her firm little chin had already taken on a look of grim determination. The odious Marquis with the oh so beguiling smile and the sparkling eyes would find her no whey-faced weakling. Lord knows she'd gotten herself out of scrapes before. She could do so again.

She began to explore her prison. There were a few tiny chinks of light coming through cracks in the roof of what she saw now was a terribly old coach. The doors were, of course, quite securely locked. The air was stuffy; it smelled of old grease and onions. By raising her face to one of the larger cracks, she could feel the slightest breeze on her face and breathe a bit of fresh air.

She must appraise her situation with a cool head and decide on a logical course of action. She examined the contents of her reticule. She found a one-pound note and a few loose shillings and crown pieces. Not much, to be sure. But it might come in handy if she found herself alone in some strange village, and it would probably cover the price of coach fare back to London, if she could once get away. She also found in her bag a handkerchief, two hairpins, a silver nail file, a card of pins, and a small pair of scissors. She was not exactly well equipped for an emergency of this sort, she realized. She didn't know where she was or even in which direction she was headed, but she would find her way out of this coach, of that she was determined. She could then find some helpful soul to aid her in getting back to London. If that failed, she would walk.

By the speed with which they were now traveling, Amy knew they must already be well out of town. From the relative smoothness of the ride, she thought they must be on a main highway. This old coach was badly sprung, and anything less than a

well-macadamized road would have caused a truly
bruising ride.

Amy was feeling ashamed of her position now.
How very sure of her response to his letter Tyrone
must have been, she thought derisively. And how
right he had been! She had come running as soon as
he had crooked his little finger, figuratively speaking.
Oh, how odious he was!

But why had he abducted her? she wondered. It
couldn't be for ransom. He was obnoxiously rich already. And she was sure he must know that he could
get no important information from her about her
brother's past spying activities. He surely knew more
about that than she possibly could.

There could be only one reason that she could
see. He knew that she suspected him of complicity in
her brother's death, of conspiring with the French.
He might also know that she had some contact, however tenuous, with her brother's organization. She
was, therefore, a threat to him. Now he would remove that threat to someplace safely out of harm's
way. He might even kill her. She had always sensed a
certain ruthlessness in his manner, she told herself
quite untruthfully. And she began to feel just the
tiniest bit afraid.

They traveled for what seemed like days, but was
probably no more than two hours, before they staggered to a stop at last. They had obviously left the
main highway some time back. For the last half hour,
the old coach had lurched and jolted over what must
have been a long-unused cart track. The ruts were
deep and perilous, and she felt bruised all over from
the knocking about. She was beginning to feel ill
from the stale air and the greasy smell that rose from
the leather squabs, and her head ached from her so
far unsuccessful efforts to think of some means of
escape.

The door of the coach was suddenly pulled open
with a wrench. Amy blinked from the light of the

still-bright sun. It was a moment before she could make out the features of the burly man who stood blocking the doorway. She was sure she had never seen him before.

Atop his head was a thick black mass of bristling hair, matted and tangled; on his chin was an equally black stubble of two or three days' growth. He wore a grimy rough cotton shirt, the sleeves rolled up to display massive arms. Amy noticed with detachment how the thick knotty veins stood out along their length. She was sure these arms could squeeze the life out of a man with barely an effort. In fact, by the look of him, they probably had. He smiled a horrible smile, showing a set of chipped and yellowing teeth, and a strange disquieting light blazed in his watery pale-blue eyes.

A direct attack is always best, thought Amy, so she faced him directly, chin up. "Where are we, and why have you brought me here?" she asked in imitation of the iciest tone her aunt had ever used.

His smile became a leer. Ignoring her question, he looked her over. "I'll say this fer the guv'nor. Yer a fair enough little gentry mort, that you are." He continued to study her with disconcerting thoroughness. Her eyes grew a little wider, and he gave a raucous laugh. "If yer hopin' to snabble me with your big green winkers, yer out, lass. I'm as peevy a cull as the guv'nor hisself, an' you'll not be gittin' by me. An' you'll hear nothin' neither. He give me a hundred yellow boys to keep my chaffer close, and so I'll do. Now get you out an' stretch yer pretty legs. You'll not be gettin' another chance."

Amy was too glad of the chance of a bit of fresh air to argue with any of this confusing speech, so she obediently climbed out of the smelly coach. As she stood beside her captor, she saw that he was well over six feet tall. And as he roughly pulled her away from the coach, she saw the sun glint menacingly on the steel of a pistol stuck in his belt. She gave an involuntary shudder. He followed her glance, and his laugh broke the air again.

"Aye, that's right, lass. Take yerself a close look at that popper there. I'd just as soon loose it off in yer direction, so you'll do as yer bid, an' you'll find me a reg'lar gen'leman." He clumsily lowered himself into a mocking bow.

Amy looked around to discover herself in front of a shack with boarded-up windows and the lonely air of a place long empty. Weeds crowded around the foundations, and a thick spiderweb curtained the doorway. Ivy grew high up the cold stone chimney. The only thing in relatively good repair was a small barn off to one side. The doors stood open, and the driver of the coach was leading out a team of fresh horses.

The burly man was pulling an old unraveling basket down from the coachman's box. "You'll be hungry. Here's bread and a bit o' cheese. It's a long ways yer goin' yet, lass, an' you'll git nothing more, so eat yer fill." He pulled down a large flask. "I misdoubt yer thirsty too. The guv'nor said as how I was to give you this to drink."

"What is it?" she asked, eyeing him suspiciously.

He made a distasteful grimace. "Tea!" he roared his disgust. Then, peering over his shoulder, he lowered his voice and said, "But if yer wishful o' somethin' a mite tastier, lass, I've some rare rum o' me own and a bit of blue ruin. I'd not mind to give you a tot."

"Thank you, no, but I should like some tea. It's terribly stuffy in the coach." He handed her a tin cup and poured out the amber liquid.

Though it was stone cold, she drank deeply, glad of the cool wetness on her parched throat. "Could you not at least open a window for me? It is unbearably hot and smelly inside. I'll not scream, if that's what you are afraid of."

He laughed yet again. "An' much good it'd do you if you did! Who's to hear you hereabouts?"

She looked around again. Her heart sank as the truth of his words became obvious. Aside from the three of them, there was not a single sign of human habitation as far as she could see. She thought of running, but she sensed he would not hesitate to shoot her if she tried it. She felt her spirits plunging to a dangerous low. She ached all over, her head was pounding, and she was so very tired. She was afraid she was about to cry from very despair.

No! she told herself firmly and turned her head away. Cry you will not, my girl, not in front of this horrible creature!

She saw the driver remount the box. A rough hand grabbed at her elbow, and she was propelled toward the lumbering vehicle again. Her feet were very heavy as she climbed the steps, as though she walked through water. To speed her along, the man gave her a firm push into the coach. The door swung closed with a thump, but she saw that the window had been lowered a few inches. A tiny breeze just brushed her cheek.

The cool air was soothing. She lowered her aching head onto the squabs. I must think, she told herself. But I'm so very tired. I will just lie here quietly a moment. The breeze will clear my head, and then I will be able to come up with a way out of this mess. I will rest just a minute.

And with that she drifted into a deep and dreamless sleep.

Chapter Sixteen

When Amelia's eyes once again fluttered open, it was many hours later. No more chinks of light filtered through the cracks in the rickety coach roof. Even the stale and stuffy air inside it had grown cooler, and she was glad of the shawl still wrapped around her shoulders. She hugged it closer.

She lifted a heavy head. With a surge of anger, she recognized this particular type of dullness and ache she was feeling. When she was ten years old and had the measles, Nurse Pennywhit had given the feverish little girl too much laudanum to lull her into an unnatural sleep. She had awakened with exactly this same sort of dull, heavy head. That villain had drugged her! It was too odious! It must have been in the tea given her by her burly captor, the tea that the "guv'nor" had so kindly insisted she be given. Her mind raged at the infamous Marquis.

She tried to clear her fuzzy head. She must have been given a very large dose. She recalled now how heavy her eyes had become almost at once. And she must have slept a very long time. The window was still open, and she pushed aside the heavy shade and peered into the darkness.

A low fog hugged the ground; a mizzle of rain dripped onto the few humble dwellings she could make out in the shred of light from a watery moon. From the fact that the cottages seemed rather close together, she guessed that they were near some town or village. The thought forced her into alertness. She

took deep gasps of the cold night air to clear the cob-
webs from her brain.

Where there were houses, there were people,
people who might help her. She must have her wits
about her and be ready to take advantage of any opportunity for escape. As she breathed in the damp air,
she tasted the traces of salt that it carried. Off in the
distance she heard a lone gull cry. They were near
the sea, and that could bode ill for her.

Unless, she thought, the Marquis was taking her
to Lyme Regis. She knew he kept his own ship anchored there. He might suppose it to be as good a
hiding place as any. But she knew every inch of that
part of the country. If she could but contrive to get
free of her captors, she would have no trouble making
her way to Standish and safety.

She looked around her more eagerly now, her
eyes trying hard to penetrate the mist and the envel-
oping darkness. It must be very late. There seemed to
be few lights burning in the thatch-roofed cottages
they passed. She tried to look at her lapel watch. Although the rain had stopped, the night-blackened
clouds still shaded much of the moon. She could not
read the delicate little watch face.

She was looking desperately for some landmark
she might recognize. As they crested a hill, the clouds
suddenly freed their hold on the full moon, and it
shone out brilliantly to reveal the panorama of sea before them.

A rippling silver moon-river shimmered on the
smooth water of a small cove. The lovely scene made
Amelia sink in despair. Here were no stately blue
cliffs, no Golden Cap looking placidly down on the
ancient Cobb. They were not at Lyme Regis.

There was, however, something familiar in the
curve of the cove and the whiteness of the moonlit
beach. The blinking light from a lighthouse out on
the headland stirred a memory. She mentally traced
the coastline on a map in her mind. She had explored

nearly the whole south coast of England at one time or another with her father, a great lover of the sea. She was sure she had been here before.

They were inching along an old road, creaking and bumping, tilting perilously in the furrowed track. They eased slowly around a curve. The sea was now behind them, but to Amy's amazement she saw water shimming ahead as well. She recognized the place with a gasp of relief. The Fleet! They were at the mouth of the Fleet, that geographically curious inland sea that ran from Portland Island to Abbotsbury. Just over that hill ahead was Fleet Village. And, more important, Weymouth stood only two or three miles beyond. She would get to Parker. She could count on a solid welcome and loyal assistance at the White Hart, if she could only get herself there.

She could hear the surf now, pounding onto the shingle reef of Chesil Bank. The coach pulled to a stop with a lurch and a shudder. Almost instantly, the door was thrown open, and the burly man stood before her again.

"Out wi' ya then, lass. You'll go no further on wheels."

She climbed slowly out, dismayed to find her legs weakened from the drug and the hours of jolting in the cramped coach. The salt air was chilling; she pulled her shawl closer about her. By the clear light of the moon she could now read the face of her watch. It was just after midnight.

They were at the very edge of the shingle beach; ahead, a small boat was pulled up, its anchor thrown carelessly out onto the beach. With alarm, she realized that they were about to take her out to a ship. She could just make out the great black hulk sitting at anchor about half a mile out to sea. She must make good her escape before they could get her into that ship.

The coachman had already crossed down the beach to the little boat and was readying the oars. The burly man nudged her in the same direction.

Before he could blink, a dainty little foot shot out and caught him squarely on the shin. As he staggered in surprise, an amazingly well-aimed blow caught him in the midsection causing him to lose his breath in a great whoosh and sending him to his knees. Not for nothing had Amelia watched her brother and Tom sparring together on many occasions.

Quick as a squirrel, she was off and running over the low dunes toward Fleet Village. Fear moved her feet. She prayed that the darkness would protect her from the pistol she had seen in the man's belt. She cursed her skirts, tangling in her legs. She stumbled on a rock, but was immediately up and running again. Her heart was pounding so loudly in her ears that she could not hear the running footsteps crunching on the gravelly beach behind her. She must have run thirty or forty yards before something round and hard came solidly down on the back of her head. Everything went black and she knew no more.

For the second time that night, Amelia's eyes fluttered open from an unnatural sleep. This time she awoke in a strange room. She was stretched out on a rough woolen blanket on a lumpy bed. She winced slightly when she tried to lift herself. Her fingers gingerly explored a very large bump on the back of her head. The brute! she thought with great indignation.

She looked around the little room. A single candle flickered on a table. The room seemed to be swaying slightly. She thought she must still be dizzy from that blow on the head. Then she realized that she was lying, quite alone, in the cabin of a ship. In great alarm and ignoring the throbbing in her head, she ran to the tiny window. With relief, she found she could still see the blinking lighthouse not far distant. And it did not appear to be receding. Apparently they had not yet set sail for wherever it was she was being taken. A brass nautical clock on the wall chimed. It was just half past twelve. She had been unconscious only a short time. But now they had her aboard, they would surely not much longer delay their embarkation. She felt a bubble of panic beginning to rise within her and pressed it ruthlessly down. It would help her not at all. She had to keep cool if she hoped to get out of the coil she found herself in—through her own folly, she reluctantly admitted.

She began to take stock of her situation. Her reticule still hung from her wrist. As she roamed the cabin she felt her strength returning to her limbs as resolution returned to her mind. She pondered the window. It was hopelessly small. There was no way she could squeeze through it. The door stood immovable at her touch, solidly locked.

Before she could think further, she heard a key turn in that lock, and the door was flung open. In the opening stood Sir Julian Deventer.

With what relief did Amelia throw herself at that gentleman! So certain had she been that her abductor was the Marquis of Tyrone that the odious Sir Julian assumed the prospect of a savior in her eyes. In her relief, resolution and control deserted her. She became nearly incoherent.

"Oh, Sir Julian, however did you find me? How did you know . . . I was sure no one could . . . oh, sir, how very glad I am that you have come."

A cruel smile stole into the man's face. He looked more sinister than ever. Peeling Amelia's imprudent hands from around his neck, he held her before him. His grip on her wrists was like steel. An equally metallic glint shone in his black eyes.

"How delightfully surprising to see this change in attitude in you, my dear. It will certainly make our marriage much more enjoyable for us both."

"Marriage!" She was studying those cold dark eyes intensely.

"Well, of course, my love. You surely do not think I have any improper designs upon you! It is a quite legal and proper marriage I am proposing we should embark upon. And after that joyous fact is accomplished, I am sure you will enjoy France, where we shall honeymoon before making a lengthy tour of the Continent."

A look of horror had stolen into Amy's face as realization came to her. "You! You have done this!" she sputtered. "You have had me brought here in this infamous fashion, you odious wretch!"

"Of course it was I, my dear Amelia. Who did you think?" A smile of treacherous satisfaction suffused his face. His voice thick with sarcasm, he added, "Surely you did not really think that Lord Tyrone. . . ?" He gave a derisive laugh. "How sorry I am to disappoint you, my dear. But have no fear. When we are legally married and the control of your fortune is securely in my hands, you will be quite free to have as many admirers as you wish. I feel sure that the Marquis will find you even more attractive when you are no longer in a position to trap him into marriage. I promise you I shall not object to your spending the occasional evening with him or any other gentleman after you are my wife."

Amelia stood listening throughout this sneering announcement, speechless with growing rage. Now the words fairly exploded out of her. "Marry you! You must be mad, sir. I'll drown myself in the sea first!"

"Tst, tsk. Such hasty words, Amelia, my love. Marry me you certainly shall, in this very room and this very night. If need be I shall drug you again," he said with maddening cool. "Oh, not enough to put you out, of course. Just enough to get the words 'I do' out of your silly mouth. A quite drunken clergyman has already been engaged to perform the ceremony. I am going ashore presently to fetch him from a very low tavern where I believe he is losing his fee to the publican. Quite adept wih a dice box is the publican, I believe." He pulled a packet of papers from a coat. Extracting one of them, he threw it on the table before her. It was a special license.

He looked through the remaining papers and turned his oily smile to her again. "I am in your debt, you know. I believe I have not thanked you for so conveniently telling me where to find this little list of your brother's French friends. Combined with such other bits of information as I have been able to pick up here and there, it will bring a tidy sum when we get to France." His tone was heavy with cynicism. He said, "The Little Emperor does like to know who his enemies are, you know. The money will tide us over until such time as your lawyers can forward us the further funds we shall require for our wedding trip."

Amelia forced a sweet smile to her lips. "Has it not occurred to you, sir, that my lawyers may have some objection to sending English money into the land of the enemy?"

"We shall not, of course, remain long in France. It is not a terribly healthy place just now. We shall move on to Brussels, or perhaps Vienna. Someplace quite unexceptionable. And since the request will be in your own hand, I think they will not refuse to send you the funds you request for your new and beloved husband."

"Who of my friends could possibly believe that I would marry you, sir?" Her voice was harsher now, and her smile had faded. Her face was etched with the first tiny lines of fear. He seemed to have left nothing to chance. "And how can you possibly hope to hold me indefinitely? I shall run away at the first opportunity and publish your ill usage to the world."

"Do so, my dear. Once you have lived with me as my wife it will not matter. I doubt you would be believed in any case. You must know that everyone has been expecting our engagement for weeks. I have taken great care to see that they should do so. You left your home today by yourself and of your own free will. It would be generally assumed that you had run off with me, then repented of your folly at some later time. Your reputation would be past salvaging."

"You have thought of everything, haven't you?" she said savagely. Her frustrated rage was beginning to get the better of her.

"As a matter of fact, I rather think I have," he said smugly. He crossed to a heavy mahogany desk that sat under the window. Depositing the papers in a drawer, he locked it securely, pocketed the key, and turned back to her. "I am going ashore to make the final arrangements for our marriage and departure. In two hours I shall return; when we sail with the tide, we shall be man and wife."

The slam of the door put a sharp period to his words. She heard a key grate in the lock, and she was alone.

Oh, infamy! Wretch! Scoundrel! Cruel, devious devil! Amelia's thoughts not unnaturally went on in this vein for some time as she paced the cabin. She kicked at the table in her fury. She threw a pillow at the door through which he had just left and generally indulged herself in a fit of useless rage. But useless it was indeed, and well she knew it. Better she should turn her energies to getting herself out of his reach.

Her first thought was for her own safety, but Amelia was also concerned about those papers. The people on that list had been Ned's friends. She could not try to save herself and leave them to be delivered to Bonaparte. She tried the desk drawer, pulling hard. The lock was quite secure. She studied it a long moment. It was not dissimilar to the lock on the door of the housekeeper's cupboard at Standish where the sweetmeats had been stored when she was a child. How many times had she watched Neddie pick that lock with one of her hairpins? In fact, he had brought the art to such a high peak that he could lock it up again with Mrs. Harbage none the wiser, or so they thought. Amy had never done the trick herself, but with little to lose at this juncture, it was certainly worth a try. She remembered the two large hairpins in her reticule and speedily extracted them. Bending a tip as she had so often seen Ned do, she inserted one of them into the lock and began to twist and turn it delicately.

For several minutes of concentrated effort, nothing happened. Her frustration grew almost unbearable, but at last she heard a beautiful and distinct little click. The drawer slid easily open.

The first paper that came to her hand was in her brother's well-loved and familiar script. A cold pang of grief clutched for a moment at her heart at the sight of it. It was indeed a list with the names of French royalists with contact points written beside them. She knew that these people would suffer and die if the list was allowed to cross the channel. And she remembered Mimms telling her what a help it could be to his organization to have that list. She must do what she could do to get it to Parker.

There were several other documents in the little pile. Most were relatively innocuous accounts of rumors or mentions of troop movements within England and the like. The last paper was in yet another hand. It looked to be a memorandum of sorts. It seemed to list arrangements and troops with shipping points and dates of embarkation. With a gasp, Amelia saw the signature at the bottom of the memorandum. "Wellington" was signed in a bold hand.

How on earth could a man like Sir Julian get hold of such a document? And in Wellington's own hand! Even the nonmilitary Amy realized that this was a very important piece of paper indeed. If it fell into French hands, it could very easily turn the tide of the war in their favor. No matter how Sir Julian had got it, it must not be allowed to leave England. She would see that it did not.

Her next problem was getting off this ship. The hairpin had worked so well on the little drawer. Perhaps it would do as well on the sturdier lock of the door. If it did not, and she heard Sir Julian returning before she could find some other means of escape, she would burn the papers with the flame from the candle. That much at least she could do for her brother and her country. She set to work on the door.

Both hairpins were hopelessly bent in a matter of minutes. Rummaging in her reticule, she pulled out a nail file. With that tool she worked for several long and frustrating minutes. A few times she felt sure she had nearly achieved her object, only to have it slip elusively away again. She threw the little silver file across the room in disgust.

Her last hope lay in the small pair of scissors that she remembered were also in her bag. With a wrenching tug, she pulled the two halves of the scissors apart. With a determined little smile, she realized that if the lock would not yield, she had at least created herself a handy little weapon. She set to work with savage precision.

A quarter of an hour inched by. Tears of frustration were dribbling down her chin as she worked on the lock, swearing at the recalcitrant thing under her breath. Then with a catch of her heart, she heard the click of the lock that heralded her possible freedom. With elation, she eased the door open a few inches and slid out and up the few short stairs.

Crouching low at the top of the steps, she surveyed the deck. Directly before her was an unknown sailor. He lay on a coil of rope, snoring stertorously, an empty brandy bottle at his hand. He very effectively barred her passage. She froze and listened hard. Snoring, lapping water, a little wind, and the creak of a mast. Nothing more. She assumed the captain must be somewhere on board, and perhaps other deckhands as well, but she could see and hear no one.

Stealing down the stair once again, she closed the door silently behind her. As she was crouching there in the darkness, a plan had sprung full-formed into her mind, but she must work quickly to carry it out. Sir Julian had been gone nearly an hour already, and she had much to accomplish before his return. She moved about the room quickly and confidently and as silent as a cat.

Moving the candle from its little table, she removed the oilskin covering from that piece of furniture. She gathered up the pile of papers, leaving aside only the odious marriage license. Wrapping them well in the oilskin, she tied the bundle securely with a ribbon pulled from her hair. Retrieving the candle from the desk, she tipped it carefully so that the melted wax dripped onto the little bundle. Her eyes flew to the brass clock as it chimed two o'clock. She futilely urged the candle to melt more quickly, her hand trembling badly.

Painstakingly, one drop at a time, she sealed the seams and edges of the oilskin packet. She only hoped her idea was sound and that the packet was now waterproof. She tucked it firmly into the bodice of her dress along with her tiny store of wealth, knotted in a handkerchief. She resolutely removed her shoes and her petticoats and tied her skirts up firmly around her waist. She knew she must look very silly, and an involuntary giggle escaped her, easing her fear a little.

Looking about the room a last time, her eye fell on the forgotten marriage license still lying on the desk. With a big smile, she tore it to shreds, scattering it to the four corners of the room.

"So, you think of everything, do you, my fine Sir Julian? But you did not think that your dear Amelia might not be quite the stupid girl you had hoped she was. A bad miscalculation, my friend."

She blew out the candle with a reckless flourish, silently opened the door, and slipped out.

She began inching up the stairs, her eyes never leaving the figure snoring there. Her own breathing seemed unbearably loud in the quiet of the night. The cold, damp air hit at her bare arms and legs. She shivered with both cold and fear. Her movements were so stealthy she might have been one of the shadows to which she carefully kept herself. At a loud snort from the drunken sailor, she jumped. He rolled over, mumbled, and snored on.

She gained the top of the stairs. Ever so slowly, she reached across the slumbering giant and picked up the empty brandy bottle. Holding it over her head, she stepped carefully over the reclining form. She was nearly clear of him when an alcohol dream caused him to toss out an arm. It struck her bare leg, and his eyes blinked up at her.

" 'Ere, you," he said thickly as he began to pull himself free from his bed of rope. The brandy bottle made no sound as it moved through the air, and it descended with a solid thump, not even breaking on his hard skull. His eyes closed as easily as they had opened. He slumped slowly back onto the rope.

Amy froze in horror at what she had done and at the thought that someone else might have heard it. She strained her mind for any new sound. Nothing. She crept silently away toward the front of the ship.

Once she reached the ship's bow, she quickly searched for what she needed. She tripped over a hatch cover and was sent sprawling. Cursing her ill luck, she recovered quickly and continued her search. At last it was successful. The anchor rope leading over the edge and down into the water was slightly frayed, but it looked strong. She was squatting low, peering over the edge of the ship and across the water toward the lighthouse. That way lay freedom.

Now it came to the point, she was decidedly nervous, and on the verge of giving up the entire scheme. She had been a strong swimmer as a child, but had not practiced the exercise for some years. It did not seem to become a Young Lady of Fashion, or so she had been told. She knew it could not be more than half a mile to the shore, but the glassy water looked very dark and threatening, the treacherous clouds had returned, and the sky was inky black.

She heard laughter coming from somewhere directly behind her. It sounded very near. Turning her head sharply, she saw the soft glow of candlelight through the window of the captain's cabin. A sharp oath, another raucous laugh, and the crash of a pewter tankard on a table. The sounds went through her like an electric shock, and she made up her mind.

Without further thought, she swung herself over the side of the ship, muttered a quick but heartfelt prayer, grabbed the rough rope in her delicate little hands, and lowered herself silently into the unfriendly sea.

Chapter Seventeen

The black water was unbelievably cold. It took Amy's breath away at once. She clung terrified to the anchor rope, trying to regain her strength as well as her composure. She was shaking savagely; her teeth chattered violently. Her fingers gripped the rope so tightly that she could not seem to force them free. With one part of her mind, it occurred to her calmly that she was about to die. I am going to faint from the cold, she thought. I will sink and drown. I wonder what it feels like to drown.

But there remained a tiny center of courage somewhere deep inside her. And a thought stole into her mind. How odd that, in her rage, it had not occurred to her before. Sir Julian had kidnapped her. Then obviously Lord Tyrone had not. He was innocent. That one tiny thought was enough. It lit a flame of hope deep within her. The flame grew to a blaze, spreading warmth throughout her soul. The frozen grip of her fingers melted; she let loose the rope and began a strong sure stroke toward the only thing she could see clearly, the blinking lighthouse.

She slid silently through the sea, but she was working hard. Her long skirt was heavy with water. Before she had gone far, it had come untied and wrapped itself about her legs, impeding her progress. The lighthouse seemed to grow no closer, and she was tiring quickly from the violent cold. The seawater stung viciously at her eyes. At intervals she would roll over onto her back to rest, being careful not to stop moving her arms and legs. She knew if once she stopped, she would never be able to begin again. She would sink peacefully into the icy water and rest there forever. It was a tempting thought, to just float here, gazing up at the now brilliant moon until she should sink. But the iron core within her made her roll over and start stroking again.

Finally, she knew she could go no further. Her adventure had come to an ignominious end. Her legs were heavy and full of sharp shooting pains. She couldn't seem to force them into movement any longer. They began to sink below her. Her right foot struck something solid. Then, excited, she let her left leg down cautiously, and it struck as well. She had touched bottom. She stood there a moment, chest deep in the swirling water, gulping in the night air. She forced herself the few more yards to the beach and collapsed in a heap beside a huge rock, gasping and laughing quietly. Her swollen eyes closed.

The moon had moved higher in the sky before she could bring herself to face the idea that her danger was still very real. What brought her abruptly to that realization was the sound of footsteps. They sounded dangerously close, just on the other side of the rock against which she leaned. She lifted her head a bit, straining her consciousness. More footsteps. And there was more than one person, she was aware. A louder crunch, as though someone had stumbled and fallen. Suddenly the familiar and detestable voice of Sir Julian Deventer came to her. He was speaking in a harsh whisper, but his imperious tone was unmistakable, and it was very close.

"Pick yourself up, you drunken fool. Get in the boat! We are late already, and I want the business over with. You'll be lucky if I don't throw you over the side to drown when we're done."

She looked frantically about her, feeling terribly exposed on the white moonlit beach, with only her rock for protection. She crouched lower behind it. A sharp edge bit viciously into her shoulder; with an effort she stifled a cry of pain.

Presently she could hear a strange sort of scraping noise. It seemed to be moving away from her. Peeking carefully around the edge of her shield, she saw three shadowy figures dragging a rowboat across the shingle beach toward the water. The first man climbed in. A second attempted it and fell face first into the foaming surf. Sir Julian muttered a stifled oath and hauled the stumbling figure roughly into the boat. The third man Amy assumed from his huge dimensions to be her burly abductor.

Her face was very near the gravelly sand. The damp salty smell filled her nostrils. To her chagrin, a sneeze surprised her, escaping before she could catch it.

" 'Ere, wot's that?" She recognized the big man's rough voice.

At once she pulled back behind her protection. Her frozen hand covered her mouth, afraid it would cry out in fear and betray her. Surely they would not find her now, not after she had come so far! It would be too unfair! And she knew she would never have the courage to try again, even if she got the chance, which she was very sure she would not.

Footsteps crunched along the shingle, moving inexorably in her direction. She was holding her breath and cursing herself for shivering so. She prayed to the shadows to keep her hidden while she listened to the wheezing of the man's breath on the other side of her boulder.

"Come, we've no time to waste on foolish fancies. There's no one there," Sir Julian whispered urgently.

"I tells ya, I heard sumin', guv'nor."

"Damn you, Jem! We're on the most deserted beach in Dorset! We're late, and we must be on our way. Now do as I say!"

"It's yer neck, guv'nor," replied the burly man.

Amy could hear the shrug in his tone, and fancied she knew the hideous grin caught on his swarthy face.

At length, she saw the little rowboat moving steadily away into the water, heading for the black hulk of the ship. Her breath escaped in a long slow sigh. She felt it was safe to start moving again, and she knew she had to hurry. She hadn't much lead time. The trip out to the ship was not a long one. And Sir Julian was bound to discover her disappearance almost at once. She would count on no more than an hour at the most before they would be on land again, searching ruthlessly for her. Her main advantage, she knew, was that they would not know in which direction she had fled, or even that she was familiar with this part of the country. The obvious course would be to go to Fleet Village. It was just over that hill ahead. She might get help from the inhabitants there.

But would that not also be the first place Sir Julian and his henchmen would search for her? It was nearing three in the morning. Her own experience had taught her that villagers are suspicious by nature and tend not to trust outsiders. In her present state, wet and muddy, barefoot and shivering, she'd be likely to have every door shut firmly and crossly in her face. She couldn't take the risk of being found wandering about the village seeking shelter. She would skirt it by a wide margin and head directly for Weymouth. She had a good chance, she felt, of getting there before her pursuers could find her. Once she reached the White Hart and Parker she would be safe.

She felt for the packet in her bodice. It was still safely tucked inside. Wringing out her heavy skirts as best she could, she set off down the beach at the briskest pace her bare feet and aching legs would allow.

Since she could not risk following the main road, the two or three miles to Weymouth soon became five or six. She had decided to follow the coastline where possible, always ready to hide among the rocks or even dive back into the rippling surf if necessary. But she felt fairly confident that she would not be sought among the shells and sand.

The wind that had earlier carried off the mist blew even stronger now. It cut mercilessly through her wet muslin gown. She shivered convulsively as she climbed over jagged rocks, seaweed, and piles of driftwood. Her hands and feet were soon cut and bleeding, but they were so numb with cold that she could no longer feel the pain. She had to strain her poor abused eyes to pick out a path among the shadows and tide pools. One unwary step caused her to disturb a large crab, who snapped his claws viciously and sidled away in disgust. She had lost her ribbon, and strands of wet hair mixed with seaweed clung to her cheeks. She resolutely pushed them back and plunged on.

With freedom, she regained a bit of her sense of humor. She looked down at the blood on her poor hands, shining darkly in the moonlight, and smiled wanly. At least her blood hadn't frozen yet, she laughed grimly as she watched it ooze slowly from a fresh cut. She wiped it on her thoroughly mutilated skirt and moved on, humming softly to keep up her spirits. Once or twice she spied an avocet or a seagull perched on a rock and eyeing the trespasser scornfully. "Good morning," she whispered to one. "Don't mind me." He didn't, but waited patiently for her to be on her way.

She slowly picked her way around a rocky point, and there at last was the lighthouse of Weymouth harbor, flashing brightly in the near distance. The horizon was already beginning to show a rosy pink; the water glinted with yellow lights. She could make out the bobbing masts of the little fishing boats in the harbor. The daub-and-wattle walls of the ancient fishermen's cottages glowed warmly as the first angled rays struck them.

By the time she'd stumbled along the last half mile of beach to the quay, the harbor was lively with the early-morning activity of a busy port. Fishwives were setting out their glistening wares at roughhewn stalls, some already hawking fresh eels and prawns with a cackle or a bellow. The words reminded Amy with a jolt how hungry she was. She had eaten nothing since the bit of dry bread and cheese of yesterday. But she would surely find breakfast at the White Hart. That comfortable inn had taken on the proportions of a castle in her mind; it called to her like the Sirens to unsuspecting sailors. The image made her giggle, and she looked at the men on the boats. These sailors looked as though they could be tempted by nothing less than a pint of rum and a warm fire!

They busied themselves with their work as she gazed across at them. Masts creaked, sails were raised, and lines cast off as the little hulks moved off into the waves. While the polite world slumbered peacefully on genteel linen sheets, their more lowly brothers at Weymouth headed happily out to catch their supper for them. The normality of the scene was for Amy a welcome return to sanity. Here were simple people going about their business as usual. And where there were people, there was safety, she believed gratefully.

She was debating the wisdom of approaching one of the less fierce-looking of the fishwives to ask the direction of the White Hart. She knew she might succeed only in frightening her away. She must look a veritable specter new arisen from the sea with her Medusa head, seaweed replacing that lady's snakes. Her gown wet and shredded, her hands and feet covered with bleeding cuts, and her eyes red-rimmed from fatigue and salt water staring from purple-shadowed sockets, she could not but appear frightful to the superstitious fisherfolk. But she must find her way to Parker, and quickly, and she had no clear idea in which direction he lay. She had put most of her

fright behind her now. But she was decidedly embarrassed by the sight she knew she presented. Well,
there was nothing for it. She screwed up her courage
and began to round the quay toward the little fish
market.

But two steps had she gone when she froze where
she stood. The blood drained from her already pale
face, a look of absolute horror spreading across it. At
the other end of the market was a menacingly familiar
burly figure, his matted hair and grizzled black beard
bobbing from stall to stall. Jem, as Sir Julian had
called him, was asking questions and searching for her
among the fishy buckets. Like the apparition she
resembled, Amy disappeared behind the stone wall of
the quay again, crouching low in an attempt to ensure
invisibility. As she cowered there in terror, like a fox
surrounded by barking hounds, she feared she would
be sick from very panic. She had been plunged right
back into the long nightmare, and she was not at all
sure she could face it any longer. She felt an almost
overwhelming desire to give in to her despair and let
herself be found. But something, she never knew quite
what, urged her to seek one last means of escape.

Directly across from her hiding place was a tiny
alley. It weaved between the leaning old buildings and
cottages and led into the town. There would be more
dark nooks and corners for hiding there if she could
just make it across the way unseen. She peeked carefully around the wall. The man was talking to a
nearby fishwife. She saw the old woman shake her
head and her fist at him, and, with a scowl and an
oath, he walked away up the street.

Now was her chance; she must seize it. With a
quick glance around and a silent prayer, she scurried
across the road and into the alley. Her bare feet made
no sound on the cobbled stones. She didn't stop running until she reached the other end of the dark little
corridor. She heard no steps behind her, and she
stepped cautiously out into a main street, remembered

from a happier visit years ago as the High Street of Weymouth. The shops were not yet open, and there were few people about. A vague remembrance of the inn she sought told her she was traveling in the right direction.

She moved stealthily down the street, darting from shadow to shadow. As she stepped out in front of a shop, she heard footsteps approaching from behind her. She darted back into the nearest alley before her heart could beat again. She willed herself to melt into the wall and was still as the stones of which it was built. A rat skittered across her bare toes, pausing to sniff at the drying blood. She winced inwardly, but not one muscle did she move. The rat ran off.

Presently, a stranger walked past on the other side of the street and disappeared. She breathed again. She peered cautiously around the corner of her wall, but she was still too frightened to leave its sanctuary.

From directly behind her came a gasp. Swinging around in alarm, she encountered two brown eyes round as saucers. They were set in a pink, dirty little face and were staring up at her in wonder.

"Be ye a mermaid, mum?" the little boy to whom they belonged asked in amazed accents.

She had to laugh from very relief. "Yes, I rather think I am," she managed at last. "But I shan't hurt you, I promise. Indeed, I'm awfully glad that you are here. Can you tell me the way to the White Hart Inn? You see, I'm lost."

Unable to speak, the awestruck boy simply pointed with a grubby little hand. Following his gesture, she realized with delight that she was but a few yards from the stableyard of the place she sought. She pulled her knotted handkerchief from her bodice to give the boy a shilling, but he had disappeared.

A few quick and silent steps brought her to the innyard. Peering in for a moment, she was relieved to see no one about. She crossed quickly to the door. It was locked but was promptly answered at her knock.

The landlord himself stood before her in a wondrously striped waistcoat, scandalized at what he found on his genteel doorstep.

"Get away with you! I'll have no beggars here," he roared with finality and turned back into the inn.

From the depths of her memory sprang a name. "Mr. Bagot!" she barked out imperiously just as the door was about to close upon her. "I am in no mood to be trifled with, I warn you. I desire to speak with Mr. Parker, whom I understand to be lodging here." She shook with rage, surprised at her own audacity.

The landlord was taken aback on hearing his name on those blue little lips. He stopped short, but quickly regained his equilibrium and stood his ground. "I run a respectable inn, my girl. I'll have no young females of your sort under my roof, and that's flat! And I'm sure Mr. Parker, who mingles with proper gentlemen, won't see you neither. Now be away gone!"

Amelia's voice was deadly calm and low in her reply. "I shall tell you once again, Mr. Bagot. I desire to speak with Mr. Parker at once. You may tell him that Miss Clerville awaits him."

"Miss Clerville! That's rich! What a brass-faced little thing it is, to be sure! As if I couldn't recognize the Quality when I saw it."

"As I am not in the habit of having to prove my pedigree to mere innkeepers, I do not intend to waste my time in trying to do so to you, Mr. Bagot. I assure you I am Lady Amelia Clerville. And I am very cold and tired. You may bring me some coffee and lay a fire for me in the coffeeroom, where I will warm myself until Mr. Parker comes."

Not waiting for an answer to this peremptory speech, she swept grandly past him into the inn. Mr. Bagot gathered up what was left of his injured dignity and followed, clucking to himself about the vagaries of the Quality and what was a poor honest man to do.

With immense relief, Amy saw that a comfortable fire was already glowing warmly in the coffeeroom. Briskly rubbing her lifeless hands before it, she tried to coax some of the warmth of the dancing flames into her deadened fingers. Exhausted though she was, she felt nervous and restless still. She could not feel safe until she gave the papers she carried into Parker's own hands. Suppose he was not here, she thought with chagrin. Suppose Mr. Bagot would indeed not allow her to stay. Her imitation of her aunt's imperious manner had gotten her in the door, but she could not honestly blame the poor innkeeper if he sent his own henchman to have her removed. She rose and paced nervously back and forth in front of the glowing hearth, unable to relax.

Her ruminations carried her to the window overlooking the yard. She stood there long moments, unseeing and unconscious of the scene before her. There were very few people about at this still-early hour to disturb her thoughts. But there was one gentleman on a horse, speaking down to an ostler. Amy's eyes focused on him with a snap. Sir Julian! Frozen with horror, she merely stared, her mouth open. His gaze rose to the window and saw her. Their eyes locked, hers seething with abhorrence, his a study in rage. She felt as though his eyes were challenging her, almost commanding her to come out and follow him away. She dared not move so much as a muscle.

Strangely, Sir Julian made no move to come in after her. He had been asking the ostler who was staying in the inn, and was not at all pleased with the answer. After a long moment of staring at Amelia, he wheeled his horse in defeat and rode savagely away as if the very furies were at his heels. She was following him with her eyes, still paralyzed with fear and perplexed at his departure, when a shocked voice from behind her caused her to turn.

"Lady Amy!" There stood the kind, loyal Parker. He took in her alarming appearance with one astonished glance. "Whatever has happened to you, Miss?" he asked in concerned tones as he crossed toward her.

She was too relieved at sight of him to speak but mutely retrieved the packet of papers from her bodice and held them out to him. He looked a question at her, then tore open the oilskin bundle. Bits of hardened wax flew to the hearth. As he read quickly through the various papers, she watched the wax melt from the heat of the flames, leaving little molten puddles on the slate. All strength seemed to be draining from her muscles. Realizing she was about to collapse, she sank into a vast wing chair before the fire, gazing dumbly into the flames.

At last Parker looked up from his reading. He was holding the memorandum from the Duke of Wellington. His look was, if possible, even more amazed than before. "But Miss, however did this paper fall to you? We learned only yesterday of its disappearance from the War Office. The loss was discovered by the merest chance. They probably thought they could show it to Borney, collect a handsome reward—for he'd be mighty impressed by the old man's signature on it—and slip it back into the file at the War Office before anyone'd miss it, and no one the wiser. We've been up all night trying to track it down and ensure that it did not leave the country. This paper is vital, Miss. Vital!" he finished with a flourishing gesture.

"Yes, I rather thought it might be," she replied wearily.

"But where did you find it?"

She recited her story like an automaton, the words coming from her mouth in a dull monotone.

With great patience and gentleness, he questioned her until he had the complete story. "You have done a wonderful thing, Miss! Wonderful! As luck would have it, the boss is here at this very moment. We've been using the inn as a command post the whole night. Very worried his lordship has been about this, I can tell you. He's put the whole of the south of England on alert. I must take this to him at once." He looked down at the shivering little creature nearly lost in the giant wing chair. His voice grew gentler still. "You stay right here and warm yourself, Miss. I'm sure his lordship will want to come in and thank you himself."

"Yes, I'll do that. Actually, I'm rather too tired to go anywhere else just now." When she looked up again, Parker was gone.

At last, relief washed over her in a flood. Her eyes closed, and the tears of panic and wrath that had been held so long in check flooded out and ran down her cheeks unabated. The combined tensions of the last several hours overcame her completely. She longed for the strong arms of her father or even the comfortable ones of old Nurse Penny to wrap themselves around her and tell her the nightmare was over, she was awake now and the sun was shining down upon her.

She was shaking with giant sobs when she heard a gentle voice beside her. "Poor little love. You've had a rather uncomfortable night, haven't you?"

Her eyes flew open, and she sat bolt upright in her chair. Kneeling beside her, unshaven and tired, but beautiful nonetheless, was the Marquis of Tyrone. Amy was certain that, in her exhaustion, her mind was playing tricks on her. Blinking the remaining moisture from her eyes, she directed him a searching look. It was indeed Tyrone, smiling a little crookedly at her.

He possessed himself of one of her trembling hands, rose, and drew her up to him. As though it were the most natural thing in the world, she melted into his strong, comforting arms.

"There now, my love. It's all over. You are safe now, quite safe," he said soothingly. They weren't her father's arms, but they seemed to do very well indeed.

When she had brought her tears under control again, as well as her fluttering heart, she turned a pair of watery eyes to look at him. "You?" The jumbled images in her mind were beginning to fall into a readable picture, one which pleased her very much.

"Yes, my love. Whom were you expecting?" he added.

How wonderful that "my love" sounded in her ears—but what could he mean by it? She looked shyly up at him again, a query in her green eyes. The answering look in his blue ones caused her to blush. He broke into an engaging grin and held her at arm's length.

"Do you remember you once told me you were perhaps not quite a lady?" he asked with a laugh. "Well, I wish you could but see yourself now. A lady? Never! You look much more like a drowned kitten!"

In her present state, that was too much. She bristled up. "Wretch! After all I have been through this night!"

"Oh, a very charming drowned kitten, to be sure." His grin broadened. "I can think of only one thing that would make you look even better." Her eyes asked the obvious question. "A marchioness's coronet would be quite the proper finishing touch for my sea queen," he finished, tweaking a wet curl.

She stared at him aghast. In spite of her dreams of him, she could not believe what she had just heard. "But you positively dislike me! I know you do!"

"No, do I? How very odd, to be sure. Is it not strange, then, that I should persist in wanting to kiss you?" he asked, his eyes dancing.

"Do not toy with me, my lord, I beg of you," she pleaded, on the verge of tears once more. "I am not in my best wits just now."

"But I am not toying with you, Amelia," he explained convincingly. "I love you. I believe I have done so since I first saw you. I can imagine no bleaker future than to go through the rest of my life without you by my side."

"Oh!" she answered weakly. She was prevented from saying anything further by his lips ruthlessly kissing hers. Fatigue, worry, pain all flew away to be replaced by a magic glow that spread slowly and deliciously into every limb. As she emerged from his embrace, it was with some difficulty that she regained her breath and her composure. He lifted her chin so that she was looking into his eyes, the flames from the fire reflected in their depths. His face held an expression of profound pride.

"You are quite incredible, you know. You have done a very brave thing. Few men I know would have shown so much courage. England must be forever grateful. When I think of the danger you were in!" He clasped her to his breast till she thought she would surely be crushed.

"Is this not carrying gratitude to the extreme, my lord?" she gasped. He eased his embrace slightly. She turned in his arms and dimpled up at him happily.

He laughed. "I can never show enough gratitude. Sir Julian Deventer is a devil, but I shall be undyingly grateful to him for bringing you here to me, my Amelia."

"Oh! Sir Julian! Oughtn't we to go after him?" she burst out.

"Most likely he is halfway to France by now, with his tail between his legs. I don't think we need worry further about him, my love. He will not be so foolish as to show his face in England again. And I do not wish to speak further of the damned fellow. He has caused me quite enough problems!" To emphasize the point, he placed another delicious kiss on her lips and one on the tip of her nose, finally brushing her closed eyelids with his warm mouth.

Her long lashes fluttered open as he spoke again. "It strikes me, sweet, that I have not yet had an answer from you." He gazed deep into the green velvet, an uncertain look on his face. "Do you love me, Amelia?"

Her smile was a caress. "Yes, Justin, I do."

He beamed all over his face. "And you will marry me?"

"Why, yes, I rather believe I shall." She tilted her head and gave him a gamine grin. "Aunt Louie will be so very pleased."

"Minx!" And he was kissing her in a manner that left no questions unanswered.

They did not hear the door openly quietly. Parker's "Oh!" went equally unnoticed, and he tiptoed out again. Lord Wellington's memorandum would wait.

ABOUT THE AUTHOR

Megan Daniel, born and raised in Southern California, combines a background in theater and music with a passion for travel and a love of England and the English. After attending UCLA and California State University, Long Beach, where she earned a degree in theater, she lived for a time in London and elsewhere in Europe. She then settled in New York, working for six years as a theatrical costume designer for Broadway, off-Broadway, ballet, and regional theater.

Miss Daniel currently divides her time between her homes in New York and Amsterdam, together with her husband, Roy Sorrels, a successful free-lance writer. She is currently working on her second novel.

Recommended Regency Romances from SIGNET

Buy them at your local
bookstore or use coupon
on next page for ordering.

Big Bestsellers from SIGNET

☐ **ELISE** by Sara Reavin. (#E9483—$2.95)

☐ **TAMARA** by Elinor Jones. (#E9450—$2.75)*

☐ **LUCETTA** by Elinor Jones. (#E8698—$2.25)*

☐ **BY OUR BEGINNINGS** by Jean Stubbs. (#E9449—$2.50)

☐ **COVENT GARDEN** by Claire Rayner. (#E9301—$2.25)

☐ **SELENA** by Ernest Brawley. (#E9242—$2.75)*

☐ **ALEXA** by Maggie Osborne. (#E9244—$2.25)*

☐ **OAKHURST** by Walter Reed Johnson. (#J7874—$1.95)

☐ **MISTRESS OF OAKHURST** by Walter Reed Johnson.
(#J8253—$1.95)

☐ **LION OF OAKHURST** by Walter Reed Johnson.
(#J8844—$2.25)*

☐ **FIRES OF OAKHURST** by Walter Reed Johnson.
(#E9406—$2.50)

☐ **ABIGAIL** by Malcolm Macdonald. (#E9404—$2.95)

☐ **ECSTASY'S EMPIRE** by Gimone Hall. (#E9242—$2.75)

☐ **LAND OF GOLDEN MOUNTAINS** by Gillian Stone.
(#E9344—$2.50)*

☐ **CALL THE DARKNESS LIGHT** by Nancy Zaroulis.
(#E9291—$2.95)

* Price slightly higher in Canada